武汉理工大学研究生教材建设基金资助出版

BRITISH&AMERICAN DRAMA: INHERITANCE DEVELOPMENT

英美戏剧：传承与发展

柯建华 著

WUHAN UNIVERSITY PRESS
武汉大学出版社

图书在版编目(CIP)数据

英美戏剧：传承与发展/柯建华著. —武汉：武汉大学出版社,2015.9
ISBN 978-7-307-15734-7

Ⅰ.英… Ⅱ.柯… Ⅲ.①戏剧文学—文学评论—英国 ②戏剧文学—文学评论—美国 Ⅳ.①I561.073 ②I712.073

中国版本图书馆 CIP 数据核字(2015)第 095830 号

责任编辑:谢群英 刘东虹　　责任校对:汪欣怡　　版式设计:马 佳

出版发行：**武汉大学出版社** (430072 武昌 珞珈山)
(电子邮件：cbs22@whu.edu.cn 网址：www.wdp.whu.edu.cn)
印刷：武汉中远印务有限公司
开本：720×1000 1/16　印张:16.5　字数:235 千字　插页:1
版次：2015 年 9 月第 1 版　2015 年 9 月第 1 次印刷
ISBN 978-7-307-15734-7　定价:32.00 元

前　言

文学，是人类心灵的历史。西方的一些真诚的心灵探险家们，以西西弗斯推石上山的胆略和勇气，在宇宙般浩瀚深邃的世界里摸索，顽强地向着它的神秘底蕴掘进。几乎没有一种痛苦与欢乐不被他们品味过、表现过。流动不已的生命现象和变幻无定的精神生态构成了西方文学多姿多彩的河流。

戏剧是一门古老的艺术形式，不管其外在形式如何千变万化，都是对不同历史时期的人的欢乐、苦闷、追求、满足的诠释。阅读戏剧作品，就是阅读人类的文明史。

戏剧既是一门文学课，同时又是一门文化课，从中学到的是智慧。文化与经济之于人类，犹如鸟之两翼、车之两轮，决非可有可无，而是不可或缺，满足人的精神需求——增长智慧、涵养德行、陶冶情操、砥砺品格，提供正确导向，丰富社会生活，归结起来便是养“心”：养智、养德、养神、养气。因此，戏剧教学，不仅应传授知识，更应关注学生的精神成长，从而实现从“英美文学教学”到“英美文学教育”的质的飞跃。

外语人才既要有扎实的专业基本功，还应具备文学和文化素养，这样，他们才能成功而有效地进行跨文化交际。因此，教材的设计与教学既要兼顾社会需求中对英语专业学生所强调的实际应用能力的培养，还应充分考虑到教材另一方面的功用，即学生通过教材接触真实的语言环境，了解社会，培养他们具有批判性的思考和创造性的表达能力和面临各种矛盾、冲突、问题时解决问题的应变能力。

近年来，我国出版了少量不同版本的英美戏剧教材，教材内容大多按时间顺序选择名家名作的全文或片段加以评析，以启迪读者的思维和提高其鉴赏能力。但与其他文学形式相比，戏剧类书籍远远不能满足读者的需要。

《英美戏剧：传承与发展》一书是作者在近十年的教学积累上反复实践、修改和补充而形成的。在编写过程中作者借鉴了国内外先进教材的编写理念，吸收了戏剧研究的最新成果。首先，教材体例新颖，话题全面而生动，信息量大，覆盖面广，难易程度得当，同时兼顾知识性、理论性与实践性相结合。本书以内容分类为中心，包括戏剧的起源、发展、传承、种类、赏析要素和戏剧家及其作品本身；其次，本书试图让学生了解戏剧不只是文学史、思想史或作者个性史，而是具有其独特特点的艺术形式，每个章节尽量挖掘文学现象背后的“what”，“when”，“how”和“why”。西方文明的源头是希腊和希伯来，因此，了解西方文学必须了解西方的另一个源头，《圣经》。一个作家如何观察现实，采用何种艺术形式固然与其所处的时代、社会环境密切相关，却同时也跟整个人类的思维发展有关。本书试图在叙述西方戏剧演变的过程中挖掘其背后的神话、宗教、政治原因，及其对戏剧的巨大影响。让学生在品评和赏析西方戏剧的同时，能从传说、历史、宗教、政治等多维度了解西方所宣传的人文精神以及对个人主义和创新进取精神的推崇，提高对英语文学的鉴赏力和思辨力，在深层次上认识中西方观念的差异，树立全球化语境中的国际视野；此外，本书还剖析了戏剧与其他文学形式如诗歌、小说等的差异，并通过对英美主要剧作家代表作品的指导性阅读、讨论、编演来培养学生欣赏和分析作品的基本能力和必要技巧。同时还引导学生探寻西方文学与宗教的紧密关系，从而更好地把握西方戏剧的发展与发展趋势。

本书还有一个创新之处是通过对戏剧的理论分析之后，让学生自编、自导、自演戏剧，培养他们的团队精神、语言表达能力和面临各种矛盾、冲突问题时的应变力和解决问题的能力，遗憾的是因涉及版权问题，有些内容没有吸纳在本书之中。

本书是第一次出版，错漏之处难免，本人怀着虔诚的心欢迎更具慧眼的读者提出批评和指正。在编撰本书的过程中，作者参考、采用、辑录了一些国内外文献的研究成果和资料，特向原作者和出版者深表谢忱，并致以诚挚的敬意！

作者

2015 年 6 月

Contents

Introduction

Drama, the mixture of performance, music, painting, dance etc., as the 3rd literature form following lyrics and epic, is an old form of arts. Western drama traces back to the 6th century BC, originating in the dithyramb — a choral hymn to god Dionysus[1] which represents love of life, joy and madness. Greece has numerous influential drama theorists and playwrights such as Plato, Aristotle, Aeschylus and Sophocles[2] etc. whose works are the treasures of all human beings.

Just like any other form of literature, drama, no matter how it changes and develops, mirrors the joy and sorrow of people of all walks of life at different periods of time. Watching drama or reading plays is to have an insight into the life of people and history. It is self-evident that drama is really important to us, which is proved by the popularity of various theatres in many countries even today when TV sets offer us main and cheap source of entertainment, with the Broadway[3], known as Great White Way in US and London's West End[4] as the most famous. American universities have thousands of drama departments, with most universities and even middle schools having their own stages for students to perform. Children drama is prosperous in the United States now, designed to cultivate children's critical thinking and creative ability.

Britain put on Shakespeare plays in multilingual languages during the Olympic Games in 2012. The "Isles of Wonder"[5] theme of the Opening Ceremony of the Games is inspired by Shakespeare's *The Tempest*[6], showing the power of literature.

As far as American drama is concerned, the USA Drama Research offers yearly conference which encourages extensive and further study on British, especially American drama, all of which present readers with rich and valuable insight into modern British and American drama here in China.

However, compared with any other forms of literature such as novels, poems and essays which have been studied at length in China, drama study both by students and scholars is, to some degree, marginalized, which is not paid enough attention to in English literature education in many universities for which there exist many reasons. One reason is that drama is a highly specialized form of literature which can do some things supremely well but which must handle matters in its own way. The novel is designed to address its audience directly: open it and you have everything you need in front of you. But a play-text addresses its ultimate audience indirectly; it is a set of instructions designed to be interpreted by theatre makers who will then stage the play before its own audience. The play-text is, actually, quite a strange incomplete object. The first thing to realize when you open a play-text is that the words in front of you are not designed to function in the same way as the words in a novel or poem. The words are designed to become a performance. So they need to be read differently, thus drama being replaced by more films and TV series. The second reason is the scarcity of plays published here in China, which spares many readers the joy of reading plays.

Actually, the popularity of drama in the West shows the necessity of drama in our life, especially for students majoring in English. Firstly, the success of drama more than anything else depends on the immediate response of the audience. Therefore, drama reflects more directly than poetry and novels the thought, society and people of a certain period of time. As the strongest and most far-reaching interpreter of our deep-felt society, drama helps us better understand the English language, history and culture. Secondly, drama can stimulate people's creativity in problem solving, critical analysis, team building and self-confidence. Besides, studying and directing drama can challenge students' perceptions about the real world, human nature and themselves, providing training in the very practical aspects of communication skills necessary in today's increasingly information-centered world.

It is known that drama is an art form which depends almost entirely on what people do and say to each other, the characteristic of which — plots move on through dialogues, is beneficial for language learning and study for English major students. Unfortunately, drama teaching in university is far beyond satisfaction because of the difficulty on the one hand and on the other hand drama is only a selective course in many universities. Pressured by the survival problem, many students prefer to have a course they think that will help in career.

There are some books about Western drama, most of which are about British and American plays and playwrights. This book attempts to start with the origin of Western drama, emphasizing the inheritance and development of British and American drama, with the ambition to present readers with a panoramic view about the origin, development, change, characteristics and trend of Western drama.

Chapter one is about the origin of Western drama, in which a lot of history and politics background of Ancient Greece is discussed, helping students to make sense why drama originated from Greece instead of being anywhere else. It is not exaggerating to say that Greek culture is one of the sources of British and American, rather the whole European culture, thus exerting great influence on British and American literature. A lot of Ancient Greek plays are still being performed in various forms on stage in the world.

Chapter two and chapter three focus on the development, inheritance and trend of Western drama which involves some knowledge about religion, attempting to help students realize the close interrelation between religion and literature and the great influence between them. Many people believe the source of Western culture lies in Ancient Greece and Hebrew, which means understanding *Bible*[7] is a must for students to get a whole picture of Western literature. *Bible* both as a religious book as well as a classic, has particular influence on literature and serves as the solid foundation of Western culture. It is known that how a writer analyzes society, observes reality and in what way he portrays his character all depend on his thinking way and the time he lives in.

Chapter four is about the genre and characteristics in which, the elements and structure of drama, and the types of drama are presented, trying to figure out the differences between drama and other forms of literature and problems of drama.

Chapter five is mainly about the nature of drama and ways of appreciating drama, cultivating students' critical analysis of some plays in the original.

Chapter six gives a brief introduction of some famous modern British and American playwrights, most of whom have won the Nobel Prize in literature, helping students to read, appreciate and perform by themselves some plays in the original.

重难点解读

[1] **Dionysus**："酒神"狄俄尼索斯。与罗马人信奉的巴克斯(Bacchus)是同一位神祇，酒神是古代希腊色雷斯人信奉的葡萄酒之神，酒神不仅握有葡萄酒醉人的力量，还布施欢乐与慈爱，是当时极有感召力的神，酒神象征新生，推动了古代社会的文明并确立了法则，护佑着希腊的农业与戏剧文化，古希腊人对酒神的祭祀是秘密宗教仪式之一。

[2] **Plato, Aristotle, Aeschylus and Sophocles**：柏拉图、亚里士多德、埃斯库罗斯和索福克勒斯。柏拉图（约公元前427—前347）是古希腊伟大的哲学家，也是整个西方文化最伟大的哲学家和思想家之一，他和老师苏格拉底，学生亚里士多德并称为希腊三贤。在雅典创办了著名的学院，主要作品包括《伊壁鸠鲁篇》、《苏格拉底的申辩》、《克力同篇》、《斐多篇》、《政治家篇》、《智者篇》、《法律篇》、《理想国》、《苏格拉底之死》等。另有其创造或发展的概念包括柏拉图思想、柏拉图主义、柏拉图式爱情、经济学图表等。亚里士多德（公元前384—前322）是古希腊哲学家，柏拉图的学生、亚历山大大帝的老师，其著作包含物理学、形而上学、诗歌（包括戏剧）、音乐、生物学、动物学、逻辑学、政治，以及伦理学，与柏拉图、苏格拉底一起被誉为西方哲学的奠基者。埃斯库罗斯，古希腊悲剧诗人，与索福克勒斯和欧里庇得斯一起被称为古希腊最伟大的悲剧作家，有"悲剧之父"、"有强烈倾向的诗人"的美誉，其代表作为《被缚的普罗米修斯》。索福克勒斯，雅典三大悲剧作家之一，其代表作为《俄狄浦斯王》。

[3] **Broadway**：百老汇。原意为"宽阔的街"，指纽约市以巴特里公园为起点，由南向北纵贯曼哈顿岛，全长25公里的一条长街。由于路的两旁分布着为数众多的剧院，是美国戏剧和音乐剧的重要发起地，"百老汇"成为美国现代歌舞艺术、美国娱乐业的代名词。每年都有几百万的来自世界各地的游客到此来欣赏歌舞剧。在百老汇大街44街至53街的剧院称为内百老汇，而百老汇大街41街和56街上的剧院则称为外百老汇。内百老汇上演的是经典的、热门的、商业化的剧目，外百老汇演出的是一些实验性的、还没有名气的、低成本的剧目，但这种区分在近年来越来越淡化，于是又出现了"外外百老汇"，其观点当然也就更新颖更先锋了。

[4] **London's West End**：伦敦西区。与纽约百老汇齐名的世界两大戏剧中心之一，是艺术家表演艺术的国际舞台，也是英国戏剧界的代名词，西区剧院特指由伦敦剧院协会的会员管理、

拥有或使用的 49 个剧院。伦敦约有 100 个剧院，剧院区就集中了 40 多个，因此，伦敦西区当之无愧地成为英国戏剧界的代称。

[5] **Isles of Wonder**：奇迹岛。2012 年伦敦奥运会开幕式的主题是奇迹岛，即英伦三岛。

[6] ***The Tempest***：《暴风雨》。莎士比亚晚年的巅峰之作，讲述了米兰公爵普洛斯彼罗因被弟弟安东尼奥篡权陷害，带女儿米兰达流亡荒岛，但他通过自己掌握的魔术精灵制造了一场暴风雨，把乘坐同一艘船的弟弟安东尼奥和与之勾结的那不勒斯国王阿隆索、国王的儿子费迪南带到了荒岛上，最终，费迪南王子和米兰达郡主一见钟情，化解了上辈的恩怨。2012 年伦敦奥运会开幕式导演丹尼·博伊尔的构想灵感来自于《暴风雨》，整个开幕式以《暴风雨》为主线，演员肯尼斯·布莱纳扮作伊桑巴德金·德姆·布鲁内尔，朗诵《暴风雨》中的选段。

[7] ***Bible***：《圣经》。圣经是犹太教和基督教(包括天主教、东正教和新教)的宗教经典，犹太教的宗教经典是指圣经《旧约》部分，即《塔纳赫》(或称希伯来《圣经》)，而基督教的《圣经》则指《旧约》和《新约》两部分。不同的基督教派别所承认的《圣经》旧约部分略有不同，天主教版本承认 46 卷；东正教版本承认 50 卷；基督新教版本承认 39 卷。《圣经》新约部分的数量比较一致，天主教、东正教、新教都承认 27 卷。

Chapter 1 The Origin of Western Drama

Why does this book begin from the origin of Western drama? This is because knowing the origin of Western drama will help students to get a whole picture of the development, inheritance and trend of drama in the future.

Section 1 Ancient Civilizations

Civilization began to appear about 5,500 years ago in the river valleys of the Nile (North Africa) and the Tigris-Euphrates[1] (the present-day Middle East); slightly later, civilization appeared in the Indus Valley (present-day Pakistan) ca. 2,400 BC and then in the Yellow River Valley in China ca. 2,000 BC. Other civilizations developed independently and considerably later in the Americas. These earliest civilizations dating back thousands of years still impress us with their achievements in art, architecture, science and techniques. What will cross your mind when it comes to the civilized countries such as India, Egypt and China?

To many people, Taj Mahal is associated with India, Pyramids with Egypt and China with Terra-Cotta. Surely the majority of people know something about pyramids and Terra-Cotta which are great and impressive mausoleums for ancient powerful emperors. What is Taj Mahal? Located in the city of Agra, India, the Taj Mahal is one of the most beautiful masterpieces of architecture in the world. It was ordered to build by Shah Jahan, the 5th Mogul emperor of India, in tribute to his wife, who died giving birth to their 14th child (You can witness the glory in the movie *Slumdog Millionaire*). All the marvelous projects mentioned above are graves for powerful people or people relevant to the power. How about Ancient Greece? Do Ancient Greeks leave us huge graves too? What do Ancient Greeks leave us?

Section 2 Ancient Greece

The plays of one ancient city 2,500 years ago by just 4 playwrights have had a profound effect on the development of all subsequent Western drama, not only on the theatrical stage, but on opera, film, television, stand-up comedy and dance — in fact, most, if not all, of the live arts owe a debt to the theatre of Ancient Greece and the city of Athens[2]. Greek tragedy grew in popularity throughout the Enlightenment, where the reading of ancient drama was part of a good classical education and Aristotle's *Poetics*[3] became a standard text for the construction of well-made tragedies.

Ancient Greeks have unparalleled achievements in various aspects such as philosophy, arts, architecture and so on. Greek sculpture is unprecedented and marvelous. The statues created by Ancient Greeks in the Classical and Hellenistic ages[4] provide the foundation not only for Roman sculpture, but also for Western sculpture as we know it today. Literature is unmatched in history too. Thucydides[5], (c. 460-400 BC) the greatest of Ancient Greek historians, gives a vivid and scientific account of the Peloponnesian War[6] between Athens and Sparta. Actually, his description of the war is one of the classic pieces of writing on war. Plato, one of the most penetrating, wide-ranging and influential authors in the history of philosophy, excels in poetic prose. In verse, Ancient Greece produces 3 of the 4 great tragedians. When it comes to epics Homer who writes the *Iliad* and *Odyssey*[7], without doubt, can not be ignored. Pindar[8] (c. 522-443 BC) produces lyrics of great beauty. Quintilian[9] writes, "Of the nine lyric poets, Pindar is by far the greatest, in virtue of his inspired magnificence, the beauty of his thoughts and figures, the rich exuberance of his language and matter and his rolling flood of eloquence, characteristics which, as Horace[10] rightly held, make him inimitable."

Ancient Greeks neither imitate the civilization earlier than theirs nor learn from the civilizations of their times. Instead they bring the world something totally new. They are the earliest Westerners, representing the Western spirit — the modern spirit. That is why we think Western civilization originates from Greece. Ancient Greece, unlike Rome, which tries to copy and imitate Ancient Greece, to some degree, belongs to modern society. Rome belongs to ancient times and is in many aspects more like the Eastern empire in the Far East where the emperor is God and subjects are slaves full of fear and awe.

People who suffer and live in a desperate situation won't play games. It is unbelievable to have so many large scale sports games in ancient Egypt and Mesopotamia[11]. Ancient Egyptians didn't have games. One Egyptian priest said, "Solon[12], Solon, You Greeks are just children!" Ancient Greeks were energetic and happy enough to enjoy life which was evidenced by the various games.

Barbarous and bloody Roman games such as gladiatorial combat and chariot racing have nothing to do with fun and enjoyment for those participating in the events. Living a joyful life and appreciating the beauty of life is the most extinct characteristic of Ancient Greeks, which is different from any other society.

But Greek literature is full of sadness too, especially the Greek

Tragedy, from which we realize that Ancient Greeks have deep insight into life which is a mixture. Happiness and sadness, joys and sorrows go together harmoniously without any conflict. People who don't understand joy of life can't really know life with sorrows. People who are depressed cannot taste happiness of life and its sadness either. It seems depression and desperation have nothing to do with Ancient Greeks. Ancient Greek literature is clear-cut, quite black and white. Ancient Greeks really know life is unpredictable and death is approaching at any moment, but they are always singing for being living.

Section 3 Ancient Greek Religion

Ancient Greek religion was polytheistic, consisting of the worship of many Gods, whom they believed appeared in human form and had the temperament like man, but were endowed with superhuman strength and ageless beauty. Each Greek city was normally under the protection of one or more individual deities who were worshipped with special emphasis, for example, Athens and the goddess Athena[13]. *Iliad* and *Odyssey*, our earliest surviving example of Greek literature, recorded men's various and impressive interactions with diverse gods and goddesses whose characters and appearances underwent little change in the centuries that followed. Though with countless temples and a variety of religious rites and ceremonies, there was no special priestly class in Ancient Greece. Any citizen could run for being a priest which in Greece was an honorary post. In fact, most of the clergy were gifted intellectual people and a new thing became apparent in Greek intellectual life — Men who were not priests but were what we should now call independent gentlemen such as philosophers, artists, musicians and poets were seeking and recording knowledge and inquiring into the mysteries of life and human beings. Greek religion had the power to elevate people.

Greek religion was quite different from any other kind of religion which just demanded people to obey without any condition instead of inspiring people to seek the truth. "Mankind must strain every nerve to be excellent." Aristotle said. People in his time were giving their minds to shrewd questionings of the world in which they lived, asking what its real nature was. And it may be noted here how important this 6th century BC was in the history of humanity. For not only were these Greek philosophers beginning the research for clear ideas about this universe and man's place in it. Isaiah[14] carried Jewish prophecy to its sublime's levels, Gautama Buddha[15] was then teaching in India and Confucius and Lao Tse[16] in China while the Hebrew prophets were working out a new sense of direct moral responsibility between the people, eternal universal and God of Right and the Greek philosophers were training the human mind in a new method and spirit of intellectual adventure.

What great philosophers said still echoes: "Let him that would move the world, first move himself", (Socrates[17]), "To find a forever through the short-lived life" (Plato) and "Plato is dear to me, but dearer still is truth" (Aristotle).

The characteristics of Greek religion mentioned above made it possible that Ancient Greeks had a more active thinking and enjoyed a more democratic life. Ancient Greek mythology offered its literature inexhaustible subject matter, with a culture reflecting a clear human consciousness.

Section 4 Greek Drama

Greek culture is one of the sources of British and American, rather the whole European culture, thus exerting great influence on British and American literature. Drama is an old form of literature, much older than novels.

The Western dramatic tradition has its origin in Aancient Greece. The precise evolution of its main divisions — tragedy, comedy and satire is not definitely known. Although the origin of Greek drama can't be known with any certainty, it is known that tragedy and comedy do have deep roots in the religious and communal life of the Greek polis and are closely connected with the worship of the god Dionysus (called Bacchus by the Romans).

4.1 Life of Ancient Greeks

Knowing how Ancient Greeks live may help us better understand the emergence of drama in Greece.

Men and races tend to swing between asceticism and indulgence in many cultures, going to the extreme occasionally. But this was not the case of Ancient Greece. Ancient Greeks had the virtue of self-restrain. They admired both Dionysus — god of wine and Apollo, god of sun and music. The religious rites were playing a significant role in people's life. Cicero[18] once said, "The religious rites teach us how to live a happy life. What's more, they let us know how to face death with dignity and best wish. The purpose of the mysterious religious ceremonies is to help people to have an elevated life, seeing spiritual purity and savior, thus making man and gods united." Gods described in Homer's writing were humanlike and sunny enough. When the night fell, the gods went to bed too. Gods were like men and men were like gods. But Greeks were not content with those lively gods. They wanted to find out something spiritual, something that made them physiologically and psychologically well being, thus Dionysus coming into their life. Wine making people ecstatic and trance-like helped Ancient Greeks free from self-restraint while Apollo, a poet and musician god representing order and harmony warned them to be gentle and dignified. In around the 5th century BC, Apollo and Dionysus came to the perfect unification, which was evidenced in Greek drama that mirrored the colorful life of both various gods in Olympia[19] and ordinary people in cities

In Ancient Greece, drama was a kind of public behavior, an important and necessary activity in people's daily life. Around the 6th century BC, Athens democracy needed and advocated a kind of collective life, which drama could perfectly offer and at the same time imperceptibly disseminate democratic idea and life style, becoming a spatial need for people step by step. In 534 BC, Athens held the first Dionysus, and Thespis[20] transformed Dithyramb[21] into tragedy. People in Athens felt it an honor to watch drama during which nobody could make noise and push around or he would be punished severely. People were encouraged to watch drama, even could get bonus in return and playwrights who won the competition were highly prized by the government.

4.2 Plays of Ancient Greece

All that was left of Greek theatre were 43 plays, Aristotle's *Poetics*, a few amphitheaters and a few theatre commentaries. Ancient Greeks liked debating, questioning and exploring new ideas. They admired logical arguments and scientific proof. They believed in justice and human dignity. But they were not all equal. Some Greeks were born free. Others were slaves with no rights. To please the gods, city-states held religious festivals, with competitions in music, dance, drama, poetry and sports. The Olympic Games began as a religious festival of this kind, probably in 776 BC. Parthenon[22] of Ancient Athens was built in the 447 BC. From 490 to 479 BC, Athens and Sparta fought together against invaders from Persia. But then they became rivals. From 431 to 404 BC, they fought each other in a bitter war which severely weakened power of both sides, all of which were caused by greed and ambition.

Greek drama was a continuation of early Greek fertility festivals to Dionysus that included music and dancing. These festivals were a plea to the god to allow life to continue into the next year as well as a chance to honor the god and thank him for everything that he had given. These festivals often included a sacrifice that was sometimes actual, sometimes symbolic.

Greek drama evolved into a more controlled worship with scheduled performances where the participants did not work themselves into a frenzied mob, but they still got the same cathartic effect by merely watching and internalizing what was going on on stage. The plays were performed during festivals and took all day to perform, much like the earlier festivals did.

During the Dionysus festival, 3 tetralogies[23] by 3 playwrights were performed and presented to a crowd of 17,000 Greek citizens. A producer was chosen to provide food, wine and amenities for the actors with all businesses being stopped while everyone attending the festival. Judges who were selected by lot watched from the front row. On the 1st day, 3 playwrights, their themes and casts were introduced. On the 2nd day, processions, sacrifices of animals and 10 dithyrambs were performed and wine were poured freely. On the 3rd day, 5 comedies, satyr plays — a short play in which the chorus was made up of Dionysus's devoted followers, the playful, violent, sensual creatures, part-human, part-animal, whose dancing and singing were in vehement contrast with the tone, style, music and costume of the choruses of tragedy from previous years were presented. The 1st tetralogy by the 1st playwright was presented on the 4th day, the 2nd tetralogy by the 2nd playwright on the 5th day and the 3rd tetralogy by the 3rd playwright on the 6th day. On the 7th day, judgment was done and the awards were given. The winning playwright was awarded a wreath of ivy, living free of the government for a whole year.

4.3 Dionysus

Greek drama, or more explicitly, Greek tragedy, originated in the dithyramb. This was a choral hymn between a lead singer and the chorus to the god Dionysus representing love of life, joy and madness at Dionysia[24]. It was thought that the dithyramb, a drunken ceremony, occurred each spring (now March 21) with sacrifice and wine offered and actors dressed in half-man, half-goat singing hymns to Dionysus.

At first there was only singing but no plot. Tradition had it that at the Dionysia of 534 BC, the lead singer of the dithyramb, a man named Thespis, added to the chorus an actor with whom he carried on a dialogue, thus initiating the possibility of dramatic action. Thespis was credited with the invention of tragedy. Eventually, Aeschylus introduced a second actor to the drama and Sophocles a third, Sophocles' format being continued by Euripides[25], the last of the great classical Greek dramatists.

As a result, with more and more dialogues and conflicts, drama evolved from deed to a story and to a play, thus Greek drama being transformed from religious ceremonial to an artistic performance.

4.3.1 Why Dionysus

From literature, art, cult titles and records of cult practice, it was clear that Dionysus was identified by Athenians as

(1) god of wine and wine miracles, fostering intoxication, which can lead both to positive release and to self-destructive passions and actions;

(2) god of wild nature, particularly associated with luxuriant plant growth and with some wild animals (lion, snake, bull) and in cult honored by phallic processions displaying the god's power over sexuality;

(3) god of ecstatic possession, characterized by the behavior of women worshippers without individual, conscious identity taking on the role of maenads shown in frenzied, trance-like states;

(4) god of the dance, in company with satyrs, nymphs and maenads as a celebration of freedom from self-consciousness and

constraint;

(5) god of masking and disguise, often represented on vases by a mask as the object of worship;

(6) god of mystic initiation, offering his worshippers the possibility of blessing in an afterlife.

It was easy to see that Dionysus was closely associated with Greek tragedy because of the major characteristics of this god. Greek drama evolved from the religious rites performed in honor of Dionysus by masked worshipers who danced and sang and worked themselves into a frenzy in order to lose their identity and merge with nature and gods. As drama slowly emerged from these ceremonies, it became more and more formalized.

4.3.2 Attitudes towards Wine and Love between Chinese and Greeks

To Ancient Greeks, Dionysus and Aphrodite[26], god of love, meant both the tragedy and comedy of desires. Gao Tse[27], an ancient Chinese philosopher in War Time thought that the desire for food and sex was part of human nature. But in the long history, Gao Mei[28], god of love and reproduction in Chinese culture, evolved into a woman serving a king in Chu state. China has Shennong[29], a god like Dionysus, who neither drank nor gathered roses, struggled between hell and heaven by tasting hundreds of herbs for people, thus desire especially sex in Chinese culture losing the artistic symbol. That is the big difference between Chinese and Greeks.

Later in the West, god of wine meant joy and fun. Churches were usually the places where wine was made and priests used to drink a lot, which made Puritans who were greatly influenced by Martin Luther[30], leader of the great religious revolt of the 16th century in Germany insisted on ban on alcohol drinking.

In China people have a very pious attitude to liqueur which is made from grains. When drinking, they tend to show their respect for heaven, thus liqueur becoming an irreplaceable tool for communication between men and gods and between people. Taoists think liqueur is nectar while Buddhists are not allowed to drink but at the same time regard liqueur as a wisdom-enhancing beverage. What is interesting is that in Chinese history those who drank too much were usually notorious tyrants or those who can cheat others into drinking more or manipulate power by means of drinking are regarded as smart, which may to some degree explain why in China people don't drink too much and there are not many drunkards wandering here and there on streets, though liqueur is not banned. Chinese people who tend to drink with friends or new acquaintance more likely try to show their smartness by not getting drunk when drinking while in the west people tend to drink alone and tend to get drunk which makes many western countries make it a policy not to drink before a certain age. Ancient Greeks placed value on truth and wisdom while ancient Chinese valued throne-loyalty and filial piety. Greeks seek real happiness in this world, appreciating the beauty of human bodies while Chinese try to reduce earthly desires, pursuing longevity.

Section 5 Greek Tragedy

The word tragedy is connected with the Greek word tragoi, meaning goats and Dionysus and his followers that are sometimes pictured with a goat. Tragedy, by common consent, is the most magnificent and profound mode of literary expression.

5.1 Tragedy

The word "tragedy" implies something intensely sad and terrible, but tragedies do not usually end upon a blackly pessimistic note. The evil forces in a tragedy most frequently destroy the tragic hero, but the tragedy rarely ends with evil triumphant. As tragedy is probably the most revealing comment upon humanity, it seems to show us that the downfall of the human individual is perhaps inescapable. The hero, like any man, is human. He deviates from morality or from a full knowledge of his situation and his deviation destroys him. Yet when they have to work out their punishment, they are also given hope. The quality of hope is affirmative. After every tragic action must come at the end of the play a reaffirmation of morality and a hope that tomorrow the world will be better. Sometimes from the very furnace of affliction a conviction seems borne to us that somehow, this agony counts as nothing against the heroism and love which appear in it and thrill our hearts. Sometimes we are driven to cry out that these mighty or heavenly spirits who perish are too great for the little space in which they move and that they vanish not into nothingness but into freedom.

So tragedy refers to a play dealing in an elevated, poetic style with events which depict man as the victim of destiny yet superior to it, both in grandeur and in misery. Tragedy characterized by seriousness and dignity involves a great person who experiences a reversal of fortune according to Aristotle. Greek tragedy originating in the Dionysian rites deals with life and death according to Aristotle and tragedy is the mixture of great joy and great sorrows.

5.2 Three Great Tragedians

Literary tragedy that was written out and that has passed down to us appeared first in the works of the three great Greek tragic writers — Aeschylus, Sophocles and Euripides in the 5th century BC. These writers set a standard for tragedy that has seldom been equaled and scarcely surpassed. About the plays of these men, the philosopher Aristotle wrote his *Poetics*, which, although it has come to us in fragmentary fashion, is perhaps the best and certainly the most influential piece of literary criticism that the world has ever seen.

5. 2. 1 Aeschylus

Aeschylus(525-456 BC), famous as "father of tragedy" was his own director, chief actor, designer, composer and choreographer. It was said he wrote 90 plays, of which the titles of 79 are known and only seven extant. It was he who introduced a second actor to the drama, allowing for conflicts among them. He witnessed the establishment of democracy at Athens and fought against the Persians at Marathon — the most glorious time in the darkest time. The war was so important to the Greeks and to Aeschylus himself that, upon his death around 456 BC, his epitaph commemorated his participation in the Greek victory at Marathon rather than to his success as a playwright winning the tragic prize at the City Dionysia 13 times between ca. 499 and 458.

Aeschylus made innovations in costuming and setting, making the costumes more elaborate and dramatic and making rules for Athens theatre. He was the first and also the last fighter in history. His plays in which heroes faced disasters with bravery, had a strong moral and religious emphasis, inspiring the Athenians to be brave and virtuous. He was good at making the utmost use of spectacle and color. He might well be regarded as one of the greatest of lyric poets in virtue of the beauty and strength of his choral odes. *The Prometheus Bound*[31], the earliest ever surviving tragedy shows an apparently irresolvable conflict between force and intelligence by presenting Prometheus as the powerless but defiant victim of an unjust and powerful god ruling by arbitrary laws and demanding blind obedience. *Oresteia*[32] comprising *Agamemnon*, *Libation-Bearers* and *Eumenides*, presents the murder of Agamemnon by his wife, the revenge taken by their son Orestes, the pursuit of Orestes by his mother's avenging Furies[33], his trial and acquittal at Athens and Athena's pacification. The *Oresteia* trilogy particularly concentrates on man's position in the cosmos in relation to the gods, divine law and divine punishment.

Aeschylus is very passionate which can be clearly noticed in his writing which is translated into Chinese:

他们奋勇向前，口中高喊：
为了自由，希腊的子孙们，
为了国家、子女、妻子的自由，
为了信仰自由，为了祖先的陵墓。

At the same time, he explored the evils of war though without any hesitation he jumped into the fight against Persians to protect his state. He firmly believed man's strength and right of freedom.

5.2.2 Sophocles

Sophocles(496-406 BC) was born into a wealthy family and highly educated, probably in Attica[34]. He was celebrated for the beauty of his voice and figure as a boy. His first plays were written later than those of Aeschylus and earlier than or contemporary with those of Euripides. Sophocles wrote 123 plays during the course of his life, but only seven have survived in a complete form. He influenced the development of drama, most importantly by adding a third character and thereby reducing the importance of the chorus in the presentation of the plot. He developed his characters to a greater extent than earlier playwrights such as Aeschylus and used female characters in his plays. He created greater opportunity for character development and conflicts between characters. He competed in around 30 competitions, winning perhaps 24 and never being judged lower than second place. Aeschylus won 14 competitions, and was sometimes defeated by Sophocles while Euripides won only 4 competitions. His plays include *Ajax*, *Antigone*, *The Women of Trachis*, *Oedipus the King*, *Electra* and *Oedipus at Colorus*[35].

Sophocles has the clearest vision of men and women struggling mightily against fate, suffering greatly and facing defeat with dignity. Though religion is always in the background, it is clear that the decisions and choices are made by human beings. His heroes are kings and leaders whose fates involve the health of the state, but their struggles are the inner conflicts of solitary souls.

Oedipus the King, the greatest tragedy ever written, is an example of a classic tragedy, noticeably containing an emphasis on how Oedipus's own faults contribute to the tragic hero's downfall, as opposed to having fate be the sole cause. Oedipus, a man who became the king of Thebes and was destined from birth to murder his father Laius and marry his mother Jocasta, was ordered to be killed with his feet bound by his parents who were scared by the oracle. The servant took the baby to a mountain top to die from exposure. A shepherd rescued the infant and named him Oedipus (meaning "swollen feet"). The shepherd carried the baby with him to Corinth, where Oedipus was taken in and raised in the court of the childless King Polybus of Corinth as if he were his own. As a young man in Corinth, Oedipus heard a rumor that he was not the biological son of Polybus and his wife Merope. When Oedipus questioned the King and Queen, they denied it. Still suspicious, he asked the Delphic Oracle[36] who his parents really were. The Oracle seemed to ignore this question, telling him instead that he was destined to "Mate with his own mother and shed with his own hands the blood of his own sire". Desperate to avoid his foretold fate, Oedipus left Corinth in the belief that Polybus and Merope were indeed his true parents and that, once away from them, he would never harm them. On the road to Thebes, he met Laius, his true father. Unaware of each other's identities, they quarreled and Oedipus threw him down from the chariot and killed him, thus fulfilling part of the oracle's prophecy.

Shortly after Oedipus solved the riddle of the Sphinx[37] "What is the creature that walks on four legs in the morning, two legs at noon, and three in the evening?" which had baffled many a diviner, he was rewarded for freeing the kingdom of Thebes from her curse with the kingship and the hand of Queen Dowager Jocasta, his biological mother. The prophecy was thus fulfilled, although none of the main characters knew it. Finally, when Oedipus found that the murderer was a native citizen of Thebes, brother and father to his own children and son and husband to his own mother, he plunged the long gold pins into his own eyes in despair, exiling himself for the rest of life.

Oedipus the King tells about an apparently irresolvable conflict between fate and free will. Oedipus's stabbing his eyes and exiling himself shows the limits of free will. Oedipus is a good and great man, making the huge mistake without intention. But he himself is the maker of his own tragedy. His annihilation is not caused by fate or god nor is by his fault. Instead, he destroys himself with his own strength and loyalty to Thebes. He is a man with free will. Stabbing himself blind and exiling himself are his won choices which elevate the theme both in grandeur and in misery.

Sophocles is a real gentleman. Aristophanes[38] mocks at many writers except him. The other playwrights are childish and womanish, quarreling or fighting with each other according to Aristophanes. Sophocles is conservative to some degree, trying to maintain established order and law. Freedom to him means disorder, chaos and greed which is the reality of Athens in his old age because his Athens is totally different from Aeschylus's though only 30 years later. Athens brings freedom to the world by defeating Persians but at the same time destroys herself by becoming a powerful and greedy empire.

Most of his plays reveal a serenity which his younger contemporary lack — serenity coming from triumph over suffering, not avoidance of it. Few moments in drama are more poignant than Sophocles' tragic climax. His characters are more fully rounded and his language is clearer and more incisive than that of Aeschylus. He is a stylist. You can't really appreciate him if you don't know Greek because great ideas can be translated into another language, thus spreading, but styles exist only in one language.

Power can lead any one to destruction. No power is justifiable but what is sorrowful is that facing power people tend to lose themselves.

Unlike Aeschylus who is passionate, Sophocles is serene. We can appreciate them when reading their describing the same woman with different styles in Chinese:

没有人可以这样命令我
我虽是个女人，但我要为他
掘好坟墓，亲手埋葬他！
勇气！我将找到行动的力量。
　　谁也不能阻止我。

——埃斯库罗斯

没有人为我哭泣，没有朋友为我送葬，
没有音乐送行，我走上这样的旅程。
请看我遭受的苦难，又是谁对我不公，
只因我不曾放弃那崇高的情操。

——索福克勒斯

Sophocles was so influential that Aristotle used his *Oedipus the King* as an example of perfect tragedy and Freud proposed "Oedipus Complex[39]" in modern psychiatry-analysis from the play which suggested the high esteem in which his work was held.

5.2.3 Euripides

Euripides (480-406 BC) was a modern man with ideas overstepping the time. He was the spokesman for all generations with theme in his plays sympathizing sufferings and having faith in individual value in an age which still venerated the ideal of duty towards one's fellow citizens. He was said to have written 92 plays, but few drama and a large number of fragments survived. Little was known of his life, but tradition represented him as a recluse living in a cave because of his reluctance to take an active part in civic life. He was the only person who saw what his contemporaries could not. So it was not surprising that he was the first to criticize the slavery. Athens and Sparta were fighting in his middle age when he had insight into the glory of victory of war which to him meant evil revealed in *The Trojan Women*[40]. He was also labeled as misogynist in spite of the obvious sympathy with women's rights and problems displayed, for example, in his *Medea*.[41]

The Trojan Women, regarded as the most powerful anti-war play ever written, was written by Euripides in 415 BC. The background was that after the Trojan War (1200 BC) where the Athenians had defeated the Trojans, the Trojan women lamented their fate. The war had lasted for ten years. It was fought because Paris had stolen Helen from her husband, Menelaus, the King of Athens and taken her back to Troy. Most of plays were about women, not men nor gods. The Trojan War was full of heroism and patriotism, but he ended his in *The Trojan Women* with a heartbroken old Trojan woman holding a dead child on ground.

Medea tells of the story of revenge of a woman betrayed through killing her own children which is a great challenge to the Athenian moral universe. Euripides created Medea, a helpless woman in the grip of violent emotion because he was hunted by the unforgivable cruelty and injustice of the world he was living in. He was shocked when Athens killed the men and enslaved the women and children of a small island that wanted to be neutral.

Euripides is critical, skeptical and interested less in the community than in the individuals. His realism brings tragedy down to earth by using more colloquial language, popular forms of music and characters, being interested in abnormal psychology though still drawn from myth and legend, which arouses great interest and great opposition. Some classical Athenians were already aware of tragedy's dangerously radical potential for giving voice and a sympathetic hearing to the citizen's subordinates and blamed Euripides for the decline of tragedy. Perhaps the most influential explanation for tragedy's death is the poison of Socratic reason, administered by Euripides. The decline of tragedy as a creative force is however as complex a phenomenon as its meteoric rising. The inter-textual play of innovation and repetition that we have seen as an important feature of tragedy can help us understand both the intense flowering of the genre in the 5th century BC and its subsequent fading.

Euripides was mocked in comedy because he inappropriately made " barbarian women and slaves " articulate philosophical opinions. Athenians at the 4th century BC, tortured by endless wars became pessimistic and began to question the faith. Losing the faith, they just seized the day by making more and more money, thus tragedy losing power of elevation. 120 BC, Dionysus celebration stopped.

Most of Euripides's plays deal with subjects usually considered unsuited to the stage which question traditional values such as Medea's loving her stepson and murdering her children. His dramatic method is often unclear such as causally related episodes with less poetic language, realistic characterizations and dialogue.

5.3 Characteristics of Greek Tragedy

The plays that have come down to us were all created in the Classical Period, when cities, particularly Athens, organized drama into large state-run festivals worshipping Dionysus — God of wine, fertility, rebirth and the plays themselves began to be written down and preserved as texts. Secondly, little action was presented on stage as well as little character development, with limited number of characters who changed masks to portray different roles (Aeschylus a single actor; Sophocles, two and Euripides three or more). Greek plays seem to be very simple both in plots and in characters. Just like Ancient Greek architecture, Greek drama is an art without ornament and disguise. It is simple, straightforward and sincere. This is because Greek culture created by sensible Greek intellectuals, is based on wisdom, sense and science.

Just like drama, Greek temples, with the Parthenon as an enduring symbol of Ancient Greek and Athenian democracy, are the mixture of scientific thought and sensible spirit. Indian temples are exquisitely carved, thus rich but seeming tangled. Egyptian temples are built with science but what is more impressive is the power reflected in the buildings which dwarf human beings. The architects in Egypt who were awed by super power of nature did not take the element of men into consideration when designing the huge buildings. Instead, the architects in Ancient Greece who created those world's greatest cultural monuments were artists who loved man and life, thus their buildings being perfect though simple but elegant with brilliance of human nature. To architects in Egypt and many other places, building temples was to admire the almighty power of God because they could do nothing else but to admire. But to ancient Greek architects, human beings were the real power of this world. They built temples to show their happiness of victory, the beauty of men and the power of strength.

世上奇迹有很多—却没有一个比得上人。
他能跨越海洋，哪怕飓风卷起一片白浪……
他是在荒山中潜行的万兽的主宰……
他是话语和像风一样快的思想。

For the same reason, Greek writers tended to be simple, straightforward and precise in expressing themselves. Hebrew poetry making readers feel instead of thinking, tried to arouse readers' emotion, "Asking for it, you will be given; looking for it, you will find; Knocking at the door, the door will be opened for you." In Greek style, Aeschylus expressed the same idea with one simple sentence, "Seeking, you will find it". Thucydides told us what people who had experienced the Sicilian Expedition[42] with one simple sentence too, "They have done what people can and suffered what people can imagine". Greek writers usually just set off a corner of the curtain on the stage so that the audience after being stirred could come to their own conclusion. Pindar led his lovers to the door of a room and didn't care what they would do next. Perhaps, leaving a secret was a wise way, reflecting the holiness of love which was dealt with in a totally different way by Shakespeare in *Romeo and Juliet*. For the same reason, characters in Ancient Greek drama were different from those at other periods. Just like designing their buildings, Greek playwrights tended to simplify characters that were only a part of the whole. Most themes of the plays centered on the conflict between the individual and the universe and not other personalities. Compared with characters in Shakespearean plays, characters in Greek plays were not so complicated. Let's take two protagonists — Aeschylus's Clytemnestra and Shakespearean Lady Macbeth as an example. The two protagonists were the classic representatives of evil women. But two great playwrights created their characters in a total different way. Clytemnestra who was already mad at her husband for sacrificing their daughter murdered him on his return from the Trojan War with the assistance of her lover Aegisthus and was later murdered herself by her son Orestes to avenge his father's death. Aeschylus didn't let audience know whether she had any hesitation when she presented her husband a knife instead of a robe right after his bath. Aeschylus did not care what she was thinking about because her tragedy was not caused by herself but by fate. No matter how strong and determined she was, she couldn't change anything which had been doomed. Mrs. Macbeth was as strong and determined as Clytemnestra. She even frowned upon her husband's timidity by saying that she would kill the king herself if the king didn't look like her own father. Lady Macbeth manipulated her husband by questioning his manhood. But Shakespeare created Lady Macbeth by describing a lot of her psychological activities in details. When Macbeth was to stab the king, she was restless, walking around and saying to herself. But such a strong and manipulative woman finally had the habit of sleepwalking and tried to wash off imaginary bloodstains from her hands, all the while speaking of the terrible things she knew and pressed her husband to do. Her belief that nothing could wash away the blood on her hands was an ironic reversal of her earlier claim to Macbeth that "little water clears us of this deed". Both plays contained powerful and manipulative female figures, which were created in different ways.

What causes this difference? Please think about it and we will discuss it in the following chapter.

Keep in mind that simply portraying characters is one thing and portraying characters simple is another thing. Greek drama presents us perfect examples of creating clear-cut characters by simply portraying them. Generally speaking, the British writing style makes audience imagine while the Greek style makes audience think. Anyway, drama originated from Greece because it was where people could think freely. Thirdly, a major part of the Ancient Greek drama was the chorus, who was a character in and of itself. The chorus provided a reflection on what was happening and was responsible for being the voice of the audience. It was also the character that appealed to the gods and asked them for help and guidance. Fourthly, it was competitive, which meant prizes were awarded for both actors and playwrights winning the competition. Finally, most plots were already familiar to the audience because the plays were closely associated with religion. The stories were based on myth or history.

Of course, playwrights varied from one to another which made them extinct and great. The characters they created were different too, from a superhuman hero in the plays of Aeschylus to refined, idealized characters with human problems (rather than religious themes) in the plays of Sophocles to ordinary characters with daily problems providing the transition from old to new ideas and from religion-myth to human passion in the plays of Euripides. The emotion theme of Euripides to portray man's beginning struggle not with fate and the gods, but with society, his mind and emotions was quite different from his contemporaries. He was critical and asking for democracy back by targeting religious authority and social injustice and evils.

Section 6 Greek Comedy

The origins of comedy are as obscure as those of tragedy. Comedy as an art form develops separately from tragedy and somewhat later.

Greek comedy appearing in the 3rd and 4th centuries BC, is divided by scholars into Old Comedy with politics and famous people as the object of satire (5th century BC), Middle Comedy of which individual, according to the law, is not allowed to be mocked at in literature (c. 404-c. 321 BC) and New Comedy with ordinary people's daily life as the main content (c. 320-264 BC). The sole literary remains of Old Comedy are the plays of Aristophanes. While there are no extant examples of Middle Comedy, it is conjectured that the satire, obscenity and fantasy of the earlier plays are much mitigated during this transitional period.

6.1 Aristophanes

The French Enlightenment writer Voltaire[43] once said, "Real comedy, is a vivid portrayal of a country's folly and weakness" which best defines Athenian old comedy. Reading the works of Aristophanes (446-385 BC), it seems you are reading a comic book. His works involve everything of ancient people in daily life, politics and economy, none of which can escape his mockery. His works reflect vividly the reality of his time which is totally different from that of Socrates.

Aristophanes is regarded as "Father of Comedy". He is the representative of Old Comedy. He created about 40 comedies with 11 available to us. Characterized by obscenity, political satire, fantasy and strong moral overtones, Aristophanes poked fun at anybody with their real names and anything he could think about such as Gods, men, local personalities and local events.

The Acharnians[44] with an anti-war stance was an attack on the politicians of the time when Athens was at war with Sparta and had declared a trade embargo on neighboring Megara. Dicaeopolis, a war veteran and representative of an average Athenian, was tired of war. Having failed to persuade the City Assembly to put an end to the conflict, which was patently being run for the benefit of political insiders, he declared an independent truce with the enemy and opened up his home as a sort of free-trade zone. The cause of a war is in this play:

Foe men of ours — I do not say the City (City Assembly),
Remember that — I do not say the City,
But worthless fellows, just bad money, coins
No mint has ever seen, kept on denouncing
The men of Megara, Trifles, I grant,
— Our way here — but some tipsy youngsters then
Go steal from Megara hussy there,
No better than they should be, caused the war.
For then in wrath Olympian Pericles
Thundered and lightened and confounded Greece.
Enacting laws against the Megarians
That sounded just like drinking songs ...
(我们这些人，我并不是说城邦，
请你们千万记住，我并不是说城邦，
而是说一些坏小子，假铜钱、冒牌货，
他们经常告发人卖了麦加拉小外套，
糟糕的是，有一些年轻小伙子喝醉了，
跑到麦加拉去，抢来了那个名叫西莲塔德妓女，
想不到这一点鸡毛蒜皮，居然扫了麦加拉人的面子，
惹动了他们大蒜劲儿，他们居然抢了阿斯帕西亚两个妓女，
好，为了三个娼妇，战火就在全希腊烧起来了。
我们的盖世英雄伯里克里斯(伯里克利)勃然大怒，

大发雷霆，大放闪电，震惊了全希腊；

他拟出一道命令，读起来就像一首酒令歌……）

The Frogs, written in 405 BC is a comedy that asks "How can Athens be saved?". *Lysistrata*[45], another anti-war play, tells of helpless and powerless women who suggest withholding sex from men that wage war. *Clouds* mocks at intellectuals like Socrates walking in cloud. Some people think Aristophanes represents both the Old Comedy and the Middle Comedy. His works also include *Knights*, *Wasps*, *Peace*, *Birds*, *Women at the Festival* and *Women in Parliament*[46]. His satire about politics, religion, morals, philosophy and arts reflects his insight into the reality of his country — deterioration which under his pen shows the stupidity and greed of men not only in his time but also at many other times of history.

6.2 Menander

Most extant examples of New Comedy were from the works of Menander(342-291 BC) who was regarded as the representative of the New Comedy. His comedies, little of which survived despite his popularity, were realistic and elegantly written, often revolving around a love-interest plot. In the New Comedy, the fiercely personal satire of real individuals disappeared and so also, to a large extent, did the Chorus. The characters of New Comedy were types rather than individuals and the plots tended to follow a certain narrow formula. New Comedy was important, however because of its great influence on the Roman dramatists Plautus and Terence[47], and through them, on our entire comic tradition. Menander was praised most highly by ancient critics for his fidelity to nature and the significant contribution to the transition from Greek to Roman comedy.

The Grouch[48] is the only one play in a relatively complete form. Menander was drowned when swimming. People can understand him and his works through the comedies of Plautus and Terence, both of whom borrowed a lot from him.

Section 7 Legacy of Greek Culture

As one of the sources of Western literature and culture, Greek drama, especially tragedy has great influence on literature all over the world.

7.1 Characteristics of Greek Thought

Western philosophy, tragedy and history started with the Greeks. What is it about the Greeks that make them so influential in the development of human thought? There are three very characteristic aspects of Greek culture that lead them to such fruitful results in so many aspects of life.

7.1.1 Curiosity

Firstly, the Greeks were very curious. Most nations in antiquity had some form of explanation for why things were as they were and on the whole people took the world for granted. But this was not the case for the Greeks. They were strongly interested in abstract questions that were not raised by others. Where did the world come from? What was the purpose of human existence? What was the best way to organize human society? This sort of inquiry never appealed much to the Roman mind. The Romans were preoccupied with conquering the whole world.

7.1.2 Power of Observation

The second characteristic of the Greeks was acuity of observation. This took place on two levels. The Greeks were keen observers of the natural world. On another level, the Greeks were aware of the variety of human institutions. This conception encouraged the Greeks to come up with their own explanations for why things were as they were and to attempt to improve upon the present state of things. The Greeks were highly intellectual, using a keen power of observation to examine the world as it was, but at the same time building elaborate theories to "explain" the world even when observable reality indicated the contrary.

7.1.3 Reliance on the Power of Reasoning

Finally, a salient characteristic of the Ancient Greeks was a wide respect for human reason and an attempt to use it as a vehicle to explain existence. On the one hand, this meant that reason was used to interpret rigorously the facts which the Greeks observed. On the other hand, the Greeks had a tendency to use abstract reasoning in astonishing disregard of observable reality. Abstract reasoning was used to reach conclusions at variance with observable reality and thus it was concluded on the basis of preconceived notions that the reality they saw was a kind of figment. But really their establishment of the modern philosophical mode of thinking was an astonishing feat in itself.

7.2 Impacts of Tragedy

Tragedy, works of art that issued a call to reflection upon our natural world in democratic Athens witnessed the complete interdependence of religion and democracy, seeking to teach citizens about the inevitability of conflict and the danger of flawed responses to it. The tragic view of politics that accepted conflict and uncertainty as an universal reality and an optimistic perspective that saw conflict as self-dissolving were of great value to man. Namely "the elevating and purifying" power of tragedy could make people accept conflict and uncertainty with dignity and an optimistic perspective. All the plays of great Greek playwrights tried to elevate audience, teaching them to be strong when facing challenge with heroism.

Thus the Greeks were the fountainhead of our modern way of viewing the world. Human reason could be used to interpret human affairs in light of a logical human development. This view was passed on to the Romans and in late antiquity the theology of the Christian church was fused with this tradition of pagan rationalism and humanism. This made medieval Western Christianity much less abstractly theological than would otherwise have been the case. During the renaissance, when direct knowledge of Greek texts was revived in the West, the Greeks exerted a more direct influence on Western thinking. It is hard to underestimate the significance of Greek thought on the modern world.

7.3 Ancient Tragedy at Present Culture and Picture

The plays of one ancient city 2,500 years ago by just 4 playwrights have had a profound effect on the development of all subsequent Western literature. Greek tragedy grew in popularity throughout the Enlightenment, where the reading of ancient drama was part of a good classical education and Aristotle's *Poetics* became a standard text for the construction of well-made tragedies.

7.3.1 Different Versions of Oedipus

Tragedy in the 16th century had a far more important role in the teaching of rhetoric and morality than in theatrical praxis. Looking at a group of versions from the 17th and 18th centuries, it was easy to find a concerted effort to improve what seemed implausible or repugnant in Sophocles' treatment of the subject. Pierre Corneille's[49] *Oedipe*, *The Oedipus* of John Dryden and Nathaniel Lee[50] and Voltaires' *Oedipe*, though sharing a number of neoclassical features, had very different emphases. In the 20th century, Greek tragedy began to regain its political form with productions such as Jean Anouilh's *Antigone*[51], produced in

Paris in 1942 when the city was under Nazi control and was taken by the Germans and Athol Fugard's[52] *The Island*, written in South Africa in 1973 about the story of political prisoners who staged Sophocles' *Antigone*. Greek tragedy and comedy had undergone something of a renaissance in the late 20th and the early 21st century, with productions all over the world. Artists restaged, translated, interpreted and deconstructed these works, often finding striking modern parallels or new ways to create on-stage ritual. While there was certainly not one way to stage a Greek play for modern audience, people were constantly drawn to those great works that stood at the beginning of Western drama and still seem to articulate so much about the human condition.

7. 3. 2 Orestes and Electra[53] in the 20th Century

Eugene O'Neill's *Mourning Becomes Electra*[54], T. S. Eliot's[55] *The Family Reunion* and Jean-Paul Sartre's[56] *Les Mouches* (the Flies) made clear how directly Greek tragic form and matter might be adapted to particular ideological ends.

O'Neill's sprawling trilogy was an Oresteia set in New England at the end of the Civil War and was at least superficially "Freudian" in its themes of love and hate within the family. Eliot's verse drama was a brittle drawing-room version of Aeschylus's *Eumernides*[57] with a specifically Christian eschatological slant. Sartre's play, the only one with the traditional characters in a more or less traditional Greek setting was at once an exposition of the existentialist ethics of freedom and a covert (not open) call to political resistance in occupied France.

7. 3. 3 Greek Tragedy and Two World Wars

Tragedy returned to the European stage with a special prestige conferred by its antiquity and its status as the loftiest form of poetic discourse. Keats[58] hoped that his reputation would at last be made by producing a tragedy. The production in British and American universities established a trend throughout the English-speaking academic world. It was in France that a significant professional production of *Oedipus the King* was staged, which laid the foundations for the eventual pre-eminence of the figure of Oedipus in Europe in the 1st half of the 20th century. W. B. Yeats[59] determined to stage Sophocle's play at the Abbey Theatre[60] in Dublin shortly after it opened at the end of the year 1904. It was not until 1926 after Yeats had completed his own version, that the Abbey Theatre finally staged Sophocle's *Oedipus the King*. So clearly could Euripides' play articulate the concerns of the war-weary Western world that it was decided in 1919, when the Versailles negotiations were taking place, to mount a production in cinema in the Cowley Road in Oxford to coincide with the Oxford Conference of the League of Nation's. In the immediate post-war period, there were a number of matinee performances of the play at the Old Vic[61], where the spirit of despair of the Trojan women struck a deep chord in the war-torn nation's psyche. Immediately after the war, *Oedipus the King* again became the Greek tragedy most responsive to current concerns and needs.

At the Deutsches Theater in Berlin at the end of 1946, the play reflected the contemporary questions of guilt and responsibility. In marked contrast, the London production at the Old Vic in 1945 (in the same month that the war ended) used the Yeats translations to highlight the sufferings of an isolated tragic hero.

More recently, O'Neill and Arthur Miller[62] staked a good part of their reputations on the possibility of a tragedy. It would perhaps be hard to find a playwright today for whom tragedy still has that kind of appeal, but there is nevertheless plenty of evidence that the old bones still live. Greek tragedy has begun to reach vast audiences through film and television.

Since the Second World War, however, the interest in Greek tragedy has become a world-wide phenomenon. It was undoubtedly the post-war Japanese production that celebrated this internationalism most fruitfully. Following the Second World War, a generation of students at Tokyo University turned deliberately towards Greek tragedy as the fountainhead of the Western humanist tradition in their search for the values of freedom and democracy that had eluded their own culture. They performed a number of Greek tragedies in translation in front of large audiences with formally cemented form and Eastern perspective. The student productions mounted at Tokyo University during the late 1950s and the 1960s were directly informed by Japan's war experiences.

Britain had multilingual versions of 38 Shakespeare's plays during the Olympic Games in 2012 as part of its culture Olympia. Now Shakespeare is clamed to belong to the world, showing the everlasting influence of literature on the power of a nation.

重难点解读

[1] **Nile and the Tigris-Euphrates：**尼罗河和底格里斯-幼发拉底河流域。尼罗河是世界第一长河，源于非洲东北部布隆迪高原，也是世界上流经国家最多的国际性河流之一，流经卢旺达、布隆迪、坦桑尼亚、肯尼亚、乌干达、扎伊尔、苏丹、埃塞俄比亚和埃及等9个国家，全长6 600多公里，最终注入地中海。尼罗河是由卡盖拉河、白尼罗河、青尼罗河三条河流汇流而成，其下游谷地三角洲是人类文明的最早发源地之一，古埃及诞生在此。至今，埃及仍有96%的人口和绝大部分工农业生产集中在尼罗河沿岸平原和三角洲地区，被视为埃及的生命线。底格里斯-幼发拉底河水系，包含了底格里斯河和幼发拉底河，两河的源头在土耳其东部山间，相距不到80公里，沿东南方向流经叙利亚北部和伊拉克，注入波斯湾。其界定的这一地区的下游以美索不达米亚知名，为文明摇篮之一。幼发拉底河全长约2 800公里，底格里斯河全长约1 900公里。

[2] **Athens：**雅典。希腊首都，位于巴尔干半岛南端，三面环山，

一面傍海，西南距爱琴海法利龙湾8公里，属亚热带地中海气候，是希腊经济、财政、工业、政治和文化中心。它是欧盟商业中心之一，也是欧洲第八大城市。市区人口330万，加上郊区人口共有380万。雅典是世界上最古老的城市之一，有记载的历史就长达3 000多年，是希腊历史上最辉煌的城邦，也是欧洲文明的源头。

[3] ***Poetics***：《诗学》。亚里士多德的作品，他在《诗学》里表达了对艺术及悲剧的观点，认为艺术的本质是模仿；而悲剧是对于一个严肃、完整、有一定长度的行动的模仿。有人认为失传的第二卷可能是讨论喜剧的。《诗学》是最早的一部文艺理论著作。

[4] **the Classical and Hellenistic ages**：古典希腊时期和希腊化时代。古典希腊时期是古希腊的一个历史时期，大约为公元前五世纪到前四世纪(一般定义为雅典最后一位僭主被推翻的年份，即公元前510年至亚历山大大帝去世时的公元前323年)。它前承古风时期，后启希腊化时代。古典希腊时期的文明影响了后来的古罗马文明，并对整个西方文明产生了重大影响，同时也对现代政治、艺术、科学、文学、哲学等方面产生了深远的影响。希腊化时代通常被认为是希腊古典时代和罗马文化间的过渡时期，甚至与辉煌的希腊古典时代相比，被认为文化上呈现下降或衰退的趋势。希腊化时期的特点是新的一波希腊殖民活动，并主要以埃及和西亚的各希腊化王国内建立殖民城市为主。

[5] **Thucydides**：修昔底德(约公元前460/455—前400/395)。古希腊历史学家，代表作是《伯罗奔尼撒战争史》。该著较翔实地记述了公元前411年以前的战争经过以及当时人对政治事件的一些看法，为研究古希腊历史提供了重要资料。

[6] **the Peloponnesian War**：伯罗奔尼撒战争。是提洛同盟与伯罗奔尼撒联盟之间的战争，战争的双方是雅典和斯巴达。该战争使雅典走出了全盛时期，结束了希腊的民主时代。

[7] ***Iliad* and *Odyssey***：《伊利亚特》和《奥德赛》。荷马(约公元前九世纪至前八世纪)，相传为古希腊的游吟诗人，生于小亚细

亚，失明，创作了史诗《伊利亚特》和《奥德赛》，两者统称《荷马史诗》。古希腊人一直将荷马史诗视作希腊文化的精华，将荷马视作民族的骄傲，但丁更称荷马为“诗人之王”。《伊利亚特》长15 693行，叙述希腊联军围攻小亚细亚的城市特洛伊的故事。《奥德赛》共12 105行，叙述伊塔卡王奥德修斯在攻陷特洛伊后归国途中十年漂泊的故事。

[8] **Pindar**：品达(约公元前 518—前 438)。古希腊抒情诗人，有“抒情诗人之魁”之称，被后世的学者认为是九大抒情诗人之首。他的作品藏于亚历山大图书馆，被汇编成册。希腊盛行体育竞技，竞技活动又和敬神的节日结合在一起，品达在诗中歌颂奥林匹克运动会以及其他希腊运动会上的竞技胜利者和他们的城邦。他写过 17 卷诗，只传下 4 卷。

[9] **Quintilian**：昆体良。古罗马帝国时期的教育大师和修辞术泰斗，也是现代西方大学的古代奠基人。

[10] **Horace**：贺拉斯(Quintus Horatius Flaccus，公元前 65—前 8)。罗马帝国奥古斯都统治时期著名的诗人、批评家、翻译家，代表作有《诗艺》等。他是古罗马文学“黄金时代”的代表人之一。

[11] **Mesopotamia**：美索不达米亚。古希腊对两河流域的称谓，意为“(两条)河流之间的地方”，这两条河指的是幼发拉底河和底格里斯河，两河之间的美索不达米亚平原上产生和发展的古文明称为两河文明或美索不达米亚文明，大体位于现今的伊拉克，其存在时间从公元前6 000年到公元前 1 世纪，是人类最早的文明。由于这两条河流每年泛滥，所以下游土壤肥沃，富含有机物和矿物质，但同时该地气候干旱缺水，所以当地人在公元前6 000年就开始运用灌溉技术，灌溉为当地带来了大规模的人力协作和农业丰产。经过数千年的演化，美索不达米亚于公元前2 900年左右形成了成熟的文字，还有众多的城市及周围的农业社会。

[12] **Solon**：梭伦。古雅典政治家和立法家，名列希腊“七贤”之一。

[13] **Athena**：雅典娜。雅典娜是古希腊神话宙斯和墨提斯的女儿，以智慧、技艺及战争女神而著名。

[14] **Isaiah**：以赛亚。希伯来的大预言家，通常被认为是写作先知中最伟大的一位。

[15] **Gautama Buddha**：悉达多·乔达摩。古印度著名思想家，佛教创始人，被后世尊称为释迦牟尼佛，还会称呼其为佛祖(佛教祖师)，出生于今尼泊尔南部。Buddha 为“觉悟者”之意。

[16] **Confucius and Lao Tse**：孔子和老子。孔子(公元前 551—前 479)，孔氏，名丘，字仲尼。祖籍宋国(今河南商丘市夏邑县)，春秋末期鲁国陬邑(今山东曲阜市南辛镇)人，春秋末期著名的思想家、政治家、教育家，为儒家学派创始人。他开创了私人讲学的风气，被后世统治者尊为孔圣人、至圣、至圣先师、万世师表、文宣皇帝、文宣王，相传其弟子三千，贤弟子七十二人，曾带领部分弟子周游列国，修订《诗》、《书》、《礼》、《乐》，序《周易》，撰写《春秋》。其弟子及其再传弟子把孔子及其弟子的言行语录和思想记录下来，整理编成著名的儒家学派经典《论语》。老子，姓李名耳(约公元前 571—前 471)，字聃，华夏族，楚国苦县厉乡曲仁里人，中国古代伟大的哲学家和思想家、道家学派创始人，被唐朝帝王追认为李姓始祖，存世有《道德经》(又称《老子》)，其作品的精华是朴素的辩证法，主张无为而治，其学说对中国哲学发展具有深刻影响。在道教中，老子被尊为道教始祖。老子与后世的庄子并称老庄 。

[17] **Socrates**：苏格拉底 (公元前 469—前 399)。古希腊著名思想家、哲学家、教育家、公民陪审员，他和他的学生柏拉图，以及柏拉图的学生亚里士多德并称为“古希腊三贤”，更被后人广泛认为是西方哲学的奠基者。身为雅典的公民，据记载苏格拉底最后被雅典法庭以侮辱雅典神和腐蚀雅典青年思想之罪名判处死刑，尽管他曾获得逃亡的机会，但苏格拉底仍选择饮下毒汁而死，因为他认为逃亡只会进一步破坏雅典法

律的权威，同时也担心他逃亡后雅典将再没有好的导师可以教育人们了。

[18] **Cicero**：西塞罗(Marcus Tullius Cicero，公元前106—前43)。罗马共和国晚期的哲学家、政治家、律师、作家、雄辩家。

[19] **Olympia**：奥林匹亚。古希腊的圣地，遗址在伯罗奔尼撒半岛西部的山谷里，阿尔菲奥斯河北岸(距河口16公里)，伊利亚州境内，具体位置为北纬37°38′18″，东经21°37′51″。距首都雅典以西约190千米，坐落在克洛诺斯树木繁茂、绿草如茵的山麓。

[20] **Thespis**：泰斯庇斯。被认为是古希腊最早的演员。

[21] **Dithyramb**：酒神颂歌。古希腊盛行的一种赞颂酒神狄俄尼索斯的祭祀歌曲。这种歌曲感情热烈、奔放，演唱者常常打破固有的形式，即兴发挥，也用于赞颂英雄或神祇。后来“酒神赞歌”喻指狂热的诗歌、演说、文章等。

[22] **Parthenon**：帕提侬神庙。希腊用以祭祀雅典娜女神的神庙，兴建于公元前5世纪的雅典卫城，现存至今最重要的古典希腊时代建筑物，长约69.49米，宽约30.78米，耸立于3层台阶上，玉阶巨柱，画栋镂檐，遍饰浮雕，蔚为壮观。整个庙宇由凿有凹槽的46根大理石柱环绕。一般被认为是多立安柱式发展的顶端；雕像装饰是古希腊艺术的顶点，此外还被尊为古希腊与雅典民主制度的象征，是举世闻名的文化遗产之一。

[23] **tetralogies**：四联剧。三悲一喜，悲剧歌队在他们露出真面目的莎提尔剧出现之前，更换三次服装，也就是演出三部悲剧，这样与随后的莎提尔剧一起就组成了完整的古希腊四联剧。

[24] **Dionysia**：酒神节。大型的祭祀酒神的宗教节日。早在公元前7世纪，古希腊就有“大酒神节”(Great Dionysia)。每年3月为表示对酒神狄奥尼索斯的敬意，都要在雅典举行这项活动。到公元前6世纪左右，酒神赞歌开始享有盛誉，并发展成由50名成年男子和男孩组成的合唱队，在科林斯的狄奥尼索斯大赛上表演竞赛的综合艺术形式。伟大的酒神赞歌时代也是

伟大的希腊抒情合唱诗盛行的时代，并导致了古希腊戏剧、音乐艺术的发展。古希腊的悲剧、喜剧和羊人剧都源于大酒神节。

[25] **Euripides**：欧里庇得斯。与埃斯库罗斯和索福克勒斯并称为希腊三大悲剧大师，一生共创作 90 多部作品，保留至今的有 18 部，如《美狄亚》等。

[26] **Aphrodite**：阿芙洛狄忒。古希腊神话中的爱与美之女神，在罗马神话中称为维纳斯。

[27] **Gao Tse**：告子。战国时思想家，名不详，一说名不害，曾受教墨子之门，善口辩，讲仁义，后与孟轲论人性问题，认为“生之谓性”，“食色，性也”。人性和水一样，“水无分于东西”，性也“无分于善不善”，其言论见《孟子·告子》篇。

[28] **Gao Mei**：高媒。中国的媒神，亦称“皋媒禖”(媒，婚姻的古称)、“神媒”、“女媒”等，为专司爱情、婚姻、生殖之神。

[29] **Shennong**：神农。神农帝即炎帝(神农氏)。炎帝，烈山氏，号神农氏，又称赤帝，华夏始祖之一，与黄帝并称为中华始祖，中国远古时期部落首领。距今6 000年至5 500年左右，生于宝鸡姜水之岸(一说湖北随州厉山)。

[30] **Martin Luther**：马丁·路德(1483—1546)。16 世纪欧洲宗教改革倡导者，基督教新教路德宗创始人。2005 年 11 月 28 日，德国电视二台投票评选最伟大的德国人，路德名列第 2 位，仅次于康拉德·阿登纳。

[31] ***The Prometheus Bound***：《被缚的普罗米修斯》。是埃斯库罗斯的代表作，作品反映的是天神普罗米修斯盗来火种送给人类，激怒了众神之主宙斯，宙斯命令威力神和火神将普罗米修斯钉在高加索的悬崖上，暴露在雨雪风霜和烈日炙烤之中，以警告他以后不要再对人类滥施同情。

[32] ***Oresteia***：《俄瑞斯忒亚》。埃斯库罗斯根据神话故事改编的戏剧，戏剧共三部，被称为《俄瑞斯忒亚》三部曲，三部分别为《阿伽门农》、《奠酒人》、《欧墨尼得》(《复仇女神》或《报仇神》)。

[33] **Furies**：复仇女神。以清算罪恶为职责，被描绘成庄严、美丽的女郎。

[34] **Attica**：阿提卡。古希腊中东部一地区。

[35] ***Ajax***，***Antigone***，***The Women of Trachis***，***Oedipus the King***，***Electra* and *Oedipus at Colorus***：《埃阿斯》、《安提戈涅》、《特拉基斯少女》、《俄狄浦斯王》、《埃勒克特拉》(迈锡尼王阿伽门农与妻子克吕泰涅斯特拉的女儿)和《俄狄浦斯王在科洛诺斯》。

[36] **Delphic Oracle**：德尔菲神谕。德尔菲在距雅典150公里的帕那索斯深山里，德尔菲神庙是世界闻名的著名古迹，主要由阿波罗太阳神庙、雅典女神庙、剧场、体育训练场和运动场组成，其中最有名的是古希腊象征光明和青春并且主管音乐、诗歌及医药、畜牧的太阳神阿波罗的神庙。古希腊人认为，德尔菲是地球的中心，是“地球的肚脐”。德尔菲神谕是古希腊有名的预言，在德尔菲神庙进入一种类似昏迷的通神状态中，由别人问问题，而由皮提亚女祭师(Pythia)传达阿波罗神的神谕。德尔菲神庙之最重要者，乃是它作为晓示神谕的地位。它的预言和指示，深刻地影响了希腊世界的文化和历史。

[37] **Sphinx**：斯芬克斯，狮身人面像。古埃及人建造于金字塔旁的巨大雕像，神话中传说它会出谜语来为难人。最为著名的谜语便是什么动物早晨四条腿，中午两条腿，晚上三条腿走路，腿最多时最无能。谜底为人。

[38] **Aristophanes**：阿里斯托芬。古希腊早期喜剧代表作家，雅典公民，写了44部喜剧，有“喜剧之父”之称。

[39] **Oedipus Complex**：恋母情结。指在精神分析中以本能冲动力为核心的一种欲望。通俗地讲是指男性的一种心理倾向，就是无论到什么年纪，总是服从和依恋母亲，在心理上还没有断乳(Electra complex：恋父情结)。西格蒙德·弗洛伊德(Sigmund Freud，1856—1939)是奥地利犹太心理学家、精神病医师，精神分析学派创始人。曾在维也纳大学医学院学习

并获医学博士学位，后作为临床精神病学家私人开业，早期从事催眠治疗工作，后创用精神分析法。他把人的心理分为意识、潜意识和无意识(又称下意识，包括被压抑的无意识和潜伏的无意识)，认为：存在于无意识中的性本能(libido)是人的心理的基本动力，是支配个人命运、决定社会发展的力量；并把人格区分为自我、本我和超我三个部分。其学说被西方哲学和人文学科各领域吸收和运用，主要著作有《梦的解析》、《日常生活的精神病理学》、《精神分析引论》、《图腾与禁忌》和《精神分析引论新编》等。

[40] ***The Trojan Women***：《特洛伊女人》。欧里庇得斯的作品。

[41] ***Medea***：《美狄亚》。欧里庇得斯的悲剧。

[42] **Sicilian Expedition**：西西里远征。是伯罗奔尼撒战争中规模最大、最为著名的一次军事行动，无疑是公元前415年至前413年间雅典对西西里岛上以叙拉古为首的诸城邦所发动的一次极其重要的远征。其失败导致雅典帝国由盛转衰。

[43] **Voltaire**：伏尔泰。本名弗朗索瓦-马利·阿鲁埃(François-Marie Arouet，1694—1778)，伏尔泰是笔名，法国文学家、哲学家、史学家，也是18世纪法国资产阶级启蒙运动的旗手，被誉为“法兰西思想之王”、“法兰西最优秀的诗人”和“欧洲的良心”。

[44] ***The Acharnians***：《阿卡奈人》。阿里斯托芬第一部成功的喜剧。

[45] ***Lysistrata***：《吕西斯特拉塔》。阿里斯托芬的喜剧。

[46] ***Knights*, *Wasps*, *Peace*, *Birds*, *Women at the Festival* and *Women in Parliament***：《骑士》、《马蜂》、《和平》、《鸟》、《地母节妇女》和《公民大会妇女》。

[47] **Plautus and Terence**：普拉图斯和泰伦斯。普劳图斯(Titus Maccius Plautus，约公元前254—前184)是古罗马第一个有完整作品传世的喜剧作家，其喜剧是现在仍保存完好的拉丁语文学最早的作品，也是音乐剧最早的先驱者之一，古代以他的名义流传的剧本有130部，现存21部喜剧，代表作有《吹

牛军人》、《撒谎者》、《俘虏》等。泰伦斯(Publius Terentius Afer，公元前190—前159)，罗马著名喜剧家，共写有6部剧本，全部保存下来：《安德罗斯女子》、《自责者》、《阉奴》、《福尔弥昂》、《两兄弟》和《婆母》。

[48] ***The Grouch***：《恨世者》。古希腊新喜剧，是米南德的早期作品。

[49] **Pierre Corneille**：皮埃尔·高乃依(1606—1684)。17世纪上半叶法国古典主义悲剧代表作家，法国古典主义戏剧的奠基人。著有喜剧《梅丽特》，悲剧《梅德》、《熙德》，《贺拉斯》(*Oedipe*)、《西拿》和《波里厄特》等。

[50] **John Dryden and Nathaniel Lee**：约翰·德莱顿和纳撒尼尔·李。德莱顿是英国诗人、剧作家、文学批评家。一生为贵族写作，为君王和复辟王朝歌功颂德，被封为“桂冠诗人”。纳撒尼尔·李是17世纪英国剧作家。他们二人合作改编古希腊剧作家索福克勒斯的《俄狄浦斯王》。

[51] **Jean Anouilh's *Antigone***：让·阿努伊的《安提戈涅》。让·阿努伊是法国剧作家。《安提戈涅》是古希腊悲剧作家索福克勒斯公元前442年的一部作品，让·阿努伊改编该剧。

[52] **Athol Fugard**：阿索尔·富加德。南非剧作家、演员及导演，被认为是南非的灵魂人物。《岛》是其作品之一。父亲可能是爱尔兰血统的白人，母亲是南非荷兰人后裔。

[53] **Orestes and Electra**：俄瑞斯忒斯和厄勒克特拉。他们是迈锡尼(Mycenae)王阿伽门农(Agamemnon)与妻子克吕泰涅斯特拉(Clytemnestra)的儿子和女儿。

[54] **Eugene O'Neill's *Mourning Becomes Electra***：尤金·奥尼尔的《悲悼》。尤金·奥尼尔是美国现代戏剧之父，表现主义文学代表作家，其主要作品有《琼斯皇》、《毛猿》、《天边外》等，于1936年获诺贝尔文学奖。《悲悼》，是一部现代心理悲剧，该剧以古希腊经典剧作家埃斯库罗斯的《俄瑞斯忒亚》和索福克勒斯、欧里庇得斯的《厄勒克特拉》为蓝本，将叔本华的悲观主义、尼采的悲剧观、弗洛伊德以及荣格的精神分析等理

论作为其悲剧思想的主要来源，堪称古希腊神话模式同现代哲学、心理学相结合的典范，剧中所表达的多重戏剧冲突为该剧增添了不朽的艺术魅力。

[55] **T. S Eliot**：T. S. 艾略特。全名托马斯·斯特恩斯·艾略特(Thomas Stearns Eliot)，一般简称其为艾略特，诗人、评论家、剧作家，现代西方开一代诗风的先驱。《家庭团聚》为其诗剧之一。

[56] **Jean-Paul Sartre**：让·保罗·萨特(1905—1980)。法国20世纪最重要的哲学家之一，法国无神论存在主义的主要代表人物，西方社会主义最积极的鼓吹者之一，一生中拒绝接受任何奖项，包括1964年的诺贝尔文学奖。优秀文学家、戏剧家、评论家和社会活动家，《苍蝇》(*Les Mouches*)是他1943年的戏剧作品，他还是20世纪70年代女权运动的重要理论家西蒙娜·德·波伏娃的伴侣，他们的哲学思想非常相近又各有千秋。

[57] ***Eumernides***：埃斯库罗斯的《复仇女神》。是其《俄瑞斯忒亚》三部曲的第三部，第一部《阿伽门农》，第二部《奠酒人》。

[58] **Keats**：约翰·济慈(1795—1821)。杰出的英诗作家之一，也是浪漫派的主要成员。

[59] **W. B. Yeats**：威廉·巴特勒·叶芝(William Butler Yeats, 1865—1939)。爱尔兰诗人、剧作家和散文家，著名的神秘主义者，是“爱尔兰文艺复兴运动”的领袖，也是艾比剧院(Abbey Theatre)的创建者之一。

[60] **the Abbey Theatre**：艾比(阿贝)剧院。爱尔兰著名剧院，全名为“都柏林艾比剧院”。1904年建于爱尔兰首府都柏林，1924年正式成为国家剧院，1951年焚于火灾。20世纪初，爱尔兰在欧洲大陆影响下，掀起了一场“爱尔兰文艺复兴”运动，戏剧繁荣，出现了一批剧作家、剧团和剧院，艾比剧院是最有影响的一个。该剧院的前身是W. G. 费所领导的爱尔兰民族戏剧剧团和由诗人叶芝、剧作家格雷戈里夫人等所创立的爱尔兰民族文学剧院，后来两家合并，成立了艾比剧院，作为

实验阵地。艾比剧院坚持演出叶芝、辛格等剧作家的具有本民族特色的爱尔兰戏剧，促进了凯尔特语剧本的创作和演出，使艾比剧院在全欧洲赢得了声誉，剧院被焚后，新艾比剧院于 1966 年 7 月重新开幕。

[61] **Old Vic**：老维克剧院。英国最著名的剧院之一，位于伦敦的滑铁卢桥路，前身是 1818 年落成的科堡剧院，1941 年由于严重受损而被迫关闭，1950 年重新启用。剧院不但演出了大量的、以莎士比亚戏剧为主的古典名剧，其所属的剧团还造就了许多杰出的导演和演员，1963 年，老维克剧院成为国家剧院的临时所在地。1979 年获老维克剧院名称的剧团曾到中国访问，演出了莎士比亚悲剧《哈姆雷特》。

[62] **Arthur Miller**：亚瑟·米勒（1915—2005）。美国剧作家，一生著有大量的戏剧评论，还写过十几部广播剧和电影剧本，以及报告文学和短篇小说。代表作为《推销员之死》、《都是我的儿子》等。2005 年 2 月 10 日深夜在位于美国康涅狄格州的家中病逝，享年 89 岁。

Chapter 2　Western Drama Development

The Roman preference for spectacle, the world domination and the Christian suppression of drama led to a virtual cessation of dramatic production during the Roman Empire and after the Roman Empire — Medieval Age when religion became the dominance of people's daily life.

Section 1　Roman Drama

When the world was ruled by Rome from England to Africa and from Syria to Spain, one in every four people on earth lived and died under Roman law. The Roman Empire in the 1st century AD mixed sophistication with brutality and could suddenly lurch from civilization strength and power to terror, tyranny and greed.

1.1　Rome and Romans

For centuries, the she-wolf[1] has been one of Rome's most powerful symbol, which to some degree, reflected the characteristics of Rome — the world domination.

According to Roman legend, the city was founded in 753 BC by

The Capitoline Wolf

Romulus and Remus, twin sons of the god Mars and a Latin Princess. The legend of Rome's founding was that the twin brothers Romulus and Remus, whose grandfather was the rightful king of Alba but had been deposed by their uncle, were abandoned by the river Tiber which was in flood. They were sucked and raised by a wolf and later were found and brought up by a swineherd. Romulus and Remus grew up into strong young men and uncovered the secret. With their own followers and their grandfather's men, they deposed their great-uncle and restored their grandfather to his throne who gave them the seven hills along the Tiber River as a gift. The twin brothers did choose different sites as their settle place and decided to seek omens for which would be better. The twin brothers fought about where to found a city and in a fit of rage, Romulus killed his brother and finished establishing a new city with his own name Rome, thus becoming the king.

In reality Rome developed because of its strategic location and its fertile soil. Rome was built on 7 rolling hills at a curve on the Tiber River, near the center of the Italian peninsula. It was midway between the Alps and Italy's southern tip. Rome also was near the midpoint of the

Mediterranean Sea. Little was known about the earliest peoples in Italy which, unlike Greece, was poor in mineral resources and surprisingly lacked useful labors but with large amount of fertile land. It was sure that Rome experienced waves of migrations from Africa, Spain and France etc. The Latins were farmers and shepherds who wandered into Italy across Alps around 1,000 BC. They settled on either side of the Tiber River. These settlers were the first Romans. Between 750 BC and 600 BC, Greek settlers established about 50 colonies on the coasts of southern Italy and Sicily[2]. The cities became prosperous and commercially active. They brought all of Italy, including Rome into closer contact with Greek civilization. In 1870, Italians attacked Rome and the next year Rome became the capital of Italy.

1.2 Roman Drama (100 BC—476 AD)

Roman cultural achievements in art, literature, philosophy and religion were greatly influenced by the Greek culture and showed very little originality. The Romans themselves had little interest in serious dramatic endeavors, being drawn toward sensationalism and spectacle. The earliest Roman dramatic attempts were simply translations from the Greek. They just imitated and actually copied much from the Greeks such as changing the names of the Greek gods and goddesses to Roman names. Dionysus became Bacchus, Athena, Minerva and Zues Jupiter[3], etc. So it was not surprising that Roman drama never approached the height of the Greek drama. Roman tragedy produced little worth. Fortunately, there was a better judgment on the comedies with farce as the dominant theatre form which was heavily influenced by Old Greek Comedy and the so-called Middle or New Comedy of Menander. Available evidence indicated that the Romans produced comedies and few, if any, tragedies in their theatre.

Drama was given mostly at harvest and wedding celebrations. The favorite entertainment for Romans were chariot races, athletic games, gladiatorial and boxing contests in arenas. For example, Colosseum[4] which was used to host gladiatorial shows as well as a variety of other events became today's one of Rome's most popular tourist attractions.

1.3 Roman Playwrights

Roman tragedy produced little of worth. Seneca[5], philosopher and statesman who was exiled, basically imitated models from the Greek tragedy playwrights with the reflection of court conflict (related to his political life). His tragedies, noted primarily for their inflated rhetoric, were gloomy and lurid, emphasizing the sensational aspects of Greek myth. Seneca became an important influence on Renaissance tragedy.

A better judgment might be passed on the comedies of Plautus and Terence. Plautus, writing comic farces in Latin, incorporated native Roman elements into the plots and themes of ancient Greek New Comedy, especially Menander, producing plays characterized by farce, intrigue, romance and sentiment. He usually depicted characters of a single emotional bent with one-dimensional stereotypes, with *The Menaechmi*[6] as his representative.

Terence, another famous comic dramatist, borrowed much from Greek New Comedy too. Terence was a more polished stylist who wrote for and about the upper class and dispensed with the element of farce. So his plays were less entertaining and more suited to cultivate audience with clear, simple and finished style. Characters in his plays contained a more lifelike human dimension and were of a slightly more complex emotional level. He was read and imitated by many writers of later generations.

1.4 Roman Legacy

Roman Empire, spreading over three continents, lasted for 2,078 years with the Eastern Roman Empire included. Though never transcending the Greek in literature, it did influence the Western civilization a lot. Europe would not be the same without the Romans. Rome was the founding father of many cities, some of which all over the continent they founded still stand today. No civilization was so identified with constructing and building things than the Romans such as aqueducts, roads, baths, walls, theatres, temples, arches, cities and palaces. They built a world from which later peoples still benefitted for a long time to come. Some of their old roads are even still in use today. Latin, the eternal language, is the language that many languages such as French, Italian, Portuguese, Rumanian, Spanish, etc., in time develope from. The Roman alphabet is what most of us still use today and Roman law is indeed a great institution. These laws form the basis of all today's justice systems in the Western world.

The amazing Rome has been attracting artists for centuries, thus a lot of books and movies about Rome being available. The famous ones are as in the following:

Ben-Hur, a Tale of the Chris[7] (in 1960) broke the record by winning 11 awards in the 32nd Oscar Award which made the Hollywood find the way to fight against TV shows.

The movie *Cleopatra*[8] was the most costly but the saddest failure in Hollywood. But the glorious fighting scenes and the queen's entering Rome ceremony left a deep impression on audience. Cleopatra VII Philopator, known to history as Cleopatra, was the last active pharaoh of Ancient Egypt, only shortly survived by her son. To this day, Cleopatra remains a popular figure in Western culture. Her legacy survives in numerous works of art and the many dramatizations of her story in literature and other media, including William Shakespeare's tragedy *Antony and Cleopatra* and the opera *Cléopâtre* of Jules Massenet[9]. In most depictions, Cleopatra was portrayed as a great beauty and her successive conquests of the world's most powerful men were taken as proof of her aesthetic and sexual appeal. She was praised by Egyptians because of the peace she earned but hated by Romans.

The Fall of the Roman Empire[10] depicted the fall of the Roman Empire. The old Roman king was going to give his power to a smart minister when dying who helped his friend, the king's son to be the new king. Unfortunately, the new king tried all means to destroy the smart minister who had given him a helping hand.

Gladiator[11], directed by Ridley Scott, was set against the splendor and barbarity of the Roman Empire in 180 AD, telling an epic story of courage and revenge. The great Roman general Maximus had been forced into exile and slavery by the jealous heir to the throne, Commodus. Trained as a gladiator, Maximus returned to Rome, intent on avenging the murder of his family by Commodus, now emperor.

Section 2 Medieval Drama

The final days of the Roman Empire were usually assigned to the year 476 AD, when the German General Odovacar[12] (or Odoacer) deposed the "last Roman Emperor", a boy ironically named Romulus Augustulus. The fall of Rome has been fascinating countless scholars who have come up with diverse causes such as depopulation, de-urbanization and barbarian invasions and so on. Although the Eastern half still survived with borders essentially intact for several centuries (until the Muslim conquests), the Empire as a whole had initiated major cultural and political transformations since the Crisis of the 3rd Century[13], with the shift towards a more openly autocratic and ritualized form of government, the adoption of Christianity as the state religion and a general rejection of the traditions and values of Classical Antiquity[14], thus a "dark age" coming.

2.1 The Dark Age

The Middle Ages or Medieval period, lasted from the 5th to the 15th centuries. It began with the collapse of the Western Roman Empire and merged into the early modern period. The Middle Ages was the middle period of the traditional division of Western history into Antiquity, Medieval and Modern periods. The Middle Ages could be classified as many different ages, from the Dark Age to the Golden Age. It could also be known as the Age of faith and the Age of feudalism. It was referred to as the Dark Age in the sense of intellectual, political and economic freedom and of advance and progress.

By the 5th century BC and indeed for many years before that, a succession of dynamic and capable foreigners coming from all ends of the Empire had kept Rome on its feet and these men were as "Roman" as anyone born or bred in the capital. Barbarians[15] who were newly adopted resident aliens were assigned to work farms or were conscripted into the Roman army in numbers so large that the late Latin word for "soldier" came to be *barbarus.* Barbarians were and had been for a long time guarding and feeding the Empire, which made it all the more difficult to claim they shouldn't also be running it. Even if the Romans of Rome still held the title to the Empire and affected superiority over the barbarians managing their domain, Roman possession of the lands around the Mediterranean Sea was, for the most part, only on paper. The reality was that the state was jointly owned by various races as second class. Roman city life and culture changed greatly in the early Middle Ages. Although Italian cities remained inhabited, they contracted significantly in size. Rome, for instance, shrank from a population of hundreds of thousands to around 30,000 by the end of the 6th century which meant a wide variety of peasant societies.

The barbarian invasion, to some degree, destroyed ancient civilization created by Romans and Greeks. If man could be classified into a natural man, a social man and a cultural man, then the barbarians belonged to the natural man based on instincts. The Ancient Greece had Athens's democratic political system in its main cities, and Rome experienced its Republican political system while the barbarians, most of whom were farmers with blood bond as dominating tie were practicing the military tribal organization form with killing and looting as their main purpose. The result of the barbarian invasion was that the agricultural way of life replaced Roman urban life, thus the glorious Greek drama tradition and achievements disappearing and even Seneca's writing only known until the 14th century. The new rulers were folding the tents of culture and quenching the fires of scholarship. The West was readying itself for its Medieval "camping trip".

2.2 Golden Age for Christianity

We have got to know the Romans have left us a lot such as the Latin language, an elaborate road system and solid cities, etc. Is there anything else left that is also very important? The answer is definitely yes. And this to some degree accounts for the disappearance of drama for centuries.

The barbarians gave up Greek and Roman culture, but there was one thing that they had carried forward and brought to a great height of development. That was Christianity. Middle Ages should be the Golden Age of faith since the religion played a major and powerful role at this time. Faith and religion had major power in the Middle Ages and was almost like a government. Why? Firstly, faith helped release people suffering. In late Rome, the intensification of social contradictions made Roman citizens lose hope of the government. They hated the government even more than the barbarians. Secondly, the barbarian's invasion worsened the life in every aspect — a world of economic collapse, a mixture of various races and chaos of the society. When people lost hope of the world they were living in, they needed something spiritual to help them through the darkness. Politically, there should be a unifying force to stabilize the society. Finally, unlike in Greece, in Rome there were no intellectuals like Plato who could hand down ancient civilization legacy. Instead, in Rome scholars were just busy with studying Christianity. Therefore, Christianity became a unifying force and a must for many people who were suffering and dissatisfied with the reality.

According to the binary thinking of the Church's early followers, everything that did not belong to God belonged to the Devil; thus all non-Christian gods and religions were satanic. Efforts were made in many countries through this period not only to convert Jews, pagans and Muslims but to destroy pre-Christian institutions and influences. Works of Greek and Roman literature were burnt, the thousand-year-old Platonic Academy was closed, the Olympic Games were banned and all theatres were shut down. The theatre itself was viewed as a diabolical threat to Christianity because of its continued popularity in Rome even among new converts. Church fathers characterized the stage as instruments in the devil's fiendish plot to corrupt men's souls, while acting was considered sinful because of its cruel mockery of God's creation.

2.3 Medieval Drama

Medieval theatre refers to the theatre at the period between the fall of the Western Roman Empire in the 5th century AD and the beginning of the Renaissance in approximately the 16th century AD (476-1550 AD). Medieval theatre covers all drama produced in Europe over that thousand year period and refers to a variety of genres, including liturgical drama, mystery plays and morality plays. While the Christian church did much to suppress the performance of plays, paradoxically it was in the church that medieval drama began.

2.3.1 Liturgical Plays

Liturgical plays evolved from liturgy[16]. Faced with the problem of explaining a new religion to a largely illiterate population, churches in the early Middle Ages began staging dramatized versions of particular biblical events on specific days of the year in order to vivify annual celebrations. Symbolic objects and actions performed by priests recalled the events which Christian ritual celebrated. These were extensive sets of visual signs that could be used to communicate with a largely illiterate audience. These performances developed into liturgical dramas, the first record of which was the trope[17] in the Easter[18] service known as the Quem Quaeritis[19]. Tropes, originally musical elaborations of the church service, gradually evolved into drama; eventually the Latin lines telling of the Resurrection were spoken, rather than sung, by priests who represented the angels and the two Marys[20] at the tomb of Jesus. The contents were taken from the *Bible* and performed by clergymen in front of churches with Latin as the language. However, by the late period, drama and theatre began to become more and more secularized and some other types of plays developed from the Liturgical Plays.

2.3.2 Mystery Plays

One important type that developed from church liturgy was mystery play referring to biblical stories that depicted biblical episodes from the Creation to Judgment Day from the Old and New Testaments[21]. The most famous of these plays was *The Second Shepherds' Play*[22].

2.3.3 Miracle Play

Another important type that developed from church liturgy was the miracle play, based on the lives of saints and martyrs[23] rather than on scripture. The miracle play reached its peak in France and the mystery play in England. The famous ones included *Mary Magdalene*, *The Conversion of St. Paul* and *The Play of the Sacrament*[24].

2.3.4 Morality play

The third type of religious drama was the morality play, appearing early in the 15th century. A morality play was a play enforcing a moral truth or lesson telling Christians how to live a good and moral life by means of the speech and action of characters which were personified abstractions — figures representing vices and virtues, qualities of the human mind or abstract conceptions in general. The famous ones were *Mankind*, *The Castle of Perseverance* and *Everyman*[25]. *Everyman*, the most famous of this kind and the only one to be seen on stage today was about the fact that when Death came to Everyman, he could not take Strength, Beauty, Wealth, Knowledge, Friends and Worldly Goods with him to Death. Only Good Deeds would come willingly to Death.

2.3.5 The Interlude

All the plays developed from liturgy gradually became more and more secularized, passing into the hands of trade guilds or professional actors. Although the theme of the plays was still about the fight between Good and Evil, ending with Good winning, stories of non-biblical materials were adopted, the simple lyric character of the early texts was enlarged by the addition of dialogue and dramatic action and more people got involved in the performance out of church. In 1240 Pope Innocent II[26] in Rome, forbade all drama performance in churches. Therefore, after 1240 all liturgical dramas were moved out of the churches into marketplaces, old Roman arenas, town squares and processions through the streets with Latin being replaced by local language such as English to entertain and relax more people, which resulted in the popularity of the Interlude.

The interlude, which grew out of the morality, was intended as its name implies, to be used more as filler than as the main part of an entertainment. As its best it was short, witty, simple in plot and suited for the diversion of guests at a banquet or for the relaxation of the audience between the divisions of a serious play. It became very popular and performed by professional actors in the late 15th and early 16th centuries. *The Four P's* of John Heywood[27] was the most popular, telling of a contest of wit between a Pardoner, a Palmer, a Peddler and a Poticary. *The Play of the Weather* was another interesting interlude, in which Jupiter and the gods assembled to listen to complaints about the weather.

The interlude popular in Britain was a kind of native farce comedy, dominating theatre to entertain more people. It was a major development in the transition from the religious plays to the great theatre of the Renaissance.

2.4 The Functions and Contributions of Medieval Drama

Plays at this time for the most part didn't transcend the level of Ancient Greek drama and added nothing new to the literature. Medieval drama seemd naive if we didn't understand the period. They had little sense of history, reflecting the limited knowledge of the people because God and his plan were the driving forces, not the characters. But it had functions and contributions in its own way to Western drama. It aimed to teach or reinforce Church doctrine, telling people how to live a "good" life and making them to believe their soul would be saved only by God. It offered a chance for all trade guilds to display their strength in various aspects and it provided people of all walks with entertainment and relaxation. It trained actors, keeping alive the dramatic spirit and preparing the way for the true drama which flourished in Renaissance. The first public theatre existed and professional actors became important in 1576 in England.

Medieval theatre brought theatre many contributions that continued to be incorporated in productions around the world to this day, the major of which were the use of the vernacular, spectacle, stage direction and the use of farce. Prior to Medieval theatre, all drama was performed in Latin or Greek. However, Medieval theatre evolved to the use of the vernacular about 1200 AD. Performances that were spoken in the vernacular provided opportunities for larger audiences, including members of lower socio-economic status, who would have otherwise been excluded from understanding the performances. Medieval theatre differed from the classical theatre for it emphasized spectacle. In addition, it presented various actions on stage in time and space and presented a combination of the sublime with detailed realism. Approximately 1400 AD, the dramas were performed with spectacle; no longer dependent exclusively on the spoken word, but incorporating music, dance, costume and set design. The spectacle of the later Medieval theatre made it necessary to have detailed stage directions. The evolution to the dependence on detailed stage direction made possible the great Shakespearean stage. Though with religious theme, the plays in Medieval time to some degree reflected the social reality which made it possible for people today to have a better understanding and study of that period. Furthermore, plays at this period, not influenced by Ancient Greeks, had its own form of drama in theme, staging and performance with originality as its main characteristics. For example, protagonists were no longer powerful or great ones. Anachronism was common which was against Ancient Greek rules such as coming to life of Jesus. In addition, the popularity of farce made it possible that Shakespeare used various forms of drama especially farce at ease.

2.5 Impacts of Religion on Literature

When it came to Medieval literature, people tended to believe there existed only four literary phenomena and one writer — the church literature, folk creation such as *Beowulf*, *Song of Roland*, *Nibelungenlied* and *Robin Hood*[28], the knight literature and townspeople literature with Dante[29] as the only writer who was both the last poet of the Medieval Ages and also the first poet of the coming age. Christianity was so important at this period that it did have great impact on development of Western culture as well as literature. Firstly, Christianity formed the foundation of Western culture. The Middle Ages was not only a transitional period. Actually, it was a process of multicultural development and influence between East and West. Though Christianity was a unifying and dominating force in the West, there existed four major geo culture plates such as the Roman Catholic culture, Constantinople's Orthodox culture, north European culture and Spain and Sicily culture. In addition, there began large-scale culture exchanges between the West and East: the prosperity and dominate influence in Spain of Muslim culture in the 8th century and the great exchange of ideas and cultures caused by the Crusades[30] in around the 12th century. Although Crusades was a failure by military standard, it brought Western Europe higher standards of Eastern medicine and learnt Greek and Muslim culture, thus bringing Europe out of the provincialism of the Dark Age. Secondly, people in the Middle Ages inherited Greek rational spirit, trying to explain the world in a reasonable way. Of course, it emphasized the importance of spiritual life of man. Finally, the fact that the reverence and awe for religion was a must for a religion-oriented world was the most obvious cultural characteristic for middle European world which went well with feudal society. Therefore, Christianity culture made people interested in and pursue their faith in God, not the life itself and the universe because of which, literature at this time was not for elevation and purifying but for the joy of religion faith and God's salvation. So it was common that there were always priests writing and literature of some kind was advocated by the ruling church.

Section 3 Renaissance Drama

Renaissance Drama (1550-1620) provided one of the richest periods of theatre history: the drama of early modern England produced for the professional theatre. It brought new insights by exploring the plays in their relation to the culture and society of the period. Drama offered us one way to understand the British culture through the unprecedented prosperity for English literature in history.

3.1 Renaissance

The Renaissance (1550-1620), meaning "rebirth" or "revival" of classical Greek thought in art and literature, marked a transition from the medieval to the modern world. Generally, it referred to the period between the 14th and 17th centuries, actually stimulated by a series of historical events such as the re-discovery of ancient Roman and Greek culture, the new discoveries in geography and astrology, the religious reformation and the economic expansion. The Renaissance, therefore, in essence was a historical period in which the European humanist thinkers and scholars made attempts to get rid of those old feudalist ideas in medieval Europe to introduce new ideas that expressed the interests of the rising bourgeoisie and to recover the purity of the early church from the corruption of the Roman Catholic Church.

3.1.1 Causes of the Renaissance

There were many reasons for the appearance of the Renascence in Europe. Firstly, the development of social productivity making the development of natural science which was meant to prove the authority of the church turned out to make people less superstitious and free to deviate from established theories, thus opening the door for a new way of looking at world and offering the possibility for further developments and rational thinking. The second reason was the decrease in the power of the Church. The Church, where corruption and abuses of power were prevalent, lost much of its power, making it a tendency to reform the religion — the movement towards more personal ways of communicating with God. Besides, a terrifying famine — black death in the 13th century in Europe made one third people dead, directly making people doubt God's ultimate authority and value life more than ever. As a result, enjoying the present became more attractive to more and more people. Thirdly, trade and education for laypeople because of printing led to the growth of the middle class which began to accumulate vast sums of money. The middle class enjoyed intellectual life exploration. They then wanted to enjoy and show off their wealth, which led to a philosophy of enjoying the real life in this world instead of simply waiting for the happiness in heaven. Fourthly, because of the Crusades and the new trade routes, Europeans began to come in contact with other more advanced civilizations, which influenced them greatly and led to study of the literature of classical antiquity and reform of education. What was more, the fall of the Byzantine[31] in 1453 made lots of ancient Roman and Greek literature known which offered the proof of enjoying life. Finally the discovery of the new world and man offered a further possibility for Renaissance. Europe in the 15th and 16th centuries had a strong desire of exploring the world and human beings. An essential element of the Renaissance was the beginning of humanism, which was frequently taken as the beginning of the Renaissance on its conscious, intellectual side for the Greek and Roman civilization was based on such a conception that man was the measure of all things. Thus, by emphasizing the dignity of human beings and the importance of the present life, humanists voiced their beliefs that man did not only have the right to enjoy the beauty of this life, but had the ability to perfect himself and to perform wonders.

3.1.2 Characteristics of the Renaissance

Renaissance sprang out first in Italy where capitalism firstly emerged with Venice as the world trade center in the 14th century, with the flowering of painting, sculpture and literature. Competition between wealthy people for status led to the development in education and art since wealthy people, wanting to be respected, would compete to see who was the most educated or had sponsored the most artists. There came the three artistic giants that dominated the art. They were Da Vinci[32] with his two oil paintings *Mona Lisa* and *The Last Supper*, Raphael[33] with his *Wedding of the Virgin* and *The School of Athens* and Michelangelo[34] with *David* and *The Scenes from Genesis* on the ceiling of the Sistine Chapel[35] in Rome. From Italy the movement went to embrace the rest of Europe. The Renaissance in Europe had two features. One was the strong curiosity for the classical literature because of dissatisfying with the Catholic and feudal ideas in Medieval Europe which had been dominating peoples' life for hundreds of years. The other was the keen interest in the activities of humanity — admiring human beauty and human achievements. The essence of the Renaissance was humanism which consisted of four aspects such as admiration and emulation of the Ancient Greeks and Romans, philosophy of enjoying this life instead of just waiting for the next one, the glorification of humans and the belief that individuals could do anything and the belief that humans deserved to be the center of attention. As a result, the European arts of painting, sculpture, architecture and literature at this period which reached an eminence and was never exceeded in any age portrayed the flesh-and-blood figures and explored their characters' pursuit of secular happiness. Humanism reflected the new outlook of the rising bourgeois who needed a beginning of political institutions with commercial economy and the encouragement of education, arts and music, hence a period of new inventions and beliefs.

3.2 Renaissance Drama on the Continent

By the advent of the Renaissance in the 15th and 16th centuries, most European countries had established native traditions of religious drama and farce that contended with the impact of the newly discovered Greek and Roman plays. Little had been known of classical drama during the Middle Ages.

3.2.1 Italian Drama

Italy, the cradling place of the Renaissance first translated and imitated the classics with Terence, Plautus and Seneca as the models. The Italians strictly applied their interpretation of Aristotle's rules for the drama and this rigidity was primarily responsible for the failure of Italian Renaissance drama. Some liveliness appeared in the comic sphere. The pastoral drama, set in the country and depicting the romantic affairs of rustic people, usually shepherds and shepherdesses, was more successful than either comedy or tragedy. The true direction of the Italian stage was toward the spectacular and the musical. A popular Italian Renaissance form was the intermezzo[36], which presented music and lively entertainment between the acts of classical imitations. The native taste for music and theatricality led to the emergence of the opera in the 16th century and the triumph of this form on the Italian stage in the 17th century.

3.2.2 French Drama

Renaissance drama appeared somewhat later in France than in Italy. The French drama initially suffered from the same rigidity as the Italian, basing itself on Roman models and Italian imitations. However, in the late 16th century, in France there was a romantic reaction to classical dullness, led by Alexandre Hardy[37], France's first professional playwright. This romantic trend was stopped in the 17th century with a return to classic forms. The great tragedies of Pierre Corneille, although classical in their grandeur and in their concern with noble characters, were decidedly of the Renaissance in their exaltation of man's ability, by force of will, to transcend adverse circumstances.

3.2.3 Spanish Drama

Renaissance drama in Spain was more successful than in France and Italy because of being able to transform classical models with infusions of native characteristics. The leading Renaissance playwright, Lope de Vega[38], famous for *The Dancing Master* set a good foundation for Spanish drama which then arrived at its culmination in Pedro Calderón de la Barca[39] famous for *Life is a Dream* and Miguel de Cervantes[40], more reputed as the novelist of *Don Quixote de la Mancha*, who wrote 30 plays with *The Siege of Mumancia* as his representative play.

3.3 Renaissance Drama in Britain

The English Renaissance was in the first half of the 16th century which was much later than Italy, but English literature at this time was usually regarded as the highlight in the history of English literature.

3.3.1 Reformation of the Church in England

The stability and prosperity came from to some degree a series of reform in England. Henry VII, founder of the Tudor Dynasty[41], came to power shortly after the War of the Roses[42], a civil war that weakened the nobles greatly. He and his successor, Henry VIII strengthened royal power and decreased noble power, thus having a centralized monarch which met the needs of the rising bourgeoisie by encouraging business and overseas trade. In 1513 Henry VIII beat invading Scottish army. England was getting richer and more powerful. In 1527 Henry

VIII pursued a divorce from Catherine to marry Anne Boleyn, but Pope Clement VII denied him an annulment which made Britain initiate a revolution when Henry VIII decided that the English church should separate from Rome, allowing Henry VIII to marry Anne in 1533. The Reformation made Henry VIII get both the woman he wanted and property from the catholic churches, becoming the most powerful both in politics and head of the Church of England. Freeing from the religion shackle and being influenced by Renascence on the continent, England became a "nest of singing birds" — a beginning to widespread knowledge and an end to ignorance because England enjoyed stability and prosperity, which made it possible that people had a thirsting curiosity for the classical literature. The study of Greek and Latin authors and the keen interest in the activities of humanity emphasized the capacities of the human mind and the achievements of human culture in contrast to the medieval value on God and contempt for the things of this world. School benefited first from Renaissance where only Grammar, Logics and Rhetoric used to be taught. At this moment, translation from classical, Italian and French works such as *Iliad* and *Odyssey* of Homer, lives of Greek and Roman Heroes, *Don Quixote* of Cervantes, *The Essays of Montaigne*[43], etc., were available. Students performed those classics first in classroom later to entertain important persons from other countries. When Queen Elizabeth[44] (1558-1603), a tact, glamorous ruler, who worked closely with Parliament and well with businessmen was in rule, Britain became the most powerful country in the world which made British more proud of their own country and more interested in its own history, thus the appearance of the *Authorized Version of the Bible*[45] and of Chronicles on English, Scottish and Irish history. Many scholars began to write plays and books of discoveries and adventures were very popular with people.

3.3.2 The Classical Drama

Renaissance period marked the end of darkness and the golden time of English drama. There appeared a group of excellent dramatists such as John Lyly, Thomas Kyd, George Peele, Robert Greene, Ben Jonson, Christopher Marlowe and William Shakespeare in Britain. Most English playwrights had certain contact with Greek and Latin drama, learning the rule and conception of Ancient Greek comedies and tragedies. Comedies and tragedies on classical model appeared in the middle of the 16th century with *Gammer Gurton's Needle* and *Gorboduc*[46] as the first English comedy and tragedy.

3.3.3 London Theatre and Audience

London became the center of English drama in the 16th century. By 1567, professional actors were organized into companies and regular playhouses were built. The Elizabethan theatres with wooden building materials were usually circular in form with the disadvantages of fire, flame and riot. London was burnt down in 1666 and many theatres were closed several times because of flame between 1592 and 1594. Later, the Globe, where many of Shakespeare's plays were staged was one of the most famous theatres which became the favorite place for both gentlemen and common people with different prices for different classes because theatre was the only source of intellectual pleasure when there were no newspapers and novels. The intimate and constant intercourse between audience and theatre made rapid progress in dramatic techniques both in performance and play writing, fostering the Elizabethan drama with hard-earned penny, tears, laughter and multitudinous applause.

Section 4 British Renaissance Playwrights

The English drama of the 16th century showed from the beginning that it would not be bound by classical rules. Elements of farce, morality and a disregard for the unities of time, place and action formed the early comedies and tragedies. William Shakespeare's great work was foreshadowed by early essays in the historical chronicle play, by elements of romance found in the works of John Lyly, by revenge plays such as Thomas Kyd's *Spanish Tragedy* and by Christopher Marlowe's development of blank verse and his deepening of the tragic perception. Companies of actors needed new and popular plays which made a group of "university wits"[47] of humble birth and struggle for a livelihood enter the dramatic circle by revising old plays and writing new ones. They sold their plays to the drama companies (6 £ per play), thus being regarded as "paid wage-laborers" by pleasing the company and audience through their writing.

4.1 Christopher Marlowe

Christopher Marlowe (1564-1593) was the representative and the most gifted of the "university wits". He was a poet of real genius, decidedly the chief dramatist among Shakespeare's early contemporaries and the one from whom Shakespeare learned the most. Marlowe was born in 1564 (the same year as Shakespeare), the son of a shoemaker at Canterbury. He studied in Cambridge for 6 years and got his B. A. and M. A. He was knowledgeable, knowing astronomy, geography, medical science and classical poetry. He turned his back on the pulpit for the stage, taking the London theatre by storm at age of 23 with *Tamburlaine*[48]— a dramatization of the stupendous career of the bloodthirsty Mongol, 14th century conqueror of the world, appealing to audience when England was fighting against Spain for ocean dominance. He was charged of "atheism" and "blasphemy" because of his association with people with independent and heretic thought and his anti-tradition, taken into prison because of fighting with others. He was killed in 1593 in a reckless and foolish brawl at 29 accidentally (suspected as a murder by some).

In his short life, Marlowe's best plays *Tamburlaine*, *The Jew of Malta* and *The Tragical History of Doctor Faustus*[49] stood respectively for ambition for power, greed for wealth and everlasting acquisition for knowledge. In *Tamburlaine*, the world conqueror who was admired for his courage and persistence declared he would scare the whole world and rule the land the light touches.

The Jew of Malta, which was to give Shakespeare suggestions for *The Merchant of Venice* had a rich merchant as the protagonist, a Tamburlaine in the narrow sphere of finance. The Jew, greedy for wealth made two guys interested in his daughter have a duel and killed four people who knew his secret. *The Tragical History of Dr. Faustus*, a treatment of the medieval story which two hundred years later was to serve Goethe[50] for his masterpiece was regarded as Marlowe's masterpiece. The hero of the play, a young and brilliant scholar was insatiable thirst for knowledge, love, arts, social ideals and political justice by selling his soul to the Devil. The following was about his pursuit of love:

It is late when he realized his wrong choice.
His last demand: meeting Helen's soul
Was this the face that launched a thousand ships
And burnt the topless towers of Ilium?
Sweet Helen, make me immortal with a kiss.
Her lips such forth my soul— see where it flies!
Come, Helen, come give me my soul again.
Here will I dwell, for heaven is in these lips
And all is dross that is not Helena
…
(就是这张脸使千帆齐发,
把伊利安的巍巍城楼烧成灰的吗?

甜蜜海伦，她一吻就使我永生。
看，她的嘴唇吸走了我的灵魂！
来，海伦，还我的灵魂来！
我住下了，天堂就在你的唇上。
凡是海伦身外的，全是粪土……）

His play *Edward the Second*, the first really artistic Chronicle History play, was ignored for a long time for its dealing with homosexuality. These plays, in spite of faults now conspicuous enough, were splendidly imaginative and poetic and were by far the most powerful that had yet been written in England. His plays revealed that he had been an ardent idealist and a representative of many of the qualities that made the greatness of the Renaissance. He created a Renaissance hero in his drama, a hero who was always individualistic, full of ambition and facing bravely the challenge from both gods and men, praising individuality freed from the restraints of medieval dogma and law. Different from the tragic hero in medieval plays, who sought the way to heaven through salvation and god's will, Marlowe was against conventional morality and contrived to obtain heaven on earth through his own efforts, even if bringing ruin to the world and sometimes to themselves. Marlowe's plays interpreted the spirit of the rising bourgeoisie: eager endless acquisition for knowledge, towering pride and insatiable appetite for power.

Marlowe was pioneer of English drama and father of English tragedy, showing the dawn of British drama gold age. He reformed the English drama and perfected the language and the verse of dramatic works, whose powerful and perfect verse without rhyme body became the most important British drama style. He was the first to analyze psychology of characters and able to learn from the both ancient and foreign classics based on the combination of native dramatic features. His creation of the Renaissance titanic hero image definitely established tragedy as a distinct form on the English popular stage and invested it with proper dignity. He was the contribution of drama development, therefore, an indelible brilliant achievement as a pioneer of English drama, paving the way for the giant of Shakespeare.

Is there any difference between Christopher Marlowe and William Shakespeare? If there is, what is it?

4.2 William Shakespeare

William Shakespeare[51] (1564-1616), of course, stood as the supreme dramatist of the Renaissance period, equally adept at writing tragedies, comedies or chronicle plays. Karl Heinrich Marx[52] regarded Aeschylus and Shakespeare as "the two greatest dramatic geniuses the world has ever known". Up to now, there are flags of 105 countries flying over the small town in Stratford-upon-Avon, hometown of this great British playwright. His plays remain highly popular today and are constantly studied, performed and reinterpreted in various languages in the world, indicating clearly this great master belongs to the whole world instead of only one period and one country.

4.2.1 His Life

There were quite few facts of Shakespeare. Born in Stratford-on-Avon, a charming little town in 1564, he was the son of a well-to-do trader who bankrupted, which made Shakespeare leave school early and become a country school-master. Later he went to London, doing many odd jobs including becoming an actor. In 1611, he retired to his native town, buying the second largest house there while many other playwrights died with no money at all. He died in 1616, leaving a legacy of 37 plays, 154 sonnets and many poems as definitely the world's pre-eminent dramatist.

4.2.2 Globe Theatre

"Totus Mudus Agjt Historionem" is Latin language, meaning "the whole world is a stage" and is translated as "Globe Theatre"[53]. Built in 1599, the first Globe Theatre which sit on south side of the Thames River and could hold 3,000 people was burnt down in 1613. The present one, called Shakespeare's Globe and only 200 meters away from the original, was built in 1997. It took 10 years to finish the construction, which imitated everything in Elizabeth's time and can hold 1,600 people at most. In Shakespeare's time most theatres were public with the disadvantages of fire and riot, which led to the appearance of private theatres that were small, inside of a house and at first for children actors — leading to the popularity of comedy with murder and money as its theme.

4.2.3 His Works

Shakespeare's career as a dramatist might be conveniently divided into three periods. The earliest period, that of apprenticeship in play-making dated from 1590 to 1600 when he was just about 30 years old, including his earliest plays, either in collaboration with or in imitation of other playwrights, nine of his ten history plays (except Henry VIII), two of his well-know early tragedies *Romeo and Juliet* and *Julius Caesar* and all his important romantic comedies. The 2nd or his most important period stretched roughly from 1601 to 1608, including all his great tragedies such as *Hamlet*, *Othello*, *King Lear* and *Macbeth* and some of his earlier tragic-comedies. The 3rd and last period dated from 1609 to 1612 or 1613, including chiefly his three last tragicomedies.

Shakespeare has been given the highest praise by various scholars and critics all over the world sometimes as the greatest playwright in the whole world, past and present. Actually, he was not so popular in his time, though Ben Johnson[54] thought he was "not of an age, but for all time". He was even attacked as an "upstart crow, beautified with our feathers, that, with his Tygers heart wrapt in a Players hide[55]" in a pamphlet, written by a well-known poet and playwright called Robert Greene, one of the University Wits. Shakespeare died silent in his hometown in 1616 while Ben Johnson eight years younger was buried in Poet's Corner[56] though penniless with people gathering around him calling themselves Sons of Ben. There are always some critics asking for more clear-headed estimates of this poet and his works. Maybe not everyone agrees that all his plays are the best ones, but some do belong to the classics.

4. 2. 3. 1 The Four Great Comedies

Undoubtedly, *A Midsummer Night's Dream*, *The Merchant of Venice*, *As You Like It* and *Twelfth Night*[57] can be regarded as great works. In these comedies, Shakespeare who was quite optimistic, portrayed young people just freed from feudal fetters struggling for their humanist ideal after struggling against all obstacles, glorifying the triumph of love and friendship over insatiable greed and brutality. These plays offered us a series of great heroines — new women of the Renaissance. They were active, vivacious, capable, clever and serious-minded, even outshining many men in many ways, their lovers and husbands included.

4. 2. 3. 2 His Mature Historical Plays

Shakespeare wrote 10 historical plays, nine of which were finished in his early period. These plays were critical of real kings except Henry V, who represented his ideal of a good king, showing the horrors of civil war, the responsibility of an efficient ruler and the necessity for national unity. *Henry IV* was the most remarkable historical play, telling the growth of Henry V who was influenced by Falstaff, one of the most brilliant creations — old, fat, selfish, treacherous and cynical, never hesitating in the least to seek profit whenever there was a chance:

Can honor set to a leg? No. or an arm? No. or take away the grief of a wound? No. Honor hath no skill in surgery, then? No. What is honor? A word. What is that word, honor? Air. A trim reckoning! Who hath it? He that died o' Wednesday. Doth he feel it? No. Doth he hear it? No. It is insensible, then? Yea, to the dead. But will it not live with the living? No. Why? Detraction will not suffer it. Therefore I'll have none of it; Honor is a mere scutcheon; and so ends my catechism.

（名誉能给我补上一条腿吗？不能。重装一条臂膀？不能。解除伤口的疼痛？不能。名誉有没有像外科手术那样救人性命的本领？没有。名誉是什么呢？一个名词。这个词又是什么呢？一阵空气，好精明的一笔账！谁有名誉？星期三死掉的那个人能感觉到名誉吗？不能。他听见名誉了吗？没有。名誉是不可捉摸的吗？对于死人确实是这样。可是它能与活人一起生存吗？不能。为什么？诽谤不好容忍它的存在。因此，我不要什么名誉，名誉只不过是送殡的勋章。我的自问自答也结束了。）

Falstaff appeared again in *The Merry Wives of Windsor*, which according to one tradition, was supposed to have been written when Queen Elizabeth wanted to see the fat old knight in love after she had enjoyed the character of Falstaff in the two parts of *Henry IV*.

Historical plays disappeared in the 17th century.

4. 2. 3. 3 The Four Great Tragedies

Hamlet, *Othello*, *King Lear* and *Macbeth*[58], generally considered his great tragedies, depicted the life-and-death struggle between the humanists and the dark power, the sunshine and laughter of the early period turning into clouds and storms in his tragedies. This showed on the one hand Shakespeare's deeper understanding of the Renaissance and on the other hand the social contradictions of his time — declining co-operation between the Crown and bourgeoisie and economic and social crises up to the English Revolution[59].

As the growth of age, Shakespeare turned from the storm to great peacefulness — a harmony of earth and heaven — storm or wrong first but well in the end when he paid more attention in plots to please audience.

4.2.4 His Position in Literature

Shakespeare is universally acknowledged to be the summit of the English literature, renaissance and the greatest of all dramatists and poet the world over now. He and the *Authorized Version of the Bible* are thought of as the two great treasuries of the English language. England up to the present-day world chiefly depends upon his penetrating exposition of human nature, his lively paintings of human life and his truthful reflections of human reality.

4.2.5 His Achievements

Any summing up of Shakespeare's achievements will be inadequate. However, the following points may be of some help to students.

(1) Shakespeare is one of the founders of realism, living in an age when the old feudal social and economic order was being destroyed and a new capitalist society was being born and when London took a leading part in that destruction and that new birth. Representing the trend of history in giving voice to the desires and aspirations for peace of the rising bourgeoisie and people, he wrote a number of plays with the history of England as their background permeated with patriotism and a feeling of national grandeur with profound insight into the social issues.

(2) The second achievement is his unrivaled subtlety of characterization and a marvelous ability to unify well-organized plot, character and imagery. His characters are round, in the sense that they have many aspects or dimensions with strong and distinct personalities. In his characters, vice and virtue commingle and that is true of the common sense of humanity.

(3) Shakespeare is original in instilling into old materials a new spirit that gives new life to his plays. He draws most of his materials from sources known to his audience, the Anglo-Saxon Chronicle and other

writers' plays, capable of transforming those materials with infusions of his own creation, thus, creating a new form of tragedy.

(4) Shakespeare is a master of the English language, with a large vocabulary of 16,000 English words — a genius for language, including the perfection of a verse form and language that captures the spirit of ordinary speech and yet stands above it to give a special dignity to his characters and situations. The popular sayings we have come more from Shakespeare than the *Bible*. He is especially successful in handling the different meanings of the same word or words having the same sound but different meanings — puns.

Then why is he looked down upon by some of his contemporaries?

4.3 Shakespeare and Marlowe

Humanists in the early Renaissance tried their best to make the shift of emphasis from religious to secular concerns on humans and their values, capacities and worth, freeing man from the feudal fetters. Shakespeare, like Christopher Marlowe, was optimistic in his early plays, no matter whether in comedies or tragedies, celebrating the victory of love and friendship and justification of the interests, needs and welfare of humans. They had firm belief in the nobility of human nature and in the power of love. Man, who had been debased in the Medieval Ages, was master. They were innocent and looking at the world with a wonderful eye. But gradually, Shakespeare became more mature and his knowledge of human nature grew in depth. The more he knew about human nature, the more he was depressed at the ugliness and baseness of human nature, thus, pessimistic outlook appearing in his tragedies. In his later and mature plays, when emphasizing the secular rights of men, he made it quite clear that evil co-existed with man's desire. Human nature, which should not be chained, should have its limits and restraints with ration. Pursuing happiness and welfare without ration would undoubtedly lead to sensual indulgence like Falstaff in *Henry IV*. Man's endless and titanic acquisition for anything he wanted, if not based on justice and love would undoubtedly result in ambition, greed and cruelty like Richard III, Macbeth etc. He tried to figure out what a real man meant in his later writings, raising a new question "how to solve the conflict between desire and ration?" Maybe that was one of the reasons that made Hamlet hesitate again and again to revenge his father on his uncle. Shakespeare, whose plays reflected the spirit of his age with his profound insight into the social issues, left us a priceless legacy with his understanding of humanism.

4.4 Shakespeare and Greek Playwrights

Shakespeare created a new form of tragedy which was mentioned above, a tragedy that has influenced the West literature ever since, thus forming a new Western tragedy style.

Tragedy understood in Western Europe had its origin in the Greek drama. The spirit of Greek writing was essentially the inevitable suffering overwhelming the characters who maintained their dignity under this suffering and proved their greatness by doing so, thus creating great power of elevation. Greek tragedy arose out of their religious interpretation of the nature or man's destiny. When Christianity prevailed over Western Europe, a much more hopeful exploration of human destiny dominated the thought of the writers then. Tragedy in the Greek sense became difficult to comprehend as it was so unreal: If good men suffer in this world, they are rewarded in Heaven and this is not tragic; wicked men happening to suffer in this world may be dammed in the next, but this also is not tragic because they are wicked. Hence medieval tragedy was on the whole reduced to a simple uninteresting conception of the Wheel of Fortune. As a result, it was unlikely to have tragedy like Ancient Greeks used to.

In the late 16th century, a tragic vision on human experience was rediscovered by some English dramatists, notably by Shakespeare. In his writing, the hero's downfall was brought about less by the hero's destiny, that was, the outside world but more by the feature of reality in which he lived and by his own character. A tragic feature was usually caused by an error or defect in characterization of the tragic hero that led to his downfall, such as greed, pride or ambition. This flaw might result from bad character, bad judgment, an inherited weakness or any other prescribed shortcoming of a character, thus more analysis on the protagonist's inner heart — psychology in Shakespeare's plays. And this was also the extinct characteristic of British drama.

Perhaps fortunately Shakespeare didn't go to elite universities such as Oxford, Cambridge as the playwrights belonging to University Wits for a further study. As a result, he was much less influenced by rigid schooling and ancient classics. Maybe that was one of the reasons that he was not liked by some University Wits like Robert Greene. With his talent of writing and profound insight into social issues, he created a new form of tragedy, a tragedy, with its everlasting life power, that had its own tradition in the West literature history. Shakespeare was original in many aspects such as the practice of combination of tragedy and comedy in *Hamlet* and *King Lear* and learning from medieval farce, interlude, thus the popularity and entertainment of his plays which in turn guaranteed his plays' financial success. Shakespeare's tragedy, more suitable for interpreting man in the modern world, reflected the conflict between man and himself — man's dilemma.

Section 5 British Drama in the 18th Century

The 17th century in Britain was marked by revolution of and restoration of the monarchy. In the 18th century, the highbrow and provocative Restoration comedy[60] lost favour, to be replaced by sentimental comedy, domestic tragedy such as *The London Merchant* of George Lillo[61] and by an overwhelming interest in Italian opera. Popular entertainment became more dominant in this period than ever before. Fair-booth burlesque and musical entertainment, the ancestors of the English music hall, flourished at the expense of legitimate English drama. By the early 19th century, few English dramas were being written, except for closet dramas and plays intended to be presented privately rather than on stage.

5.1 The Unrest Situation

Oliver Cromwell[62], who came into power after the only execution of a king — Charles I[63] in 1649, was actually a dictator too. He ordered to close all pubs and theatres, banning sports and Christmas celebration for religious and ideological reasons, even sending soldiers to people's houses to get away gifts for Christmas, thus a real end of the gold age of British drama and the time of drama as an entertainment of all people.

Charles II, whose restoration to the throne in 1660 marked the end of republican rule in England, spent years in exile until Oliver Cromwell died and returned to the monarchy. The accession to the throne of Charles II brought a fun-loving, woman-loving and theatre-loving king to power. He became known as the Merry Monarch for his lifting of Puritan restrictions on entertainment and his own love of pleasure. Wide and socially mixed audiences were attracted by topical writing and by the introduction of the first professional actresses (in Shakespeare's time, all female roles had been played by boys). It was said he was quite interested in plays and his best-known mistress was an actress. Dramatic activity flourished again. Audiences attending the Restoration theaters were predominately the aristocracy who demanded heroics in their tragedies and imitation of their own manners in their comedies.

5.2 Restoration and Sentimental Drama

The second half of the 17th century was distinguished by the achievements of the French neoclassicists and the Restoration playwrights in England where restoration tragedy degenerated into bombastic heroic dramas by such authors as John Dryden and Thomas Otway[64] with the characteristics such as full of love intrigue, seduction and promiscuity. Theaters were open again but most of them were private — a place for gathering for the privileged few. Restoration comedy or comedy of manners[65] was preeminent on the English stage form 1660 to approximately 1710. The English aristocracy was enthralled with the accurate imitation of their customs and manners mirrored on the stage. Restoration actors and actresses captured their audience with a flamboyant display of witty bluntly sexual dialogues; boudoir intrigues sensual innuendos and rakish behavior. A narrow set of conventions entirely dominated Restoration comedy: constancy in love, especially in marriage, was bore; sex should be tempting; love thrived on variety; genuine sexual feelings had no place on the stage. In the play, characters clashed with other characters in situations selected to produce love entanglements and intrigues. Drama became witty but to a large degree immoral for the entertainment of the few and court, writing almost exclusively to and about a small segment of society — the highest. The audience at this time was, according to George Etherege[66] like, "from one theatre to another, if they dislike the play and have no interest in any female present, they have no intention of staying any longer. At most they comb their wigs or have some greetings with friends and then just leave nosily with hats on askew"[67].

But Restoration comedy achieved a perfection of style and cynical upper-class wit that was still appreciated.

The influence of Restoration comedy could be seen in the 18th century in the plays of Oliver Goldsmith and Richard Brinsley Sheridan[68]. This century also ushered in the middle-class or domestic drama, which treated the problems of ordinary people. This period was marked by sensationalism and rhetoric in tragedy, spectacle in the form of the masque and a gradual turn to polished wit in comedy.

By the beginning of the 18th century, the number of people attending the theatre had increased, including many middle-class patrons. As interest in the court's activities lessened, middle-class self-awareness grew. No longer were theatre audiences predominately aristocratic. The purpose of sentimental drama was to show the middle class the disparity between the real world and the ideal world. The sentimentalists believed that it was a part of Christian morality to see oneself as a moral paragon whose behavior was in many respects Christ-like. Playwrights stressed the rewards of virtue and need for gentility. Great emphasis was placed on arousing sympathetic response to the misfortunes of others and it was considered healthy to display emotion and to test one's virtues.

The 18th century's Enlightenment movement and industrial Revolution[69] which resulted in unprecedented technical innovations led to a new class — the rising bourgeoisie. More theatres for new audience were open because of English middle class that grew rapidly both in power and influence. The 18th enlighteners of classicism wrote for the rising bourgeoisie to tidy up the capitalist social order — a new code of social morality for the rising bourgeoisie. Consequently came a debased kind of comedy — the sentimental drama in which romantic love was predominant and virtue was rewarded.

Such playwrights as Sir Richard Steele and Colley Cibber[70] in England contributed to the development of the genteel, sentimental comedy. While the political satire in the plays of Henry Fielding and in *Beggar's Opera* of John Gay[71] (1728) seemed to offer a more interesting potential than the sentiment of Cibber, this line of development was cut off by the Licensing Act[72] of 1737, which required government approval before a play could be produced, restricting the freedom of dramatists and driving Fielding out of the theatre whose plays were filled with political, theatrical and social satire — mercilessly exposing the English courts of law, the parliamentary system and the corruption of state officials. The stage lost power as a criticism of society, thus declining with a brief flowering in the 2nd half of the 18th century for the comedies of Sheridan whose *The School for Scandal* was the masterpiece of comedy in the 18th century and Goldsmith with the most famous *She Stoops to Conquer*. The 18th century also saw Romanticism, Neoclassicism and novel with Realism on the continent, paving the way for critical realism in the 19th century.

5.3 Characteristics of the 18th Century British Drama

Why did British drama at this time aim at criticizing and mocking at evil practice and moral fashion of the upper class of the bourgeois upstarts instead of feudal nobles and privileged priests? This was because after the Glory Revolution which was also called Bloodless Revolution, though actually not, in 1688, Constitutional Monarchy was put into practice in Britain, which limited the power of the monarchy and made Parliament supreme, leading to the enactment of the Bill of Rights[73]. The big bourgeoisie and new upstarts came into power earlier than those on the Europe continent, thus anti-feudalism less urgent and important in Britain. The new audience of the 18th century — the newly rising middle class had a desire to see their attitude and idea reflected on stage.

So sentimental and Restoration drama tended to focus on eulogizing the beauty of life with obvious ethical preaching, emphasizing pity and sympathy. Most drama catered to the audience enthusiastic response, not their ration, usually with a lot of exaggerations and also romantic love stories.

5.4 The Enlightenment Movement

The Age of Enlightenment (or simply the Enlightenment or Age of Reason) was a cultural movement of intellectuals in the 17th and 18th centuries, which began first in Europe and later in the American colonies. Its purpose was to reform society away from irrationality; specifically, away from superstition, dogmatism of all kinds, unfounded intolerance of all kinds; and, gross abuses of power by both the Catholic Church and by despotic kings. The ideas of the Enlightenment have had a major impact on the culture, politics and governments of the Western world. The ideas of social equality, human right and liberty and atheism had spread all over Europe, greatly shaking the foundation of royal autocracy and its status in people's mind. The Enlightenment provided the theoretical and ideological preparation for critical ideas, such as the centrality of freedom, democracy and reason as primary value of society. No brief summary could do justice to the diversity of enlightened thought in the 18th century Europe because it was a value system rather than a set of shared beliefs. The tendency of philosophers in particular to apply rationality to every problem was considered the essential change. In his famous essay "What is Enlightenment?" (1784), Immanuel Kant[74] described it simply as freedom to sue one's own intelligence. More broadly, the Enlightenment period was marked by increasing empiricism, scientific rigor and reductionism, along with thorough and direct questioning of religious orthodox. Enlighteners such as Voltaire, Denis Diderot, Jean-Jacques Rousseau, David Hume[75] etc., whose attacks on the established Catholic Church and whose advocacy of freedom of religion and freedom of expression had made religious orthodox face a real crisis tried to establish a new system of thought that was totally different from the religious one. That was why the late 18th century witnessed a flowering of thinkers and philosophers in Europe who were very active both in literature and philosophy.

重难点解读

[1] **the she-wolf**："母狼乳婴"，也称为"the Capitoline Wolf"。著名的"母狼乳婴"与罗马古城的历史传说有关。这座赫赫有名的"母狼乳婴"青铜雕像原作，收藏在罗马市政厅所在地坎比多里奥山顶广场的博物馆里。走进这个世界上最古老的博物馆之一，很容易就能找到那尊著名的"母狼乳婴"雕像，意大利首都罗马的城雕也是"母狼乳婴"雕像。贝尼托·墨索里尼，意大利法西斯党魁、独裁者，第二次世界大战元凶很喜欢"母狼乳婴"，送了一些仿制品给美国的城市。

[2] **Sicily**：西西里岛。地中海最大和人口最稠密的岛，属意大利。

[3] **Athena, Minerva and Zues Jupiter**：雅典娜成了弥涅尔瓦、宙斯成了朱庇特。雅典娜是希腊的智慧女神，罗马人改为弥涅尔瓦，成为罗马神话中的智慧女神。宙斯是希腊神话中的主神，奥林匹斯众神之王，也是宇宙之王，罗马人改为朱庇特，成为罗马神话神王的名字，也用来为木星命名。

[4] **Colosseum**：罗马斗兽场，亦译作罗马大角斗场、罗马竞技场、罗马圆形竞技场、科洛西姆等。是古罗马帝国专供奴隶主、贵族和自由民观看奴隶与猛兽搏斗的地方，建于公元 72 至 82 年间，现已成为古罗马文明的象征。遗址位于意大利首都罗马市中心，在威尼斯广场的南面，古罗马市场附近。从外观上看，它呈正圆形；俯瞰时，它是椭圆形的。其占地面积约 2 万平方米，最大直径为 188 米，最小直径为 156 米，外墙高 48.5 米，可以容纳45 000观众。

[5] **Seneca**：塞涅卡(Lucius Annaeus Seneca，约公元前 4 或 1—公元 65)。古罗马时代著名斯多亚学派哲学家和作家，留下 9 部悲剧，均取材于希腊神话传说。

[6] ***The Menaechmi***：《孪生兄弟》(*The Twin Brothers*)。普拉图斯的喜剧作品。

[7] ***Ben-Hur, a Tale of the Christ***：《宾虚》。1960 年，《宾虚》获得 32 届奥斯卡奖 11 项大奖，创下该奖历史最高纪录。宾虚本是一位犹太王子，后被朋友出卖，沦为奴隶，几经磨难，终于重获自由，向仇人发起了挑战。

[8] ***Cleopatra***：《埃及艳后》。埃及艳后即克莉奥佩特拉七世，古埃及托勒密王朝的最后一任法老。在文学和电影里，她被刻画成了保卫国家免受罗马帝国吞并而色诱恺撒大帝及他的手下马克・安东尼。

[9] **Jules Massenet**：儒勒・马斯内(1842—1912)。法国作曲家，音乐教育家，尤以歌剧出名，从小显露出音乐上的天赋，11 岁时进入巴黎音乐学院，毕业时获得罗马大奖，1878 年开始在巴黎音乐学院教授作曲，同年被选为法兰西学院院士，1899 年荣获二级勋位。

[10] ***The Fall of the Roman Empire***：《罗马帝国的衰亡》。是安东尼・曼导演的史诗巨片，由派拉蒙公司制作。本片描写的是罗马帝国逐步走向灭亡的过程，罗马皇帝卡斯奥里路，晚年决定将王位传给贤臣利比亚斯，而不是传给王子康莫德斯，因而被毒死，辅佐好友康莫德斯登上王位的利比亚斯却引来新皇的忌恨。

[11] ***Gladiator***：《角斗士》。导演雷德利・司各特将宏伟的古罗马角斗场，再现于银幕之上，为人们讲述了一个有关勇气与复仇的故事。

[12] **Odovacar**：奥多瓦卡(435—493)。日耳曼首领，公元 476 年被他统率的驻守罗马的日耳曼雇佣兵拥立为国王，同时将西罗马帝国的最后一位皇帝，年仅 6 岁的罗慕路斯・奥古斯图卢斯废除，从而结束了西罗马帝国。后被西奥多里克率领的东哥特人击败，并且被西奥多里克指使的人谋杀。

[13] **the Crisis of the 3rd Century**：三世纪危机，又名军事无政府状态或帝国危机。指罗马帝国在 235 年(皇帝亚历山大・塞维鲁被杀)至 284 年(皇帝戴克里先即位)之间受到三项同时发生的危机而衰落甚至接近崩溃的过程。这三个危机分别是：

外敌入侵、内战及经济崩溃。在此期间，罗马帝国的组织、社会、日常生活以及宗教均产生了根本的转变，包括承认基督教，因此该危机被视为古典时代前期和后期之间的分水岭。

[14] **Classical Antiquity**：古典时代(或称为古典时期、古典古代、古风时期)。是对希腊罗马世界以地中海为中心，包括古希腊和古罗马等一系列文明的文化史的一个广义称谓。在这个时期，古希腊文明和古罗马文明十分繁荣，对欧洲、北非、中东等地区具有巨大影响。通常认为古典时代起始于古希腊最早的文字记录，即公元前 8—前 7 世纪荷马史诗，一直延伸至基督教出现以及罗马帝国的衰落。古典时代的结束伴随着古典时代晚期(公元 300—公元 600 年)古典文化的崩溃，欧洲历史随后进入中世纪前期(公元 600—公元 1000 年)。这段历史时期涵盖了广袤的领土、多种不同的文化与历史分期。爱伦·坡的一句诗很好地诠释了“古典时代”一词的含义：“光荣属于希腊，伟大属于罗马!”

[15] **Barbarians**：野蛮人。奴隶制社会后期，罗马人建立了一个横跨欧亚的大帝国—罗马帝国。罗马人把居住在罗马帝国北方的外族部落称为“蛮族”。这些外族部落人数最多的除了凯尔特人和斯拉夫人，最著名的就是日耳曼人了。日耳曼人是一些语言、文化和习俗相近的民族的总称。这时的日耳曼人，还处于氏族社会末期，到了公元 1 世纪至公元 3 世纪，各日耳曼人部落开始结成联盟，其中较大的一支就是法兰克。随着罗马帝国陷入危机和来自东方匈奴人带来的压力，公元 4 世纪末，日耳曼人各部族相继卷入欧洲民族大迁徙的洪流，他们从北方多瑙河一带不断进入罗马帝国境内并展开袭击，从而加速了西罗马帝国的灭亡。那些进入罗马帝国境内的日耳曼人，纷纷在西罗马帝国的废墟上建立起日耳曼人王国。

[16] **Liturgy**：礼拜仪式(英国国教的祈祷书)。早期中世纪戏剧的内容和形式与基督教崇拜中的弥撒及圣餐仪式有着密切联系。

[17] **trope**：转义，衍文。弥撒或圣餐仪式充满戏剧性，但不可能真正转化为戏剧。于是研究者将关注点逐渐集中在附加在圣

餐仪式之中的一些“衍文”。最初的“衍文”包括另外添加在弥撒仪式上的开场白、插话或结束语。比如在弥撒结束时，执事要说一句，“好了，弥撒结束，哈利路亚，哈利路亚”，众人则说，“感谢，哈利路亚，哈利路亚”。据记载，一位热情的修士最先使用另外一种直接关联到中世纪戏剧的“转义”。大约在基督教刚刚站稳脚跟的时候，这位修士在弥撒的结束语之后又添加了16个词，以强化圣餐仪式对于众人感情的诉求，并为原来的祈祷书增色，随后，它很快普及开来。这或许是因为当时的基督教尚处于“发展”阶段，圣餐仪式还没有太多定则，所以4世纪以后的宗教会议和教皇颁布的教令中不仅提及这一类“衍文”，而且并未加以制止。润色文字越来越多，以至于不得不单独列作附件，于是有了最早的“衍文”作品。至公元9世纪加洛林王朝时期，“衍文”已作为一种准文学活动而占有相当显著的地位。

[18] **Easter**：复活节(主复活日)。西方的重要节日，在每年春分月圆之后的第一个星期日。基督徒认为，复活节象征着重生与希望，为纪念耶稣基督于公元30至33年之间被钉死在十字架之后第三天复活的日子。

[19] **Quem Quaeritis**：“你要找谁?”(拉丁文)。最初是在做复活节弥撒开始时唱的四行赞美诗的一部分，由两组相同人数的合唱组以应答的方式咏唱，在公元10世纪成为一个独立的复活节演出的礼仪剧，是中世纪戏剧的萌芽。

[20] **two Marys**：两个玛利亚。这里指到过基督墓地的妇女。

[21] **the Creation to Judgment Day from the Old and New Testaments**：旧约和新约中的从创世纪到最后的审判。

[22] ***The Second Shepherds' Play***：《第二牧羊人剧》。英国中世纪威克菲尔德连环组剧最著名的戏剧，也是英国中世纪宗教剧的代表。该剧在叙事结构和内容安排方面与圣经故事之间存在着结构的类比性，而且第一部分与第二部分之间还存在着一定的类型学和隐喻结构。

[23] **saints and martyrs**：圣徒和殉道者。圣徒是追随某一宗教或某

一宗教流派而受到该宗教派别推崇的人。殉道者一词又译为致命圣人、殉教者，来自希腊文的 martys，本意为见证、作证的人，在基督徒心目中耶稣基督是第一位殉道者。

[24] ***Mary Magdalene*** , ***The Conversion of St. Paul*** **and** ***The Play of the Sacrament***：《从良妓女玛丽》、《圣保罗的皈依》和《圣礼剧》。

[25] ***Mankind*** , ***The Castle of Perseverance*** **and** ***Everyman***：《人类》、《坚忍堡垒》和《每个人》。

[26] **Pope Innocent II**：教皇英诺森二世。在位时间为 1130—1143 年。

[27] ***John Heywood***：约翰·海伍德(1497—1580)。宫廷乐师，也是英格兰首部非说教性质的插剧作者，主要活动于 16 世纪，写作戏剧和讽刺诗。

[28] ***Beowulf*** , ***Song of Roland*** , ***Nibelungenlied*** **and** ***Robin Hood***：《贝奥武夫》、《罗兰之歌》、《尼伯龙根之歌》和《罗宾汉》。《贝奥武夫》是英国古代史诗，公元 5 世纪已开始口头传诵，约 8 世纪时成书。《罗兰之歌》是法国英雄史诗，中世纪口头流传的“武功歌”的代表作品，全诗共分为 291 节，长4 002行，以当时民间语言罗曼语写成。《尼伯龙根之歌》是著名的中世纪中古高地德语叙事诗，全诗共 39 歌，9 516行，讲述的是古代勃艮第国王的故事，大约创作于 1190—1200 年，作者不详。《罗宾汉》是英国民间传说中的侠盗式的一个英雄人物，相传活跃在 1160—1247 年间的英国，人称汉丁顿伯爵，他武艺出众、机智勇敢、仇视官吏和教士，是一位劫富济贫、行侠仗义的绿林英雄。

[29] **Dante**：但丁(1265—1321)。13 世纪末，意大利诗人，现代意大利语的奠基者，欧洲文艺复兴时代的开拓人物之一，以长诗《神曲》留名后世。

[30] **the Crusades**：十字军东征(1096—1291)。在罗马天主教教皇的准许下，由西欧的封建领主和骑士对地中海东岸国家发动的持续了近 200 年的宗教性侵略性战争，战争期间屠杀无辜穆斯林不计其数。由于罗马天主教圣城耶路撒冷落入伊斯兰

教徒手中，十字军东征大多数是针对伊斯兰教国家的，主要目的是从伊斯兰教教徒手中夺回耶路撒冷。东征期间，教会授予每一个战士十字架，组成的军队称为十字军。十字军东征一般被认为是天主教的侵略，尽管如此，十字军东征使西欧直接接触到了当时更为先进的拜占庭文明和伊斯兰文明。这种接触，为欧洲的文艺复兴开辟了道路。

[31] **Byzantine**：拜占庭。拜占庭帝国(395—1453)，即东罗马帝国，是一个信奉东正教的君主专制国家。位于欧洲东部，领土曾包括亚洲西部和非洲北部，极盛时领土还包括意大利、叙利亚、巴勒斯坦、埃及和北非地中海沿岸，是古代和中世纪欧洲最悠久的君主制国家。在其上千年的存在期内一般被人简单地称为"罗马帝国"。拜占庭帝国共历经 12 个朝代，93 位皇帝，首都为新罗马(君士坦丁堡)。1453 年，被奥斯曼土耳其攻入君士坦丁堡(现已更名为伊斯坦布尔)而灭亡。

[32] **Da Vinci**：达·芬奇(1452—1519)。意大利文艺复兴三杰之一，也是整个欧洲文艺复兴时期最完美的代表。他是一位思想深邃、学识渊博、多才多艺的画家、数学家、天文学家、预言家、发明家、医学家、生物学家、建筑工程师和军事工程师。《蒙娜丽莎》和《最后的晚餐》是其代表作。

[33] **Raphael**：拉斐尔(1483—1520)。文艺复兴时期意大利著名画家，"文艺复兴三杰"中最年轻的一位，代表了文艺复兴时期艺术家从事理想美的事业所能达到的巅峰。他性情平和、文雅，创作了大量的圣母像。和他的画作一样，他的作品充分体现了安宁、协调、和谐、对称以及完美和恬静的秩序。代表作《圣母的婚礼》、《雅典学院》等。

[34] **Michelangelo**：米开朗基罗(1475—1564)。意大利文艺复兴时期伟大的绘画家、雕塑家、建筑师和诗人，文艺复兴时期雕塑艺术最高峰的代表。与拉斐尔和达·芬奇并称为"文艺复兴三杰"，一生追求艺术的完美，坚持自己的艺术思路，小行星 3001 以他的名字命名以表达后人对他的尊敬。代表作有雕塑《大卫》和世界上最大的壁画——西斯廷教堂天顶壁画

《创世纪》。

[35] **Sistine Chapel**：西斯廷教堂。位于梵蒂冈宫殿内的天主教教堂，紧邻圣伯多禄大殿。西斯廷教堂始建于1445年，由教皇西斯廷四世发起创建。西斯廷教堂是罗马教皇的私用经堂，也是教皇的选出仪式的举行之处。教堂内的天顶画，是文艺复兴三杰之一的米开朗基罗的绘画艺术丰碑，它与同一教堂的另一幅壁画《最后的审判》并列为米开朗基罗一生最有代表性的两大巨制。西斯廷教堂因为米开朗基罗创作了《创世纪》和《最后的审判》而名扬天下。

[36] **Intermezzo**：间奏曲。原指16、17世纪在意大利歌剧的两幕之间演出的轻松愉快的喜剧表演，后发展为意大利喜剧。

[37] **Alexandre Hardy**：亚历山大·阿尔迪(1570—1631)。法国较有名的戏剧家，据说创作了约六百部戏剧，可惜仅存的只有三十四部。

[38] **Lope de Vega**：洛佩·德·维加(1562—1635)。文艺复兴时期西班牙黄金时期最重要的诗人和剧作家。有"西班牙民族戏剧之父"，"天才中的凤凰"以及"大自然中的魔鬼"(出自塞万提斯)之称，他革新了西班牙戏剧的模式，直到今天，他的作品也一直被搬上舞台，这些作品代表了西班牙文学和艺术的最高峰之一。

[39] **Pedro Calderón de la Barca**：佩德罗·卡尔德隆·德·拉·巴尔卡(1600—1681)。西班牙军事家、作家、诗人、戏剧家，西班牙文学黄金时期的重要人物。代表作为《人生如梦》。

[40] **Miguel de Cervantes**：米格尔·德·塞万提斯(1547—1616)。西班牙小说家、剧作家、诗人，被誉为西班牙文学世界最伟大的作家，评论家称他的小说《堂吉诃德》是文学史的第一部现代小说，同时也是世界文学的瑰宝之一，悲剧历史剧《奴曼西亚》(*The Siege of Mumancia*)是其戏剧代表作。

[41] **Tudor dynasty**：都铎王朝(1485—1603)。是在亨利七世1485年入主英格兰、威尔士和爱尔兰所开创的一个王朝，统治英格兰王国及其所属的周围地区。伯爵亨利·都铎于1485年8

月，在法国援助下杀死理查三世，夺取王位，建立都铎王朝，史称亨利七世。都铎王朝统治英格兰王国直到 1603 年伊丽莎白一世去世为止，历经 118 年，共经历了五代君主。都铎王朝处于英国从封建主义向资本主义过渡时期，被认为是英国君主专制历史上的黄金时期。

[42] **War of the Roses**：玫瑰战争或称蔷薇战争(1455—1485)。是英王爱德华三世(1327—1377)的两支后裔：兰开斯特家族和约克家族的支持者为了争夺英格兰王位而发生的内战。两大家族都是金雀花王朝王室的分支，约克家族是爱德华三世的次子的后裔、兰开斯特家族是爱德华三世的第三子的后裔。“玫瑰战争”的名称当时并没有使用，而是在 16 世纪，莎士比亚在历史剧《亨利六世》中以两朵玫瑰被拔标志战争的开始后才成为普遍用语。此名称源于两个家族所选的家徽，兰开斯特的红蔷薇和约克的白蔷薇。贵族力量在整个战争期间被大大削弱，导致了都铎王朝统治下中央集权君主专制的发展。战争最终以兰开斯特家族的亨利七世与约克家族的伊丽莎白联姻结束了战争，也结束了法国金雀花王朝在英格兰的统治，开启了新的威尔士人都铎王朝的统治，也标志着英格兰中世纪时期的结束并走向新的文艺复兴时代。为了纪念这次战争，英格兰以玫瑰为国花，并把皇室徽章改为红白玫瑰。

[43] **Montaigne**：蒙田(1533—1592)。法国文艺复兴后期、16 世纪人文主义思想家。主要作品有《蒙田随笔全集》(*Les Essais de Michelde Montaigne*)，是启蒙运动以前法国的一位知识权威和批评家、人类感情的冷峻的观察家，他对各民族文化，特别是西方文化进行冷静研究。

[44] **Queen Elizabeth**：伊丽莎白女王(1533—1603)。都铎王朝最后一位君主，英格兰与爱尔兰的女王，也是名义上的法国女王。她是英王亨利八世和他的第二任妻子安妮·博林的女儿。1558 年，伊丽莎白的同父异母姐姐玛丽一世去世，伊丽莎白继承王位。1559 年 1 月 15 日，伊丽莎白正式加冕成为英格兰的女王。伊丽莎白即位之初成功地保持了英格兰的统

一。经过近半个世纪的统治后，英格兰成为欧洲最强大的国家之一。英格兰文化也在此期间达到了一个顶峰，涌现出了诸如莎士比亚、弗朗西斯·培根这样的著名人物。英国在北美的殖民地也在此期间开始确立。伊丽莎白一世统治时期，在英国历史上被称为“黄金时代”，她终身未嫁，因此被称为“童贞女王”，也被称为“荣光女王”、“英明女王”。

[45] ***Authorized Version of the Bible***：《钦定版圣经》(*King James Version of the Bible*，简称 KJV)，是《圣经》的诸多英文版本之一，于 1611 年出版。《钦定版圣经》是在英王詹姆斯一世的命令下翻译的，所以在中文里，称之为英王钦定版、詹姆士王译本或英王詹姆士王译本等。

[46] ***Gammer Gurton's Needle*** **and** ***Gorboduc***：《盖墨·格顿的针》和《高布达克》。前者为英国最早的喜剧之一，该剧在 1552 年至 1563 年之间多次被上演，该剧的主题和人物与典型的中世纪讽刺剧相同，在技巧上则借鉴了罗马喜剧。后者被认为是英国的第一部悲剧，由托马斯·塞克维尔和托马斯·诺尔顿合写。1561 年，在神殿学院上演，翌年，该剧在怀特霍尔宫上演，伊丽莎白女王也出席观看。

[47] **“university wits ”**：“大学才子派”。指 16 世纪 80 年代英国出现的一批人文主义剧作家，他们多数是在伦敦牛津或剑桥接受过人文主义教育的青年知识分子，从事在当时被视为并不十分光彩的戏剧行业，致力于英国戏剧改革，把戏剧艺术提升到了一个新高度，这些剧作家包括约翰·黎里、乔治·皮尔、克利斯托弗·马洛、托马斯·基德、罗伯特·格林等(John Lyly，George Peele，Christopher Marlowe，Thomas Kyd，Robert Greene，etc.)。

[48] ***Tamburlaine***：《帖木儿大帝》。克里斯托弗·马洛(1564—1593)创作的戏剧，马洛是英国诗人、剧作家，人称黑夜派和无神论者，曾一度入狱，后被人刺死。该剧讲述了 14 世纪一个普通牧民帖木儿，如何登上国王宝座，成为一个野心勃勃、残暴无情的鞑靼统治者的故事，马洛通过刻画一个百战

百胜的枭雄，表达了文艺复兴时期的人们渴望获得无穷力量与权势的心情。马洛革新了中世纪的戏剧，在舞台上创造了反映时代精神的巨人性格和“雄伟的诗行”，为莎士比亚的创作铺平了道路。

[49] ***The Jew of Malta* and *The Tragical History of Doctor Faustus*：**《马耳他岛的犹太人》和《浮士德博士的悲剧》。

[50] **Goethe：**歌德(1749—1832)。德国著名思想家、作家、科学家，魏玛的古典主义最著名的代表。作为诗歌、戏剧和散文作品的创作者，他是最伟大的德国作家之一，也是世界文学领域的一个出类拔萃的光辉人物，最著名的是书信体小说《少年维特之烦恼》、诗体哲理悲剧《浮士德》和长篇小说《威廉·麦斯特》。

[51] **William Shakespeare：**威廉·莎士比亚(1564—1616)。欧洲文艺复兴时期最重要的作家、杰出的戏剧家和诗人，被喻为“人类文学奥林匹克山上的宙斯”，他跟古希腊三大悲剧家埃斯库罗斯、索福克勒斯及欧里庇得斯合称戏剧史上四大悲剧家。

[52] **Karl Heinrich Marx：**卡尔·马克思。全世界无产阶级的伟大导师、科学社会主义的创始人，德国政治家、哲学家、经济学家、革命理论家、社会学家、革命家，社会学三巨头之一。主要著作有《资本论》、《共产党宣言》，其最广为人知的哲学理论是他对于人类历史进程中阶级斗争的分析。

[53] **the Globe Theatre：**环球剧场。位于英国伦敦，最初的环球剧场由威廉·莎士比亚所在的宫内大臣剧团于 1599 年建造，1613 年毁于火灾，1614 年环球剧场重建，并于 1642 年关闭。1997 年，一座现代仿造的环球剧场落成，命名为“莎士比亚环球剧场”或“新环球剧场”，距离公园街(Park Street)的原址约 205 米远。

[54] **Ben Jonson：**本·琼森(1572—1637)。英国文艺复兴剧作家、诗人、评论家和演员，成为当时学识最渊博的剧作家之一，其作品以讽刺剧见长，《福尔蓬奈》(*Volpone*)和《炼金士》

(*The Alchemist*)为其代表作。

[55] **"upstart crow, beautified with our feathers, that, with his Tygers heart wrapt in a Players hide"** "一只暴发户式的乌鸦，用我们的羽毛装点了起来，用一件演员的外衣保藏了他的虎狼之心"……这是"大学才子"派之一的罗伯特·格林在其《格林的小智慧》中对一个演员和作家的批评，人们普遍认为他批评的是莎士比亚。

[56] **Poet's Corner**：诗人角。伦敦"诗人角"位于泰晤士河畔古老的威斯敏斯特教堂中，因许多诗人、剧作家和作家在那里埋葬和纪念而得名。迄今为止，这里已经安息了 120 名英国历史上最有影响的艺术精英们的亡灵，诗人角靠近教堂的中殿，是一个独立的空间，当教堂举行宗教仪式时，整个正殿烛光熠熠，连耳厅里都坐满了虔诚的教徒。站在诗人角的任何一个位置，都可以看到墙上布满了大小不一的墓碑和依墙而立的石棺。

[57] ***A Midsummer Night's Dream*, *The Merchant of Venice*, *As You Like It* and *Twelfth Night***：《仲夏夜之梦》、《威尼斯商人》、《皆大欢喜》和《第十二夜》，莎士比亚的四大喜剧。

[58] ***Hamlet*, *Othello*, *King Lear* and *Macbeth***：《哈姆雷特》、《奥赛罗》、《李尔王》和《麦克白》，莎士比亚的四大悲剧。

[59] **the English Revolution**：英国资产阶级革命。从 1640 年查理一世召开新议会的事件开始到 1688 年詹姆斯二世退位的事件结束，以新贵族阶级为代表推翻封建统治建立起英国资本主义制度的社会革命。其间经历了议会斗争、以查理一世为代表的国王的军队和资产阶级为代表的议会之间的内战、英吉利共和国成立。克伦威尔独裁时期、查理二世复辟和 1688 年"光荣革命"，导致 1689 年的《权利法案》，英国确立了君主立宪制的资产阶级专政。

[60] **Restoration comedy**：复辟时期喜剧。讽刺性的风俗喜剧，讽刺对象是当时的英国上流社会，但讽刺不深刻，以轻松的心情和愉快的反讽来表现生活，俏皮幽默的对话为突出特点。

喜剧最常见的主题是上流社会男女之间的爱情纠纷，反映出宫廷环境中轻浮放荡的时尚。

[61] **George Lillo**：乔治·李洛(1693—1739)。英国剧作家，著有《伦敦商人》和《致命的好奇心》，前者是英国文学中第一部用散文写成的市民悲剧，反映了资产阶级改善道德的要求。后者以无韵诗体写成，采用乡间背景，打破了古典戏剧的传统。这些家庭悲剧在欧洲大陆相当流行，并且影响了狄德罗、莱辛等剧作家。

[62] **Oliver Cromwell**：奥利弗·克伦威尔。英国资产阶级革命家、政治家、军事家、宗教领袖。在17世纪英国资产阶级革命中，是资产阶级新贵族集团的代表人物、独立派的首领，他信奉清教思想，在1642—1648年两次内战中，先后统率“铁骑军”和新模范军，战胜了国王的军队。1649年，在城市平民和自耕农压力下，处死国王查理一世，宣布成立共和国。1653年，建立军事独裁统治，自任“护国主”。

[63] **Charles I**：查理一世(1600—1649)。唯一一位被以国王身份处死的英格兰国王，在位期间卷入了与国会的权力斗争，还干扰英格兰和苏格兰的教会活动，未征得国会同意就任意收税，与国会之间爆发了战争，史称英国内战。同时他又利用自己英国教会领袖的身份制定了一系列的宗教政策，引起了以清教徒为代表的加尔文教派的不满。查理一世在第一次英国内战(1642—1645)中被击败后，国会希望他能够接受君主立宪制，但他却与苏格兰结盟，逃到了怀特岛郡，这种行为彻底激怒了国会，从而导致了第二次英国内战(1648—1649)，随后被捕、审判、定罪，并以叛国罪被处死。

[64] **Thomas Otway**：托马斯·奥特韦(1652—1685)，英国王政复辟时期剧作家，作品有《阿尔西比亚德斯》、《西班牙王子堂·卡洛斯》、《威尼斯得免于难》等悲剧，《友谊时尚》、《士兵的好运》和《无神论者》是其讽刺效果强烈的喜剧。

[65] **comedy of manners**：风俗喜剧或风尚喜剧。英国王政复辟时期的喜剧，不同于伊丽莎白时代的浪漫喜剧，而是不太深刻的

讽刺性的风俗喜剧，讽刺对象是当时的英国上流社会，以轻松的心情和愉快的反讽来表现上流社会的生活。

[66] **George Etherege**：乔治·埃斯里奇(1636—1692)。英国喜剧作家，以《滑稽的复仇》(1664)开创了复辟风尚喜剧，后来由康格里夫修改完善。他在《摩登人物》(*The Man of Mode*，1676)中塑造了许多舞台上纨绔子弟的鼻祖——福普林·福拉特爵士。

[67] 文中这句话译为"……从一个剧场到另一个剧场，如果他们既不喜欢这个剧目又对周围的女士没有兴趣，他们很少会多待一会儿，最多梳理一下他们的假发或和一个朋友私语几句，然后歪戴着帽子，大步走了出去"。

[68] **Oliver Goldsmith and Richard Brinsley Sheridan**：奥利弗·哥德史密斯和理查德·布林斯莱·谢立丹。哥德史密斯(1730—1774)是18世纪英国著名的剧作家，作品包括《威克菲尔德的牧师》(*The Vicar of Wakefield*)、《委曲求全》(*She Stoops to Conquer*)、《世界公民》(*The Citizen of the World*)等。谢立丹(1751—1816)是18世纪英国最有成就的喜剧家，代表作是《造谣学校》(*The School for Scandal*)，《情敌》(*The Rivals*)等。

[69] **Enlightenment Movement and Industrial Revolution**：启蒙运动和工业革命。启蒙运动(又称理性时代)，指在17世纪和18世纪欧洲地区发生的一场知识与文化运动，该运动相信理性发展知识可以解决人类生存的基本问题。人类历史从此展开在思潮、知识及媒体上的"启蒙"，开启现代化发展历程，德意志哲学家康德以"敢于求知"的启蒙精神来阐述人类的理性担当。工业革命，又称产业革命，指资本主义工业化的早期历程，即资本主义生产完成了从工厂手工业向机器大工业过渡的阶段。工业革命发源于英格兰中部地区，1769年，英国人瓦特改良蒸汽机之后，由一系列技术革命引起了从手工劳动向动力机器生产转变的重大飞跃。随后自英格兰扩散到整个欧洲大陆，19世纪传播到北美地区。工业革命是以机器取代

人力，以大规模工厂化生产取代个体手工生产的一场生产与科技革命。

[70] **Sir Richard Steele and Colley Cibber**：理查德·斯蒂尔和柯莱·西柏。斯蒂尔(1672—1729)是英国作家，其《葬礼》、《撒谎的情人》、《温柔的丈夫》及《互相谅解的情人们》为其代表作，这些感伤喜剧不同于复辟时期喜剧的轻佻，在对婚姻、爱情的描写中表现了中产阶级的道德观，但他的主要贡献在于期刊文学，尤其是《闲话报》和《旁观者》。西柏(1671—1757)，英国自编、自导、自制片的兼任经理的男演员，他为自己的公司写了24部剧，自认为首先是演员，并以喜剧角色见长。《盲孩》是其诗作。

[71] **Henry Fielding and John Gay**：亨利·菲尔丁和约翰·盖伊。菲尔丁(1707—1754)是18世纪英国启蒙运动代表之一，最杰出的英国小说家、戏剧家，被沃尔特·司各特称为“英国小说之父”，其戏剧作品主要属于笑剧、模仿嘲讽剧和讽刺剧，一度主持小剧场，先后写了《堂吉诃德在英国》、《历史纪事》等25部政治讽刺喜剧，均遭禁演。盖伊(1685—1732)，英国诗人兼剧作家，死后葬在诗人角，其最有名的叙事歌剧是《乞丐歌剧》，前后共演出62场，是当时演出最久的剧目，至今是轻歌剧中的保留剧目。此剧大部分演员是乞丐、娼妓、强盗、赌徒，意在反映社会道德的堕落。

[72] **the Licensing Act**：戏剧审查法案。1737年，英国国会通过了“戏剧审查法案”，菲尔丁和其他一些作家从此转入小说创作。这一法案极大地阻碍了英国戏剧的发展，此后100多年中，伦敦只剩下两座剧院，戏剧基本上处于萧条冷落的状态。

[73] **the Bill of Rights**：《权利法案》，又译《人权法案》。全称《国民权利与自由和王位继承宣言》，是英国资产阶级革命中的重要法律文件，奠定了英国君主立宪政体的理论和法律基础，确立了议会所拥有的权力高于王权的原则，具有宪法的性质，标志着君主立宪制开始在英国建立，为英国资本主义的迅速发展扫清了道路，以法律的权力监督国王的权力。

[74] **Immanuel Kant**：伊曼努尔·康德。出生于柯尼斯堡，德国哲学家、德国古典哲学创始人。他被认为是对现代欧洲最具影响力的思想家之一，也是启蒙运动最后一位主要哲学家。其一生深居简出，终身未娶，过着单调刻板的学者生活，直到1804年去世为止，从未踏出过出生地半步。

[75] **Denis Diderot, Jean-Jacques Rousseau, David Hume**：丹尼斯·狄德罗、让·雅克·卢梭和大卫·休谟。狄德罗(1713—1784)，法国启蒙思想家、唯物主义哲学家、无神论者和作家，百科全书派的代表，其最大成就是主编《百科全书》，此书概括了18世纪启蒙运动的精神。卢梭（1712—1778)，法国伟大的启蒙思想家、哲学家、教育家、文学家，是18世纪法国大革命的思想先驱，启蒙运动最卓越的代表人物之一，著有《论人类不平等的起源和基础》、《社会契约论》、《爱弥儿》、《忏悔录》、《新爱洛漪丝》、《植物学通信》。休谟(1711—1776)是苏格兰哲学家、经济学家和历史学家，苏格兰启蒙运动以及西方哲学历史中最重要的人物之一。最先是以历史学家成名。其所著的《英格兰史》一书在当时成为英格兰历史学界的基础著作长达60至70年。

Chapter 3 Modern Drama

Modern Drama (1880-present) refers to an international development or movement centered in Europe and North America, which directs against many of the conventions and institutions of the 19th century drama and theatre. From 1880 to 1960, a number of foundational figures broke with inherited dramatic conventions, instituting new forms of drama and creating different values for performance. After World War I, Western drama was more internationally unified and less of the product of separate national literary traditions. New plays quickly circulated through translation and new production techniques through touring companies established an international standard for modernism in drama. With numerous dramatists' miscellaneous plays, there were roughly two large groups: realistic and anti-realistic drama including symbolic, expressionistic, surrealistic, existentialistic, absurd drama etc.

Section 1 The Realistic Drama in the 19th Century

After a century of emphasis on nature and reason, the late 18th century and the early 19th century, often called the Romantic Age was an emotional, passionate time. The term romance implied emotional(1798-

1832) attractions, affairs of the heart, religious ideals, freedom and strong emphasis on the needs of both the masses and the individual. This was the time Napoleon Bonaparte and the French Revolution[1], a time in which the aristocracy was challenged by the middle and lower classes. It was well a century of scientific innovation leading to the Industrial Revolution, to the evolutionary theories of Charles Darwin[2] and to the psychological insights of Sigmund Freud. In England, it was the era of the great Romantic poets such as Wordsworth, Coleridge, Byron, Shelley and Keats[3]; in Germany of the poets and dramatists Johann Von Goethe and Friedrich Schiller[4]; in France, of the Romantic poet, novelist and dramatist Victor Hugo[5]; in America, of Henry Wadsworth Longfellow[6].

Romanticism encouraged the exploration of fantasy in juxtaposition to the world of natural phenomena. Romanticism reflected a belief in religious transcendentalism or the affinity of man and spirit and of man and nature. The Romantics believed in the autonomy of inspired genius, the necessity of releasing the imagination, the spontaneity of intuitive feeling, the freedom of artistic expression and a vision of nature as part of unified cosmos. Romantic idealism culminated in the notion of organic growth and development arising from an interest in the past, particularly in the Middle Ages.

The romantic movement did not blossom in French drama until the 1820s, while in England the great Romantic poets did not produce important drama. Burlesque and mediocre melodrama reigned supreme on the English stage. Although melodrama was aimed solely at producing superficial excitement, its development, coupled with the emergence of realism in the 19th century, resulted in more serious drama.

1.1 Realism

The development of capitalism and imperialism asked for a

widespread demand for social reform of every kind. Fast developed new science and appearance of various philosophical ideas such as Karl Marx's theory of scientific socialism, Darwin's theory of evolution and "survival of the fittest", Freud's theory of analytical psychology, Nietzsche's[7] doctrines of power and superman and Einstein's theory of relativity needed writers to make new explorations on human natures and human relationships. Nearly all successful novelists wrote plays also as an instrument of social reform with Henrik Ibsen, Oscar Wilde, G. B. Shaw[8], etc. as major representatives.

Realism in the arts, allied with the origins of modern science, might be generally defined as the attempt to represent subject matter truthfully, without artificiality and avoiding artistic conventions, implausible exotic and supernatural elements — the goal of realism. Realism revolted against the exotic subject matter and exaggerated emotionalism and drama of the Romantic Movement in the 18th century. Instead it sought to portray real and typical contemporary people and situations with truth and accuracy, not avoiding unpleasant or sordid aspects of life. Realist works depicted people of all classes in situations arising in ordinary life, and often reflected the changes wrought by the Industrial and Commercial Revolutions. The popularity of such 'realistic' works grew with the introduction of photography — a new visual source that created a desire for people to produce representations which looked "objectively real". Theatre was based on natural, rational explanation as evidenced and experienced through the 5 senses instead of on emotional or mystic explanations. Characters were based on real life, three dimensional human beings and the plots were concerned with the problems of daily life — the environmental and social forces that encroached on man. Realistic playwrights tended to emphasize outward action more than inner psychology, telling us to stop dreaming and start solving problems by taking a serious, practical and scientific attitude. They turned away from the far away and long ago of the romantics to a concern with the here and now, from fantasies of heroic adventure to a journalistic study of ordinary people and from idealistic speculation to pragmatic concern with actual problems, with the illnesses of society presented and the nature of family, social relationship explored and exposed. The "theatre of the 4th wall removed" became popular as audience peered into the lives of the character on stage. Thomas William Robertson[9] was the first man letting actors sit in real chairs and really drink tea on stage.

1.2 Realistic Playwrights

Realism had perhaps its most profound expression in the works of the great 19th century Russian dramatists Nikolai Gogol, Ivan Turgenev, Anton Chekhov, Leo Tolstoy[10], etc. The Norway playwright Henrik Ibsen brought to a climax the realistic movement of the 19th century. Some of his late plays served as a bridge to the 20th century symbolism, marking a trend away from realism. His works such as *A Doll's House*, *Ghosts*, *The Wild Duck*, *The Enemy of the People*, and *The Master Builder*[11] were translated into many different languages. His realistic drama of ideas with the theme of man's unending conflict between duty to himself and duty to others surpassed others for blending a complex plot, a detailed setting and middle-class yet extraordinary characters in an organic whole.

Another great representative of realistic playwrights dealing with social problems was George Bernard Shaw who brought the play of ideas to fruition with penetrating intelligence and singular wit. He was the 1st modem man of the English drama, and undoubtedly the most prolific, witty and influential comic dramatist that England had seen in two hundred years who anticipated by half a century the time when the world would try to use power and money to abolish poverty and help individuals find a higher spiritual life.

Related to realism is naturalism, which can be defined as a

selective realism emphasizing the more sordid and pessimistic aspects of life. Naturalism is the application of the principles of scientific determinism to literature. It gains from Newton's[12] mechanistic determinism, from Darwin's biological determinism, from Marx's view of history as a battle ground of vast economic and social forces and from Freud's view of determinism of the inner and subconscious self. Naturalists see human beings as the victims of destiny or fate, who are portrayed as animals driven by fundamental urges — fear, hunger and sex. The naturalistic movement is most commonly identified with the "slice-of-life" theory of Émile Zola[13], which has a profound effect on the 20th century playwrights.

Anyway when the Victorian idealist said, "keep your eyes on the stars" the naturalist added, "And fall into a ditch!"

1.3 Atheistic Playwrights

The playwright that was making unique contribution to English theater was Oscar Wilde, born in Dublin and educated in Trinity College[14]. He became under the influence of old aesthetic theories of John Ruskin and Walter Pater[15], a writer and a spokesman for the school of Aestheticism (art for art's sake).

Aestheticism is an art movement that focuses on the idea that art exists for the sake of its beauty alone. It studies beauty in nature, art and literature. The aesthetics in literature concerns the sense of the beautiful, rather than on moral, social or practical considerations. Wilde made a lecture tour to America and Canada on the aesthetic movement in 1882, where he met Walt Whitman[16] and then went to Paris where he met Zola and Balzac[17]. In 1895, he was suddenly put into jail because of a homosexual relationship which ruined him and the aesthetic movement itself suffered a severe setback not only with the public but among writers as well. He followed the literary theory advocated by Walter Pater and stated that art was amoral and totally separated with morality and art was above life and the function of real art was to attract, to please and to provide enjoyment. He produced comedies of manners, with *The Importance of Being Earnest*[18] as his representative — with an unimportant plot, well-etched character types and witty dialogue of remarkable excellence, seeming a direct throwback to Restoration comedy.

Section 2 The Anti-Realistic Drama in the 20th Century

Realism still occupied a dominant position in literary techniques in the early 20th century. Some writers followed the 19th century realistic trend and focused on the post-war reality of society, with naturalism, aestheticism etc. But when modernism, which began in the late 19th century and flourished until 1950s, was getting more influential, more literary tendencies and schools came into being like mushrooms after rain, making this period named "the Era of Isms" such as symbolism, surrealism, impressionism, expressionism and futurism. So many "-ism" literary and artistic movements developed into two opposing facets: positive to promote growth and negative to depict man's inhumanity. Modernist writers took the irrational philosophy and the theory of psychoanalysis as its theoretical base. They concentrated more on the private than on the public, more on the subjective than on the objective. They were mainly concerned with the inner being of an individual, with the distorted, alienated and ill relationships between man and nature, man and society, man and man and man and himself as the major themes, paying more attention to the psychic time than the chronological time. Namely, in their writings, the past, present and future mingled together and existed at the same time in the consciousness of an individual.

War, as a psychological wound, was omnipresent. The terrible destructive force of science and the disillusionment and dissatisfaction with the drift of material civilization made people doubt the real meaning of life. Theatre-goers looking for fun and light entertainment decreased much. Theatres for small and particular groups came into being.

2.1 The Surrealistic Drama

Anti-realistic drama, whose forms or ideas actively or implicitly opposed realistic ones, was a kind of distortion — genuine realistic results from the deepened, broadened and reverse interpretation of the reality, thus a new reality.

Surrealism referred to a movement in art and literature which began in Paris in 1924 to improve poetry and prose writing of conscious mental control and aesthetic technique, allowing the subconscious and all irrational impulses the freedom to express other traditional principles of standards. It was regarded as an outgrowth of Dadaism[19] and influenced by Freud. Dada, meaning "hobby horse" in French, proposed to free the plastic and graphic arts and the verbal arts from traditional ways of seeing and feeling, stressing the unpredictable. Surrealistic drama promised to free the mind of rational control by exposing the subconscious mind of man, preaching a new psychology based on combining the dreaming state with the waking state with the goal of finding a new reality, a kind of sur (above) reality. This kind of drama provided audience with vaguer scenery, fragmentary and unmotivated characters with minimal conscious activity and disjointed events in general a chaotic universe. Surrealism was the philosophical forerunners of the Absurd.

2.2 The Symbolic Drama

Symbolism is the use of one object to represent or suggest another in literature, the use of symbols in writing, particularly the serious and extensive use of such symbols, stressing the autonomy of art, measured entirely in terms of aesthetic standards. Symbolist writers use symbols to transcend what is normally considered "realistic" in everyday life, hoping the symbols will take them beyond the truth. Characters in symbolic plays have no personality of their own — just symbols of some qualities, offering readers an opportunity to read between the lines and interpret the piece according to personal desire and feeling response.

2.3 The Expressionistic Drama

Another important movement in the early 20th century drama was expressionism which had its roots in a German political movement against mass industrialization and dehumanized mechanization. It was used to describe any art that raised subjective feelings above objective observations. In literature, writers attempted to exhibit the distortion of the objects of the outer world and the violent dislocation of time sequence and spatial logic by the impressions or moods of characters, conveying the dehumanizing aspect of the 20th century technological society through devices such as minimal scenery, telegraphic dialogue, talking machines and characters portrayed as types rather than individuals. Expressionist writers, Franz Kafka and James Joyce[20] developed a particular style of expressionists — "stream of consciousness"[21] writing technique. The notable expressionist playwright, Eugene O'Neill was able to combine fantasy, symbolism, fragments of realism as well as naturalism, tending to represent anonymous human types instead of individualized characters.

2.4 The Existentialistic Drama

The most influential expression of Western philosophy over the post-war years is Existentialism[22] which is a school of European philosophy distinguished by its emphasis on human existence. The destructive force of science and the possibility of self-annihilation set people thinking about the meaning of existence and life. The English literary situation looked depressingly bleak after the wars. The men of letters showed the absurdity and emptiness of existence, the human anguish, despair and the inner vacancy of self on the one hand, showed a serious concern for the future and affirmed the need for a moral regeneration on the other hand. Existentialists tend to emphasize the unique and particular in human experience. They place the individual person at the center of their picture of the world. Each man is the source of all value and obliged to choose for himself what to do and what standards to adopt or reject, and consciousness of such freedom is a condition of authentic existence, giving priority to sincerity and creativity in the moral life.

The pessimism and despair of the 20th century found expression in the existentialist dramas of Jean-Paul Sartre, who was awarded the Nobel Prize for literature in 1964 but refused. He claimed each one should be responsible for his own acts and for the consequences of those acts, which was manifested in his drama *The Flies*[23]. His existentialism was an atheist philosophy of human freedom conceived in terms of individual responsibility and authenticity, believing that all human interaction was a living hell.

2.5 The Absurd Drama[24]

The theater of the absurd achieved popularity when World War II highlighted the essential precariousness of human life — primarily probably because of both traumatic experience of the horrors of wars and a reaction to the disappearance of the religious dimension of contemporary life. World War II and its attendant horrors produced a widespread sense of the utter meaninglessness of human existence. This sense was brilliantly expressed in the body of plays that have come to be known collectively as the theater of the absurd, a term coined by the critic Martin Esslin[25] for some playwrights who mostly wrote in the 1950s and 1960s. By abandoning traditional devices of the drama, including logical plot development, meaningful dialogues and intelligible characters, absurdist writers sought to convey modern humanity's feeling of bewilderment, alienation, meaninglessness of existence and despair — the sense that reality was itself unreal. They took a highly unusual, innovative form: anti-theatre, creating meaningless speeches, illogical plots and even just silence to directly aim to startle the viewer and shake him out of this comfortable, conventional life of everyday concerns. One of the most important aspects of absurd drama was its distrust of language as a means of communication, believing words failed to express the essence of human experience. In their plays human beings often portrayed as dupes, clowns who, although not without dignity, were at the mercy of forces were inscrutable. Representative playwrights included Eugene Ionesco, Samuel Beckett, Jean Genet, Arthur Adamov, Harold Pinter, Edward Albee, etc.,[26] with *Waiting for Godot*[27] as the first and perhaps the most characteristic play in this style.

2.6 Drama of Other Kinds

Of course, there were many other kinds of drama forms though not as influential as mentioned above. The overwhelming revival of ideologically oriented theories since the 1980s with British cultural materialism, American New Historicism and Feminist Theory and Criticism among the great variety of approaches provided impetus for new plays with new forms. British cultural materialism studied drama, along with other literary forms as a cultural phenomenon from a basically Marxist perspective. American New Historicists were influenced more by the French poststructuralists, showing particular interest in power, authority and subversion underlying the dramatic texts. Feminist theory showed greater diversity both in source and attitude while postcolonial theory (Edward Said[28]) lent perspective to the analysis of plays written by imperialist and third-world authors. The civil rights and women's movements, gay liberation, and the AIDS crisis made it possible for new plays to explore the lives of minorities and women. Feminist and other women-centered themes dramatized by contemporary female playwrights were plentiful in the 1970s and extended in the following decades. Keep in mind we can also understand people and life through the realistic and symbolic dramas of Arthur Miller at this period. The last third of the 20th century emphasized creative directing, too.

In the United States and England, however, many dramatists old and new continued to flourish, with numerous plays of the later decades of the 20th century and the early 21st century, echoing the trends of the years preceding them.

Section 3 Christianity

The core of Humanism in the West focuses on the value of human beings and the pursuit of freedom individually and collectively and generally prefers critical thinking and evidence (rationalism, empiricism) over established doctrine or faith, which seems against Christianity that emphasizes the absolute obedience to God.

Actually, humanism and Christianity are in a dialectic relationship, neither in a total agreement nor in a simple confrontation. Christianity is not the Humanities, but it does not oppose or repel the humanities. On the contrary, the emergence and evolution of the humanism attributes to or owns debt to Christianity. Generally, humanism and Christianity are different from each other and at the same time mutually complementary. Therefore, with no knowledge of Christianity and without a sight into Christian culture, it is no easy task for students to get a clear picture of

Western culture and literature.

3.1 The Origin of Christianity

Christianity began in the 1st century AD as a Jewish sect in Palestine[29], following the life, death and resurrection of Jesus[30]. Christianity continued to spread to Europe, especially to the poor, becoming a dominant religion of the whole Roman Empire in the 4th century AD after mixing with many other sects of religions. The fall of Rome gave rebirth of Christianity which became an international religious organization, known for its caesaropapism[31]. Actually, it was the integration of various Western cultures that formed the Christianity, which in turn laid the foundation of politics, spirit and culture of Europe.

3.2 The Importance of Christianity

Christianity plays a dominant role in shaping the cultural tradition and value in the West. First of all, without Christianity, there could never have formed the Western thinking way and their attitude towards the relationship between man and the nature, let alone the Western civilization in today's sense. Secondly, without Christianity, our world would never have seen the ancient Western culture's modernization process. Ancient European culture is best represented by Greek and Roman cultures, whose basic value is to meet human's nature. Marx once compared the Ancient Greeks to normal human beings in their childhood, which means the Ancient Greeks have always lived following their human nature and primitive desires. However, the emergence of Christianity has brought human beings' spiritual life and mental needs to an all-time high level. Therefore, it is the Christianity that raises the ancient concept of "Natural Person" to "Spiritual Person". Finally, Christianity and its striking conflicts between flesh and spirit, sensibility and rationality, life in heaven and life on earth, offer undoubtedly the strong driving force for the Western culture's self-development.

As one kind of religious faith, Christianity is featured by three elements which include a faith in "God-Jesus", the purpose of gaining "redemption" and the emphasis on human' spiritual power.

Christianity focuses on the four elementary issues. Firstly, it tries to figure out the essence of the world we live in. The first chapter *Genesis in the Old Testament*[32] offers its answer to this question, that is, the essence of the world is spiritual and the world is created by God and that God exist undoubtedly as the "primary driving force". The Ancient Greeks explain the world to some degree from the perspective of human's instinct while Christianity does from rational theology. This mode of thinking, casting aside human beings' instinctive desires and regarding of their feelings and experience in life, is a completely new thinking way. By focusing on human beings' spirit, this kind of thinking mode indicates that human beings are making efforts to shake off the yoke of their instincts, heading for rationality eventually, though hard.

Secondly, Christianity takes pains to find an answer to what man is. According to *Genesis*, God make man with dust, which manifests that man's essence lies in God, not in themselves. Therefore, man is, on the one hand, the outcome of spirits because of being created by God and on the other hand, has the property of materiality because of being made of mud. Materiality plays no important role at all in Christianity for the reason that dust is the most useless material in the world. Only after God breathe into the man's nostrils the breath of life and endow him a soul, is man given a spiritual commonness with God, which indicates that human beings are the integrity of flesh and soul as well as spirit and material. As a result, man has to face the challenges: to rise or to fall. The conflicts between spiritual needs and sensual desires are human being's major contradiction. Those who are addicted to physical and instinct desires will fall while those who make unremitted efforts to meet their spirituality will rise.

Thirdly, Christianity wants to get to know the relationship between man and the world. The absolute predominance of God is valued in *The Old Testament*. Later, there exist different explanations of the relationship between man and the world. One rather extreme point of view is that man should accept God's salvation unconditionally and passively while the opposite extreme is the position that whether one will go to the heaven or the hell depends on his faith in God and belief in Christianity, focusing on man's pursuit of Heaven in his inner heart.

Finally, Christianity places value on the ideology of fairness and justice. According to Christianity, the greatest justice in the world lies in the justice of love, which reflects Christianity's concept of fairness and justice, enriched continuously during the process of Christianity development. "Freedom, equality and fraternity", advocated during the period of Enlightenment, actually originate from ideology of Christianity.

3.3 The Crises of Christianity

From the late 13th century to the early 14th century, the development of the European social productivity gave rise to the flourishing of natural science, which offered the historical and cultural opportunities for the rise of the Renaissance. The natural science, which served as the means to prove the rationality of theology, finally became the powerful ideological weapon against religious theology during the Renaissance, accelerating the collapse of theological ideas. The appearance of the natural science, in fact, ushered in a new way of thinking and perceiving the world — the approaching of the era of rational thinking.

3.3.1 The 1st Crisis Christianity Facing

Why did the first crisis of Christianity appear in the 13th century? Firstly, in the 13th century, a great plague — the Black Death swept the whole Europe. About one-third of the Europeans died from this plague, which influenced people greatly. Some people began to question the "Almighty God", which provided an opportunity to people's ideological emancipation, accelerating the collapse of ideological ideas formed in the Middle Ages. Witnessing the great loss of life of the beloved, many people began to realize the value of life, thus believing in the importance of enjoying the present life. The second historical and cultural chance was the fall of the Byzantine and the rediscovery of the ancient classics. In 1453, the Turks attacked the Byzantine and destroyed a large number of historical relics. Fortunately, many Ancient Greek and Roman classics were found, which made the people, living through the Middle Ages, come to realize that their ancestors had lived thus a glorious, happy and beautiful life based on their own desires without Christianity. These Ancient Greek classics offered the proof and reason for them to enjoy life instead of abiding by God unconditionally and unsuspectingly. The third opportunity was that, in the 15th and 16th century, the Europeans loved exploring the outside world. The great discoveries of geography promoted the Renaissance movement, which let people realize the strength and ability of man.

3.3.2 The 2nd Crisis Christianity Facing

The prevalence of science and ration and the Enlightenment in the 18th century in the West liquidated theology on a large scale ideologically, culturally and politically. Christianity in the 18th century faced for the first time a real challenge. Industrial Revolution in Britain stimulated the development of science and technology. People's understanding of the connotation of rationality had undergone profound changes. From the late 17th century, people began to value science and wisdom in Europe.

In the Renaissance, the rationality we are talking about refers to the "erotic rationality". It was not until the late 16th century and the early

17th century that people began to doubt "erotic rationality". People began to place value on "wisdom rationality", which meant that with the wisdom and strength, man could judge and deal with things independently. In the 18th century, there came a marriage of "wisdom rationality" and "scientific thought", thus resulting in a great leap of rational thinking way in the West. In the essay *Answering the Question: What is Enlightenment*? Kant defined the Enlightenment as an age shaped by the Latin motto Sapere aude ("Dare to be wise"). Kant maintained that one ought to think autonomously, free of the dictates of external authority. He said, "Enlightenment is man's emergence from his self-imposed nonage. Nonage is the inability to use one's own understanding without another's guidance. This nonage is self-imposed if its cause lies not in lack of understanding but in indecision and lack of courage to use one's own mind without another's guidance. Having the courage to use your own understanding is therefore the motto of the enlightenment."

3.4 The Reform and Evolution of Christianity

After the 13th century, the religious circles also called for a reform. From the day when Christianity was born, conflicts and struggles regarding the doctrinal explanation and other relevant religious issues have never ended. From early Paul to Abelard[33] to Martin Luther, they all insisted that God be in the heart of people, emphasizing man's ability to pursue the God by themselves instead of with the help of priests while many priests stressed the decisive role of God, believing people should obey God unconditionally and wait for the salvation passively.

In the 14th century, Martin Luther's religious reform advocated the promotion of human self-consciousness and pursuit of rational spirit. *Bible* used to be Latin, which could be read, understood and explained only by learnt priests. Believing that the voice of God should reach the heart of all people, Martin Luther translated *Bible* from Latin to local language, making it possible that ordinary people could also communicate with God with heart. Actually, the concept of "God" was keeping changing all the time. At the very beginning it was the symbol of power and salvation. In the dark age of Middle Ages, it meant order and then began to have the meaning of "Almighty Love", which evolved into "eternal love" and "eternal justice" until the end of the 19th century. The fact was that the Christianity in the eyes of many thinkers and men of letters in the 19th century had become part of the bourgeois ideology and culture system, thus the connotation of God having been changed and enriched. The "eternal love" and the "eternal justice" were the core and essence of Christianity. Therefore, the renaissance of the Christian in the 19th century was the renaissance based on love and justice. God was the symbol of supreme love and absolute justice in the world, which was the major theme of the novel of Jane Eyre[34].

Various modern and postmodern theories sprang out like mushrooms around the 20th century when "God" as "a relation structure of noble spirit" began to become the trend of a new explanation. When the connotation of "God" was being enriched day by day, "God" in Christian culture developed into "God in heart" and "God of the combination of both internal and external relation" from the only external logos[35] in the premier understanding, the change of which reflected man's cognitional changes of God from "the objective mechanism" theory to "epistemology" then to "sensualism" theory. It is the continuous change and adaption of "God" in its original concept and system by Christians that makes it keep up with the times, thus becoming an important component of Western spirit and culture no matter how the world is changing over the time, which can be sensed from the fact that Christianity emerged as the world outlook of the poor, developed into a feudal world view, then was adapted into the bourgeois' world outlook and now attempts to become one of all human beings.

Section 4 Christianity and Literature

Undoubtedly Christianity and literature is closely related. Actually, a lot of early famous writers came from churches.

4.1 Christianity as the Foundation of Literature in Medieval Europe

The budding of dramatic art after Carolingian Renaissance[36] was the most important harvest of medieval European Christian literature. The ancient civilization was drastically devastated when the barbarians invaded European continent. As a result, the glorious drama tradition and achievements of the Ancient Greece and Rome lost and disappeared at the beginning of the Middle Ages. The Greek drama was hardly known to people and Roman Seneca's written materials, though close to them in time didn't appear in a few literature works until the 14th century. Instead of imitating, adapting and inheriting the tradition, the medieval drama, to a great extent, was created with originality. Therefore Christian drama had its own value. Firstly, though it was of little value as far as the theme and content those Christian dramas reflected and advocated were concerned because they were supposed to propaganda Christianity and consolidate Christian consciousness in people's mind, they actually mirrored the typical social and cultural characteristics of the medieval Europe. This, undoubtedly, offers precious materials for the present researchers to do some further researches on basic situation in cultural and ideological field of the medieval Europe. In addition, medieval drama had a great impact on the Renaissance drama though looking superficial and crude compared to the grand Greek and Roman drama of the old days. Secondly, without being influenced by the Ancient Greek and Roman drama, the medieval Christian drama preliminarily developed its own dramatic art form which was exclusive to the medieval time. The ingenuity was that there existed no hierarchy of characters of all walks of life and God could talk directly on the stage, which challenged the concept of class in classical drama which insisted that characters should be classified according to their status, personality, occupation and many other factors. Besides, the medieval drama which paid little attention to form and logistics differed greatly from classical drama that had very strict rules for drama. For example, Jesus came to life from the grave, God appeared on the stage in person and some characters even jumped off the stage to join the audience. In the mystery and miracle plays, time yesterday, today and tomorrow appeared simultaneously. Finally, religious drama had enriched people's spiritual life to get rid of the infertility and tediousness of daily life when people had little cultural entertainment and recreation, enlightening people culturally and upgrading their art taste though in a limited way.

4.2 Rebellion and Inheritance of Christian Culture in the 18th Century Literature

Men of letters before the 18th century rebelled against and negated religion with expressions of personal experience. However, when the 18th century writers fought against religious theology with their own works, they acted consciously with the guidance of rationality. Literary rebellions against Christian theology could be divided into allegorical one and direct one. Daniel Defoe[37] was a representative writer who fought against theology in the 18th century literature. *Robinson Crusoe* was a cultural fable that eulogized the wisdom and creativity of human beings, revealing the essence of freedom of man and denying the creation of the world and the history of God. The "Little Paradise" in the Desert Island was created by Robinson himself with his wisdom, his hands and unremitting labor, with which God had nothing to do. "His philosophy is action and is not afraid of difficulties." The protagonist believed that the Christian passion would no longer be found in his time.

Writers who attacked and negated the thought and culture of theological system directly and relentlessly were Enlightenment writers such as Voltaire, Diderot, Rousseau and Hume. "Just as the 17th century was the century of Louis XIV[38], the 18th century was the century of Voltaire." In his youth, Voltaire used to study religion in the Jesuit school where he declared that he learned only "Latin and stupidity". Later, he devoted his life to criticizing the oppression of feudal superstition and despotism.

A further negation of the feudal theological system will inevitably make people rethink about the relationship between man and the world, causing a new ideological system of human beings. Anyone who is familiar with the world cultural and thought history knows that from the late 18th century to the early 19th century, there sprang out a large number of great thinkers and philosophers who were famous for their efforts of constructing a new and huge thought system. Kant, Fichte, Schelling and Hegel[39] were the world-renowned representatives. Regardless of the huge differences their respective theories revealed, it was obvious that they were taking pains to establish a new theoretical system which was completely different from the religious theological system of Christianity. Kant, widely considered to be a central figure of modern philosophy, was the founder of German classical idealism philosophy. He argued that human concepts and categories structured our view of the world and its laws and that reason was the source of morality. Based on the contradiction between good and evil, he established a new ideological system of human beings different from the existing religious one. German and European thinking progressed after him until a philosophy giant, Hegel appeared. Hegel brought the philosophy pioneered by Kant to a new height and established the hugest and the most complicated objective idealism in the European philosophy history, which was even adopted by quite a few Protestant theologians. In short, in the second half of the 18th century, it was a cultural fashion to establish a new thought system to negate theology in both philosophical and literary fields. The achievements of Hegel and Goethe's goals to reconstruct a new thought system in their respective fields indicated that the rebellion to and negation of theological system from European progressive thinkers and writers since the Renaissance had reached a new height.

4.3 Literature Development and Christian Culture in the Early 19th Century

Chance favored Christianity in the 19th century in Europe. Firstly, the reason that people began to value Christian culture once again in the early 19th century was closely relevant to the widely spread overwhelming desperation brought by the cruelty and bloodiness of the French Revolution and the brutal dictatorship after it. For those intellectuals with humanitarian thoughts, the social disorder caused by Revolution violence, the revolution terrorism and dictatorship during and after the French Revolution ran counter to their living morals. The last straw was the disillusionment of a rational society painted by the enlightened thinkers, thus making them disappointed, distressed and skeptic of what was going on. Coleridge regarded as the most creative British from 1770 to 1830, was sympathetic with the French Revolution at his early ages, writing *The Fall of the Bastille*. His masterpiece *The Rime of the Ancient Mariner*[40] which reflected his change of attitude towards revolution, depicted the mental torture vividly caused both by the indiscriminate killing of the innocent and the lack of faith during and after the French Revolution, seeking salvation from religion. Secondly, the disillusionment of enlightenment and detest of tyranny made many thinkers go back to Christianity for strength and spiritual comfort. Thirdly, what the industrialization and urbanization along with the ills of then emerging capitalist industrial civilization had taught people was class consciousness. What was worse, the vulgarity and viciousness of Bourgeois smashed the ethics, rules and value system that had been formed and tested by the influence of Christian culture. In a capitalist society, the relationship between people was totally based on economic benefits, no longer supported by moral obligations and emotional factors, thus worsening interpersonal relationship even within a family. Facing moral corruption and the loss of human nature, some men of letters tried to direct people to the right direction, turning to religion for spiritual comfort. The human anguish and despair and the inner vacancy of self on the one hand and a serious concern for the future on the other urged a need for a moral regeneration.

In the 20th century, the two world wars brought tremendous hurt to people. Writers of modernism insisted that literature should turn inwardly — man's inner world due primarily to their sickness of the absurd world and their retreat and escape from the ugly reality. Unfortunately, they didn't find God in the heart of men. What existed in the heart of human beings was the animal instinct that indulged in pleasure. This kind of instinct was gloomy, blind, selfish and extremely devastating. A lot of literature works in the 1950s and 1960s reflected the beast-like hidden evils in man's inner heart. Chained by materialism spiritually and feeling overwhelmed by the outside world, the modernists in the first half of the 20th century shared a heavy sense of crisis and disillusionment by presenting depression, pessimism and desperation. Novelists of stream of consciousness described people's inner world as confusing and frivolous as possible; writers of expressionism depicted people as humble and lonely; writers of surrealism portrayed characters as empty and bored, showing the absurdity and emptiness of existence, all of which indicated that after the death of "the external God" (claimed by Nietzsche), "the internal God" also died (claimed by William

Faulkner, Golding[41] and so on). In the 1960s and the 1970s, the thought "God in the heart" yielded no God but devil in man's heart. Therefore, the tradition of searching God in literature came to an end.

In the latter half of the 20th century, Western literary thoughts and Christian cultural spirits began to integrate, though many writers were no longer Christians. Even those who still claimed to be were obviously different from earlier writers. When writing, what they advertised were no longer just preaching religious ideas, but the universal value shared by the whole contemporary society. "It is something immortal in religion that can survive." Any society can find it necessary to regularly consolidate and verify the collective emotion and consciousness, which assures a society of its unity and harmony. That is why literature is interwoven with Christianity in the West.

重难点解读

[1] **Napoleon Bonaparte and the French Revolution**：拿破仑·波拿巴和法国大革命。拿破仑也被称为"拿破仑一世(1769—1821)"，出生于科西嘉岛，法国军事家与政治家、法兰西第一共和国第一执政(1799—1804 年)、法兰西第一帝国及百日王朝的皇帝。拿破仑一度让法国变得强大无比，曾占领过西欧和中欧的广大领土，使法国资产阶级革命思想得到了广泛的传播，被称作奇迹缔造者，也是法国人民的骄傲。法国大革命是 1789 年在法国爆发的资产阶级革命，统治法国多个世纪的君主制封建制度在三年内土崩瓦解。法国在这段时期经历着一个史诗般的转变：过往的封建、贵族和宗教特权不断受到自由主义政治组织及上街抗议的民众的冲击，旧的观念逐渐被全新的天赋人权、三权分立等民主思想所取代。

[2] **Charles Darwin**：查尔斯·达尔文(1809—1882)。英国生物学家、进化论的奠基人。曾乘坐英国皇家海军的贝格尔号舰艇进行历时 5 年的环球航行，对动植物和地质结构等进行了大量

的观察和采集，出版了《物种起源》，提出了生物进化论学说，从而摧毁了各种唯心的神造论以及物种不变论，其理论对人类学、心理学、哲学的发展都有不容忽视的影响。

[3] **Wordswoth, Coleridge, Byron, Shelley and Keats**：华兹华斯、柯勒律治、拜伦、雪莱和济慈。华兹华斯(William Wordsworth, 1770—1850)，英国浪漫主义诗人，湖畔诗人之一，桂冠诗人，代表作有与柯勒律治合著的《抒情歌谣集》、长诗《序曲》、《漫游》。柯勒律治(Samuel Taylor Coleridge, 1772—1834)，英国诗人和评论家，一生在贫病交困和鸦片成瘾的阴影下度过，诗歌作品相对较少。拜伦(George Gordon Byron, 1788—1824)，英国19世纪初期伟大的浪漫主义诗人，代表作有《恰尔德·哈洛尔德游记》、《唐璜》等，他积极而勇敢地投身革命，参加了希腊民族解放运动。雪莱(Percy Bysshe Shelley), 1792—1822)，英国浪漫主义民主诗人、第一位社会主义诗人、小说家、哲学家、散文随笔和政论作家、改革家、柏拉图主义者和理想主义者。济慈（John Keats, 1795—1821)，杰出的英诗作家之一，浪漫派的主要成员。

[4] **Friedrich Schiller**：弗里德里希·席勒(1759—1805)。德国18世纪著名诗人、哲学家、历史学家和剧作家，德国启蒙文学代表人物之一，德国文学史上著名的"狂飙突进运动"的代表人物，也被公认为德国文学史上地位仅次于歌德的伟大作家。

[5] **Victor Hugo**：维克多·雨果(1802—1885)。法国作家，19世纪前期积极浪漫主义文学代表作家，人道主义代表人物，法国文学史上卓越的资产阶级民主作家，被人们称为"法兰西的莎士比亚"。一生写过多部诗歌、小说、剧本、各种散文和文艺评论及政论文章，在法国及世界有着广泛的影响力，其代表作有《巴黎圣母院》和《悲惨世界》，短篇小说有《"诺曼底"号遇难记》。

[6] **Henry Wadsworth Longfellow**：亨利·沃兹沃斯·朗费罗(1807—1882)。19世纪美国最伟大的浪漫主义诗人之一。1839年出版第一部诗集《夜吟》，包括著名的《夜的赞歌》、《生命颂》、

《群星之光》等音韵优美的抒情诗。其主要诗作包括3首长篇叙事诗，或"通俗史诗"：《伊凡吉林》、《海华沙之歌》和《迈尔斯·斯坦狄什的求婚》，并致力于介绍欧洲文化和浪漫主义作家的作品，成为新英格兰文化中心剑桥文学界和社交界的重要人物。

[7] **Nietzsche**：尼采（Friedrich Wilhelm Nietzsche，1844—1900）。德国唯心哲学家，西方现代哲学的开创者，其著作对于宗教、道德、现代文化、哲学，以及科学等领域提出了广泛的批判和讨论，写作风格独特，经常使用格言和悖论的技巧，尼采对于后代哲学的发展影响极大，尤其是在存在主义与后现代主义，主要著作：《悲剧的诞生》、《不合时宜的考察》、《扎拉图斯特拉如是说》、《希腊悲剧时代的哲学》、《道德的世系》等。

[8] **Henrik Ibsen, Oscar Wilde, G. B. Shaw**：亨利克·易卜生、奥斯卡·王尔德和乔治·伯纳德·萧。易卜生（1828—1906）是挪威著名戏剧家，现代现实主义戏剧创始人。王尔德（1854—1900），爱尔兰最伟大的作家与艺术家之一，唯美主义代表人物，19世纪80年代美学运动的主力和90年代颓废派运动的先驱。萧伯纳（1856—1950），爱尔兰剧作家，诺贝尔文学奖获得者。

[9] **Thomas William Robertson**：托马斯·威廉·罗伯逊（1829—1871）。英国剧作家，革新派舞台导演，以在伦敦导演一系列现实和自然主义戏剧而闻名。

[10] **Nikolai Gogol, Ivan Turgenev, Anton Chekhov and Leo Tolstoy**：尼古莱·果戈理、伊凡·屠格涅夫、安东·契诃夫和列夫·托尔斯泰。果戈理（1809—1852）是俄国现实主义文学奠基人，其创作与普希金的创作相配合，奠定了19世纪俄国批判现实主义文学的基础，是俄国文学自然派的创始者，最著名的作品是《死魂灵》和《钦差大臣》。屠格涅夫（1818—1883）是19世纪俄国享有世界声誉的现实主义作家、诗人和剧作家。契诃夫（1860—1904），俄国的世界级短篇小说巨匠和俄国19

世纪末期最后一位批判现实主义艺术大师，世界三大短篇小说家之一，其作品对20世纪戏剧产生了很大的影响。托尔斯泰是19世纪末20世纪初俄国最伟大的文学家，也是世界文学史上最杰出的作家之一，代表作有长篇小说《战争与和平》、《安娜·卡列尼娜》以及《复活》。

[11] ***A Doll's House*, *Ghosts* , *The Wild Duck* , *The Enemy of the People*, and *The Master Builder***：《玩偶之家》(1879)、《群鬼》(1881)、《野鸭》(1884)、《人民公敌》(1873)和《建筑大师》(1892)。挪威作家易卜生的戏剧作品。

[12] **Newton**：牛顿(Sir Isaac Newton，1643—1727)。英国物理学家、数学家、天文学家、自然哲学家和炼金术士，被认为是历史上最具影响力人的人。

[13] **Émile Zola**：埃米尔·左拉。19世纪法国最重要的作家之一，自然主义文学流派的领袖。亦是法国自由主义政治运动的重要角色，从28岁到54岁，勤奋写作26年，终于写完了一部巨著《鲁贡玛卡一家人的自然史和社会史》，其中包括20部长篇小说，登场人物达1 000多人。

[14] **Trinity College**：三一学院。Trinity的含义是(神学)三位一体，即圣父、圣子、圣灵，英国很多大学都有三一学院，最有名的是剑桥大学三一学院(Trinity College，Cambridge)，这里指都柏林大学三一学院(Trinity College，Dublin)。

[15] **John Ruskin and Walter Pater**：约翰·拉斯金和瓦尔特·佩特。拉斯金(1819—1900)是英国作家、艺术家、艺术评论家、哲学家、教师和业余地质学家，维多利亚时代艺术趣味代言人。佩特(1839—1894)是英国作家、批评家，提出"为艺术而艺术"的美学主张。

[16] **Walt Whitman**：沃尔特·惠特曼(1819—1892)。美国诗人、散文家、新闻工作者及人文主义者。在超验主义与现实主义间的变革期，著作兼有二者的文风，美国文坛最伟大的诗人之一，有自由诗之父的美誉，代表作是《草叶集》。

[17] **Balzac**：巴尔扎克(1799—1850)。法国19世纪著名作家，法

国现实主义文学成就最高者之一。他创作的《人间喜剧》共 91 部小说，写了2 400多个人物，是人类文学史上罕见的文学丰碑，被称为法国社会的“百科全书”。

[18] ***The Importance of Being Earnest***：《认真的重要》(1895)。王尔德的作品。

[19] **Dadaism**：达达主义。达达主义兴起于一战时期的苏黎世，涉及视觉艺术、文学(主要是诗歌)、戏剧和美术设计等领域的文艺运动，是 20 世纪西方文艺发展历程中的一个重要流派，也是第一次世界大战颠覆、摧毁旧有的欧洲社会和文化秩序的产物，其主要特征包括：追求清醒的非理性状态、拒绝约定俗成的艺术标准、幻灭感、愤世嫉俗等。达达(Dada)一词的含义，历来众说纷纭。有些人认为这是一个没有实际意义的词，有些人则认为它来自罗马尼亚艺术家查拉和詹可频繁使用的口头语“是的，是的”。最流行的一种说法是，1916 年，一群艺术家在苏黎世集会，准备为他们的组织取个名字，他们随便翻开一本法德词典，任意选择了一个词，就是“Dada”。法语中，“达达”一词为儿童玩耍用的摇木马。因此，这场运动就被命名为“达达主义”，以昭显其随意性，而非一场一般意义上的“文艺运动”。

[20] **Franz Kafka and James Joyce**：弗兰兹·卡夫卡和詹姆斯·乔伊斯。卡夫卡(1883—1924)，奥地利小说家，出生于犹太商人家庭，主要作品为 4 部短篇小说集和 3 部长篇小说，代表作为《变形记》，是欧洲著名的表现主义作家，20 世纪各个写作流派纷纷追认其为先驱。詹姆斯·乔伊斯(1882—1941)，爱尔兰作家和诗人，20 世纪最重要的作家之一，代表作是成为英语意识流文学奠基之作的《尤利西斯》(1922)。

[21] **stream of consciousness**：意识流。原是西方心理学的术语，最初见于美国心理学家威廉·詹姆斯的论文《论内省心理学所忽略的几个问题》。他认为人类的意识活动是一种连续不断的流程，意识并不是片断的衔接，而是流动的。意识流文学泛指注重描绘人物意识流动状态的文学作品，既包括清醒的

意识，更包括无意识、梦幻意识和语言潜意识。这一术语是1918年梅·辛克莱评论英国小说《旅程》时引入文学界的。意识流文学是现代主义文学的重要分支，主要成就局限在小说领域，在戏剧、诗歌中也有表现。

[22] **Existentialism**：存在主义。哲学的非理性主义思潮，认为人存在的意义是无法经由理性思考而得到答案，强调个人、独立自主和主观经验。唯意志论的尼采和神秘主义克尔凯郭尔为其先驱，20世纪流传非常广泛，其哲学思想还延续到了60年代兴起的人本主义，雅斯贝尔斯和海德格尔、保罗·萨特和作家加缪是其代表人物。其最突出的命题是：世界没有终极的目标；人们发现自己处于一个隐隐约约而有敌意的世界中；人们选择而且无法避免选择他们的品格、目标和观点；不选择就是一种选择，即是选择了"不选择"，世界和我们的处境的真相最清楚地反映在茫然的心理不安或恐惧的瞬间。

[23] ***The Flies***：《苍蝇》(*Les Mouches*，1943)。萨特根据古希腊神话故事改编的一部存在主义悲剧，作者借用这出浓郁的古代神话悲剧的诗意，艺术地破除了人对自然之谜的恍惚感，传递出人能战胜"上帝"，自由选择生活道路的现代意识，《苍蝇》创作于全世界反法西斯战争期间，是一部利用古典题材影射现实的杰出作品。

[24] **The Absurd Drama**：荒诞派戏剧。现代戏剧流派之一。荒诞一词，由拉丁文的sardus(耳聋)演变而来，在哲学上指个人与其生存环境脱节。"荒诞派戏剧"一词，最早见于英国戏剧评论家马丁·艾思林1961年发表的《荒诞派戏剧》论著，对20世纪50年代在欧洲出现的贝克特、尤内斯库、阿达莫夫、惹内、品特这类剧作家的作品进行了系统的概括。荒诞派戏剧作家拒绝像存在主义的剧作家那样，用传统的、理智的手法来反映荒诞的生活，而是用荒诞的手法直接表现荒诞的存在，表现在艺术上的特点是：①反对戏剧传统，摒弃结构、语言、情节上的逻辑性、连贯性；②通常用象征、暗喻的方法表达主题；③用轻松的喜剧形式来表达严肃的悲剧主题。

[25] **Martin Esslin**：马丁·艾斯林(1918—2002)。英国著名荒诞派戏剧理论家。1961年，他发表了题为《荒诞派戏剧》的论著，在理论上给荒诞派戏剧这一流派正式定名。代表作品有《荒诞派戏剧》、《戏剧剖析》等。

[26] **Eugene Ionesco, Samuel Beckett, Jean Genet, Arthur Adamov, Harold Pinter, Edward Albee, etc.**：欧仁·尤内斯库、塞缪尔·贝克特、尚·惹内、阿瑟·阿达莫夫、哈罗德·品特、爱德华·阿尔比等。尤内斯库(1909—1994)，罗马尼亚及法国剧作家，荒诞派戏剧最著名的代表之一。贝克特(1906—1989)，20世纪爱尔兰、法国作家。创作的领域包括戏剧、小说和诗歌，尤以戏剧成就最高，荒诞派戏剧的重要代表人物，1969年，因"以一种新的小说与戏剧的形式，以崇高的艺术表现人类的苦恼"而获得诺贝尔文学奖。惹内(1910—1986)是法国当代著名小说家、剧作家、诗人、评论家、社会活动家。阿达莫夫(1908—1970)俄裔法国剧作家，其剧本显示了荒谬剧的特色。品特(1930—2008)，英国剧作家、导演，曾获诺贝尔文学奖。阿尔比是美国荒诞派剧作家，代表作《动物园的故事》,《三个高个子女人》等。

[27] ***Waiting for Godot***：《等待戈多》(1952)。贝克特的代表作，也是荒诞派戏剧的奠基之作。1953年在巴黎巴比伦剧院首演，立刻引发了激烈的争议，在比较不宽容的伦敦上演后，备受嘲弄，甚至引发评论家群起而攻之，1956年在纽约百老汇上演，被美国评论界讥称为"来路不明的戏剧"。直到20世纪70年代才开始被评论界接受并赞誉，成为20世纪最重要的剧本之一。

[28] **Edward Said**：爱德华·萨义德(1935—2003)。巴勒斯坦裔美国文学理论家、乐评家、歌剧鉴赏家、钢琴家，创立后殖民主义批评理论，代表作：《东方学》，成为巴勒斯坦在西方世界最雄辩的代言人。

[29] **Palestine**：巴勒斯坦。位于亚洲西部，地处亚、非、欧三洲交通要冲，战略地位重要。由加沙和约旦河西岸两部分组成。

[30] **resurrection of Jesus**：耶稣复活。耶稣是《圣经旧约》中所预言的救主，又称基督，是神的儿子，常被称为"拿撒勒人耶稣"。两千多年前出生于以色列的伯利恒，三十岁左右开始传天国福音，在总督彼拉多执政时受难被钉死在十字架上，照《圣经》所说，耶稣为人类的罪孽而赴死，第三天复活了，并向众门徒显现，复活后第四十天升天。

[31] **caesaropapism**：政教合一。该制度在中世纪时期拜占庭帝国、沙俄、阿拉伯帝国、印度、意大利等国家或地区实行过。当时封建统治阶级为了维护和加强自己的政治统治，需要利用宗教为其执政服务。

[32] ***Genesis in the Old Testament***：《旧约全书》的创世纪。《旧约圣经》是基督教对《圣经》全书前一部分的常用称呼，原是犹太教主要经籍《塔纳赫》。《旧约》从摩西带领以色列人出埃及时开始撰写，直到耶稣降生前大约500年完成，前后经历大约1 000年左右。创世记是全部圣经的第一卷，也是圣经中最重要的一卷：关乎神自己的启示、宇宙和万物的来历、神和人的关系、神拯救的计划等。

[33] **Abelard**：阿伯拉尔(1079—1142)。法国哲学家、神学家，人称高卢的苏格拉底，中世纪最富才华的经院哲学家之一，坚持理性和试验，在《自我认识》一书中，强调动机决定行为之善恶，上帝所考虑的是人的意图，行为本身无所谓好坏。

[34] **Jane Eyre**：《简·爱》。19世纪著名英国作家、诗人夏洛蒂·勃朗特(1816—1855)的代表作，展示了当时社会的政治风貌和地位差异所带来的不平等，倡导人的价值与尊严。

[35] **logos**：逻各斯。出自古希腊语，因有多重含义，汉语里很难找到对应的词。是欧洲古代和中世纪常用的哲学概念。一般指世界的可理解的规律，因而也有语言或"理性"的意义。赫拉克利特最早将这个概念引入哲学，在他的著作残篇中，这个词也具有多种含义，但他主要是用来说明万物的生灭变化具有一定的尺度，虽然它变幻无常，但人们能够把握它。在这个意义上，"逻各斯"一词属于西方哲学史上最早关于规律

性的哲学范畴。

[36] **Carolingian Renaissance**：加洛林文艺复兴。是公元 8 世纪晚期至 9 世纪，由查理曼大帝及其后继者在欧洲推行的文艺与科学的复兴运动，被称为“欧洲的第一次觉醒”。加洛林一词，来自拉丁文 Carolus，即查理。查理曼大帝(742—841)，法兰克王国加洛林王朝国王，欧洲中世纪史上一位赫赫有名的人物，当时，除了教士以外，几乎没有人会读书，为了改变这种状况，查理曼大帝广纳欧洲的优秀学者来到帝国，恢复和兴办学校与图书馆，形成了文艺复兴的局面，史称加洛林文艺复兴，其标志是：开始了基督教教义和宗教活动的初步规范工作；改革拉丁文，学习新文字和形成了君主奖励学习者和研读的风气。此间，宗教性的文学艺术也有了初步的发展。体裁大多是一些圣经故事、圣徒传以及用拉丁文写作的教诲诗、圣歌、赞美诗和传记等等，水平虽不高，但毕竟已经出现了中世纪宗教文学的作品。

[37] **Daniel Defoe**：丹尼尔·笛福(1660—1731)。英国启蒙时期现实主义小说奠基人，被誉为“欧洲小说之父”，其作品介绍了主人公个人通过努力，靠智慧和勇敢战胜困难，表现了当时追求冒险，倡导个人奋斗的社会风气。其代表作《鲁滨孙漂流记》创造了与困难抗争的典型人物。

[38] **Louis XIV**：路易十四(1638—1715)。波旁王朝的法国国王和纳瓦拉国王，自号太阳王，1680 年接受巴黎市政会献上的“大帝”尊号，在位长达 72 年。路易十四在法国建立了一个君主专制的中央集权王国，把大贵族集中在凡尔赛宫居住，将整个法国的官僚机构集中于他的周围，以此强化法王的军事、财政和机构的决策权。亲政期间，法国发动了三次重大的战争和两次小规模的冲突，使他在 1680 年开始成为至高无上的欧洲霸主。

[39] **Fichte, Schelling and Hegel**：费希特、谢林和黑格尔。费希特是(Johann Gottlieb Fichte，1762—1814)前康德主义、德国唯心主义哲学家，以主张绝对自我而著名，常被认为是连接康

德和黑格尔两人哲学间的过渡人物。谢林（Friedrich Schelling，1775—1854）德国哲学家，在哲学史上，谢林是德国唯心主义发展中期的主要人物，处在费希特和黑格尔之间。黑格尔（Georg Hegel，1770—1831）是德国哲学中由康德启始的那个运动的顶峰，德国近代客观唯心主义哲学的代表、政治哲学家。他对德国资产阶级的国家哲学作了最系统、最丰富和最完整的阐述，19世纪末，在美国和英国，一流的学院哲学家大多都是黑格尔派。

[40] ***The Rime of the Ancient Mariner***：《古舟子咏》。柯勒律治的音乐叙事诗，讲述了一个生动的罪与赎罪的故事。

[41] **William Faulkner，Golding**：威廉·福克纳、戈尔丁。福克纳（1897—1962），美国文学史上最具影响力的作家之一，是美国意识流文学的代表人物，1949年诺贝尔文学奖得主。一生共写了19部长篇小说与120多篇短篇小说，最有代表性的作品是《喧哗与骚动》。戈尔丁（William Gerald Golding，1911—1993）是英国小说家、诗人，1983年诺贝尔文学奖获得者，其小说富含寓意，广泛地融入了古典文学、神话、基督教文化以及象征主义，第一本小说《蝇王》（1954）突出了他一直不停探讨的主题：人类天生的野蛮与文明理性的斗争。

Chapter 4 Genre and Components of Drama

All the world's a stage,
And all the men and women merely players;
They have their exits and their entrances;
And one man in his time plays many parts[1].

…

The phrase above that begins a monologue from William Shakespeare's *As You Like It* and one of Shakespeare's most frequently-quoted passages shows somewhat similarity between our real life and stories and the glamour of plays to people who may be illiterate. Yet life in reality and life on the stage are not the same. Everyone knows that the theatre, its false front and painted canvas, its masks and its disguises, is illusion created by sleight of hand. But everyone still is glad to make believe, to participate in the deception that deceives no one because the theatre offers rich and deep experience. The theatre relates us to the great archetypal patterns of human purpose and destiny expressed in the great myths. It is an extension of life. Like religious conversion, the theatre brings the joy of enlightenment, a new health, a revelation that makes order of confusion and doubt. Andrei Serban[2], the brilliant young New York director, said, "Theatre is a manifestation of the essence of life." That essence is more than pleasure in entertainment, more than role-playing, more than any personal emotion of love, hate, anger or jealousy. The essence of life is a deep sense of wonder and awe, of a common human destiny. The very center of the theatrical experience is the confrontation between two unstable, unpredictable elements: the living actor and the living audience. For most ordinary audience, they just love plays and go to theatres, but for those who are studying literature, they should know something more.

Section 1 Genre of Drama

Each kind of play presents a different attitude toward life, a different way of answering some of the age-old questions that are still very pertinent to our lives today.

1.1 Tragedy

Tragedy, the oldest literary form, the one that gives us our model of what we mean "dramatic" still fascinates us, as it did the Athenians of 2,500 years ago. Tragedy refers to a play dealing in an elevated, poetic style with events which depict man as the victim of destiny yet superior to it, both in grandeur and in misery. Tragedy is the oldest literary form, characterized by seriousness and dignity, which involves a great person who experiences a reversal of fortune according to Aristotle, exalting the spirit with pride and showing a man daring to pursue his spiritual destiny when facing a challenging universe. Aristotle is basically the first person to clarify what makes a "true" tragic character. He believes (1) the character must be of noble stature, such as a person of royalty — think of Sophocles' *Oedipus the King* for example; (2) the character must have some tragic flaw, such as excessive pride, impulsiveness, rejecting the Gods, etc.; (3) the flaw must somehow lead to his death; (4) he must have a catharsis or a cleansing of emotions, before he dies, which is kind of like a lesson to the audience, like a "Don't make a mistake like I did" kind of message.

1.1.1 Aspects of Tragedy in Greek Drama

For Aristotle, drama is the imitation (i. e. representation) by impersonators of an action (i. e., a sequence of happenings). The action in tragedy is serious and important and is often the heroes' or heroines' perception of a great mistake they have made; they suffer intensely and perhaps die, having exhausted all the possibilities of their life. But tragedy is not what many of us think it is — a sad play with an unhappy ending. The root of tragedy has nothing to do with death or sadness. The whole concept of tragedy is a product of Greek civilization founded upon a very special view which the Greeks hold concerning mankind and their relationship to the gods.

Ancient Greek tragedy has some common aspects. One is crisis feeling, a painful or harmful experience that may upset or depress the audience. The second is catharsis, which means the audience cleanse their emotions through watching the tragedy, the protagonist's painful experience. They may feel uplifted or get a new sense of spiritual understanding or tragic pleasure. The final aspect is the so called reversal, that is, the hero or heroine goes through a significant change in fortune for the worse. Reversal may happen after a discovery or recognition of something previously not known to the hero or heroine. *Oedipus the King* has been regarded as the best representative of tragedies since its appearance because the protagonist experiences great upheavals in his life — totally falling to victim of his doomed fate although he desperately wants to escape from it.

1.1.2 Characteristics of Greek Tragic Drama

Plots of Ancient Greek plays were usually based on myths which the audience knew quite well with little action. Much flexibility made it a variety for the dramatists in handling the story. The hero who was unconscious of his fate and heading for it made audience interested in the struggle of the hero into inevitable doom. Tragedy was a disaster that happened to other people. In Greek tragedy the tragic situation, in which the characters found themselves, was always one in which man seemed to be deprived of all outward help and was forced to rely entirely on himself. It was a situation of extraordinary tension and of utmost conflict. There were two basic tragic situations. One was the case of man's miscalculation of reality which brought about the fatal situation. The other was that man found himself "between two conflicting principles". The hero or heroine was suddenly put at the crossing point of two duties, both of which claimed fulfillment. This was the most compelling tragic situation. The greater the person was, the more acute was their tragedy; the bigger they were, the harder they fell.

Tragedy seldom ended on pessimistic note, though sad and terrible. For the tragic protagonists, there was no escape. They were doomed and audience watched in awe as they moved toward that doom. Thereafter came a balance of forces and tranquility. Tragedy did not deal with the incidental which could be avoided; it tackled the inevitable. It was not saddening and depressing in the sense of a fatal accident or some destructive catastrophe. Tragedy was positive and optimistic in its view of the heights human beings could reach. The tragic hero might be destroyed but failed in a way that might evoke admiration for him and the play rarely ended with evil triumphant. Bloody or violent events didn't occur on stage — chorus or actors related such events to the audience. The theme of plays was religious in nature in Ancient Greece, though it might also have been good entertainment but audience remained aware of its religious nature. Drama helped to explain the relation of the human to the divine, to the material world, violence and its origins, reasons for suffering and attempts to control the irrational and material world. As a result, by identifying with issues presented on stage, audience vicariously participated in the grief, pain and fear of the tragic hero or heroine and then left changed and thrilled by the sense of having gone through a great experience, thus being more civilized.

1.2 Comedy

The word "comedy" has a Greek origin as well. The primitive festival from which comedy grows is a joyous and happy one, marked by jokes and laughter. Today, "comedy" is a term broadly applied to a light, humorous play that ends happily.

Comedy is a play that shows the humorous actions of characters when they try to solve social, personal or religious problems. Comedy refers to a play written chiefly to amuse its audience by appealing to a sense of superiority over the characters depicted, with a happy ending for the leading characters. Comedy is normally closer to the representation of everyday life than a tragedy by exploring common human failings rather than disastrous crimes.

Comedy is often considered inferior to tragedy in insight and power, but in some cases — in the romantic comedies of Shakespeare, for example, or in the penetrating social comedies of Bernard Shaw — the comic vision comes very close to that of tragedy. The ultimate significance of great comedies is that they, too, provide an insight into the nature of the human condition and deepen our understanding and experience of life.

1.2.1 Aspects of Comedy in Greek Drama

There are some common aspects of Greek Comedy. Firstly, the action and conflict of comedy usually leads to a happy ending. Secondly, the plays usually include ridiculing and violent personal attacks on contemporary personalities, with Aristophanes, the representative of Old

Comedy as a good example. Thirdly, the play involves acting out of bawdy personal and social relationships. Finally, as opposed to Ancient Greek tragedy, a change in fortune is almost always for the better. Comedy lives in the very world that tragedy transcends. Clothing, manners, physical appearance, money, possession etc., are the very stuff of comedy. It is the genre of plays that make us laugh at humanity's vices and follies. Comedy is most concerned with our social being, while tragedy with our philosophical being. Comedy concentrates, not on people's destiny, but on their follies, foibles and vices. Frequently, comedy exaggerates or distorts these deviations for greater effect.

1.2.2 Types of Comedy

Comedy has subdivided terms in a broad sense such as romantic comedy, satiric comedy, comedy of manners and farce.

1.2.2.1 Romantic Comedy

Romantic comedy represents a love affair that involves a beautiful and engaging heroine. The course of this love does not run smooth, yet overcome all difficulties to end in a happy union. Such kind of plays invites us to forget the drab everyday world and follow the charming paths of romance into the dream world of the primitive unconscious. Shakespeare's *A Midsummer Night's Dream* is a famous romantic comedy, in which the problems and injustices of the ordinary world are dissolved, enemies reconciled and true lovers united.

1.2.2.2 Satiric Comedy

Satiric comedy usually ridicules political policies or philosophical doctrines or else attacks deviations from the social order by making ridiculous the violators of its standards of moral or manners. Ben Jonson makes the greed and ingenuity of one or more intelligent in *The Alchemist*[3] grotesquely or repulsively ludicrous rather than lightly amusing.

1.2.2.3 Comedy of Manners

Comedy of manners refers to a kind of comedy representing the complex and sophisticated code of behavior current in fashionable circles of society, where appearances count for more than true moral character. Its plot usually revolves around intrigues. Richard Brinsley Sheridan's *The Rivals* is one of the best English comedies of manners, in which the author satirizes traditional practice of the parents to arrange marriages for their children. Oscar Wilde's *Lady Windermere's Fan*[4] is another comedy of manners, but he is more famous for being aesthetic representative.

1.2.2.4 Farce

Farce is a type of comedy designed to provoke the audience to simple, hearty laughter. Farce commonly employs highly exaggerated or caricatured types of characters, putting them into improbable and ludicrous situations by making full use of sexual mix-ups, broad verbal humor, physical bustle and horseplay. Shakespeare's *The Comedy of Errors*[5] is his shortest and one of his most farcical, with a major part of the humor coming from slapstick and mistaken identity, in addition to puns and wordplay.

1.2.3 The Functions of Comedy

"Comic Spirit", the "sunlight of the mind", corrects the faults of mankind through gentle laughter, without the "pain of satiric heat" or the "bitter craving to strike heavy blows". There are at least three reasons for the popularity of comedy. In the first place, it is a release of pent-up dormant life, like the arrival of spring. A second reason for people's pleasure in comedy is that it brings the great reassurance that all the great clowns have brought and the reassurance that a person can take it. The clown in comedy takes his beating and survives by his wisecrack and his comeback, proving his spiritual superiority to his fate. He is always the butt, the victim, the fall guy, the little fellow that something always happens to. Actually, he is all of us — unlucky and mistreated, but refuses to give up. In addition, comedy serves as a device for accepting the basic incongruity of everyday living, spanning the ideal and the real without denying either.

Some critics think without the relaxation of farcical laughter, whose function is to release chemical that is life-enhancing, life-elongating and wounds healing, human beings would long ago have torn themselves and their neighbors apart.

1.3 Tragicomedy

Tragicomedy, as the name indicates, refers to a play that combines elements of tragedy and comedy, either by providing a happy ending to a potentially tragic story or by some more complicated blending of serious and light moods. Tragicomedy applies to almost any kind of drama that does not conform strictly to comic or tragic conventions in its broadest sense with a fairy tale ending happily such as *The Cinderella*[6]. In such plays, the action, serious in theme and subject matter, seems to be leading to a tragic catastrophe until an unexpected and often arbitrary turn in events brings about the happy denouement. For example, Shakespeare's *Merchant of Venice* [7] develops threat of death to Antonio but suddenly reverses at the end by Persia's ingenious casuistry in the trail scene.

1.4 Melodrama

Melodrama refers to theatre in which music is used to increase the spectator's emotional response or to suggest character types. Now very often it applies to some of the typical plays, especially during the Victorian Period[8], that were written to be produced to musical accompaniment. Music in melodrama is used in rigid structure, indicating the unambiguous quality of the staging characters which are either villains or heroes with a happy ending. For example, heroes' entrance is heralded by heroic-sounding trumpets and martial music while villains are greeted with dark-sounding, ominous chords.

1.5 Dark Comedy

Dark comedy, also known as black comedy, refers to a kind of drama in which disturbing or sinister subjects like death, disease or warfare are treated with bitter amusement. In dark comedy topics and events for satire that are usually regarded as taboos are treated in a satirical or humorous manner but retain their seriousness, including an element of irony or even fatalism. The most famed *Waiting for Godot* in Theatre of Absurd is grouped into dark comedy by representing man's meaninglessness in life in absurd ways — exemplified by a scene in the play that a man takes off his belt to hang himself and his trousers fall down.

1.6 History

History here refers to a play representing events drawn wholly or partly from recorded history. It usually refers to chronicle plays, especially those of Shakespeare, his *Henry IV* for example. History is most frequently associated either with the short phase of the great Elizabethan histories of Marlowe and Shakespeare in the 1590s or with the historicism of the 19th century, continuing to be one of the main themes of contemporary drama.

1.7 Musical

Musical is the abbreviation of musical comedy, called simply musicals since the early 20th century. Musicals, developing out of British comedy at the end of the 19th century, are stage productions that use popular-style songs and dialogues. They put together music and play, as well as song and dance. In Europe, the US and Japan, the musical is a popular form of performing art. The emotional content of the musicals such as humor, pathos, love, anger and the story itself is communicated through the words, music, movement and technical aspects of the entertainment as an integrated whole. *Show Boat*, *West Side Story*[9] etc., are famous musicals with *Cats*[10] as the most successful one and *The Black Crook*[11] (1866), considered by some historians, the first one. An opera singer is primarily a singer secondarily an actor (rarely needing to dance), but a musical performer is an actor first and then a singer and dancer. Musicals have achieved great success on Broadway in New York City as well as in London's West End, both of which are famous for their musicals. The musical has become an important form of art in these countries.

1.8 Documentary

Documentary is a play revealing the artfulness of life. It dated impulse back to 492 BC when the Greek playwright Phrynichus produced his play *The Capture of Miletus*[12] about the Persian War[13]. It grows out of an impulse to explore the boundaries of reality. The text of documentary is found by documenting words that are spoken in the realm we call "life" and then transferred to the realm we call "art". Interview, court trial transcripts, print, media articles, broadcast transcripts, recordings of live speeches and public hearings are used to create a script about actual rather than imaginary events.

Section 2 Components of Drama

Aristotle, the great Greek philosopher and drama theoretician, categorized drama into six elements, which were listed in his *Poetics*, in order of importance as he viewed them plot, character, thought, diction, music and spectacle. *Poetics* not only sets the cornerstone of understanding Western drama but also defines most topics of subsequent discussions in this field. The first serious challenge to his authority came from the rise of Romanticism in the late 18th century and the early 19th century, then the 20th century when various forms of drama that were anti-traditional came into being. But traditional and well-made plays are still fascinating to most audience.

2.1 Plot

Plot is another term for structure, the things happening and the ways in which those incidents connect with each other. It is the entire action and sequence of events in a play, providing the basic framework of the action and telling who, what, when, where, why and how.

2.1.1 Plot and Conflict

Plot is the way the story is told. Different ways of arranging the same story often yield different plays. The weakest type of plot, according to Aristotle, is the episodic plot where one event follows another with little or no causal effect or relationship. The strongest is the involved plot, such as the plot of *Oedipus Rex*[14], where each action flows out of some preceding one, where the very struggle of the tragic heroes or heroines to free themselves becomes the force that destroys them. That is, any plot of a dramatic work necessarily has to do with conflicts between characters. The two sides of the conflict, the pros and cons of the argument, are usually represented by the protagonist and the antagonist in the play. *A Street Car Named Desire*[15] has a neat structure plot — the protagonist Blanch, a delicate southerner goes to visit her younger sister Stella in New Orleans after the loss of the family's plantation, thus having constant conflicts with Stanley, her brother-in-law, who is a coarse factory worker. Finally, Blanche is driven mad and sent to madhouse.

2.1.2 Action or Plot

Drama in Greek root means "to do" or "to act". In drama, something happens before the eyes of audience. Drama portrays the present moment, but that moment is full of promise and threat, pregnant with the future. There is delay, but the critical moment does arrive and a fate is determined, a choice is made and a door is closed forever. The audience is caught up and carried from crisis to crisis in a rhythmic pattern of tension and relaxation, swept to a climax by an irresistible momentum, leaving at the end changed and thrilled by the sense of having gone through a great experience.

The confrontation of two minds can create conflict as tense and exciting as a physical fight on the stage. Plots in Ibsen's plays are often the gradual revelations of some long-hidden truth about the past. Discoveries explode one by one like carefully placed time bombs, shaking and sometimes destroying those forced to hear.

2.2 Character

Character refers to the people in a play with the cast names, ages, professions, and relationships to each other.

2.2.1 Characteristics of Character in Drama

The nature of drama and the conventions of the physical theater exert great influence on characterization. Dramatists must select a few key incidents occurring in a short space of time and in a few locales and they must reveal character by speech and behavior. Dramatists usually have no means of commenting directly on character. For example, *A*

Street Car Named Desire focuses on three characters including Blanche, Stella and Stanley.

Ibsen, Strindberg[16] and Chekhov, the three masters of modern Western drama, are particularly successful in creating life-like figures. Dramatists in the 20th century have continued to strive for the creation of solid characters whose motivations are subtle and complicated.

2.2.2 Ways to Portray Characters

Characters are usually portrayed through their appearance, ages, manner, languages, action, decisions, feelings etc., through which the characterization and the theme are completed and expressed. Generally, character may be portrayed in the following 4 ways.

2.2.2.1 Being Delineated by Appearance

Firstly, character is delineated by appearance. The actor's physical qualities give an immediate stimulus to the audience. Many modern playwrights have a very specific image in mind, describing the character's appearance in considerable detail. For example, in the play *The Hairy Ape*[17], Yank's appearance is demonstrated as ugly and muscled. In the play, *Endgame*[18], Hamm, an aged master, can't walk and is without legs while Clov, a servant, can not sit down, both of whom quarrel every day but can not live without each other.

2.2.2.2 Being Revealed by Speech

Character can be revealed by speech. The kind of language employed by the personate, their manner of speaking and their voice quality and so on all say something about them. The dramatist takes great care to write dialogue that makes an immediate impression about the characters. So dialogues that make an immediate impression about the characters are very important. For example, in *Mrs. Warren's Profession*[19], Mrs. Warren said to her daughter that money could buy beautiful dresses, buy big houses and they could have parties every night which immediately pictures a money-orientated woman.

2. 2. 2. 3 Being Established by Action

Character is established by his action. On stage, a dramatist can not give direct comments on his characters frequently. He can not describe them in details either. What a person says and how he says give us clues to their inner motivation. In addition, what a person does and how he does, that is, action is a fundamental technique for depicting character. For example, the author mirrors Hamlet's hesitation by his delaying actions of revenge from time to time. When Hamlet's friends told him that his father's ghost was up and about, he doubted it and resolved to see the Ghost himself. After the Ghost appeared to Hamlet and told him that Claudius murdered the old king by pouring poison in his ear and demanded that Hamlet avenge him, Hamlet was, however, uncertain of the Ghost's reliability. Then he staged a play, re-enacting his father's murder, which offered him proof positive of his uncle's guilt. But Hamlet still hesitated to kill him, reasoning that killing Claudius would send him straight to heaven, while his father was still in hell or purgatory. Only after Claudius's murderous plot on Hamlet himself was revealed, did Hamlet manage to kill Claudius and name Fortinbras as his heir in his own last moment.

2. 2. 2. 4 Bing Revealed Indirectly

Finally, character may be revealed indirectly by what others say about and how they react to the person. Often, dramatists use other people's comment as a method of revealing the truth about an absent character. For example, in Arthur Miller's *Death of a Salesman* audience may know what a kind of person Willy Loman is from what his wife's comments, "I don't say he is a great man. Willy Loman never made a lot of money. His name was never in the paper. He's not the finest character that ever lived. But he is a human being and a terrible thing is happening to him..."

2.3 Thought

Thought refers to the reasoning aspect of drama, the central idea and message of a play communicated to the audience, usually an abstract concept a play is about such as ambition, revenge, love, fate, greed, jealousy, justice, faith etc. Thought also concerns a play's theme which summarizes the moral and indicates the symbolic meaning of the play as a whole.

2.3.1 Variety and Arbitrariness of Theme

A given play may have different meanings to different audience, some conveying more than one theme. *A Street Car Named Desire* as suggested by the title is of course about desire and fate, but it has other significant themes too.

Dramatists are reluctant to discuss theme unless their purpose is didactic. Ask playwrights what their plays are about and some of them will answer, "About two and a half hours." When Alan Schneider, who was to direct the 1st American production of *Waiting for Godot*, asked Beckett who or what was meant by Godot, he received the answer, "If I knew, I would have said so in the play".

Theme is an abstraction, but writers are concerned with the concrete. They may be hostile to questions about theme. Unlike the medieval writers, most of the modern playwrights do not point to clear-cut solutions to the problems they raise in their plays. Their purposes are to provoke thought rather than to persuade the audience to adopt a specific plan of action.

2.3.2 Theme Understanding

Countless young readers have been soured on poetry and drama because pedagogues have taught them that the purpose of reading a poem or play is to find out what it "means", as if it were a puzzle or code to be solved and as if poetic or dramatic expression were a communication obstacle to be surmounted. But as Archibald MacLeish states in *Arts Poetica*[20] that a poem should not mean, but be.

Investigation of theme, a poem's or a play's, is not an attempt to discover what the work means. A play doesn't mean anything. Its artistic expression is meaning in and of itself. It doesn't translate or decode or puzzle or compute into anything but itself.

Theme is a result. Look for it last. First analyze with care the action, characterization, images and other components. By then theme will be manifestly apparent almost by itself. If you simply see the motivation that drives Hamlet once the Ghost has told its terrible tale in act one, you cannot miss the revenge theme.

Some elements of a play can be abstract topics that emerge from or are important to the action. One theme of *Hamlet* is revenge. This does not mean that the play's purpose is to study or examine or explore revenge. It only means that revenge is an abstract concept made concrete by the play's action. For example, *Macbeth* is not a treatise on ambition. It is a play in which one theme is ambition. Another theme is power and another is guilt. There are more. For some audience, *King Lear* has the theme about parent-child relationship, for some, about power and for some, about madness and much, much more. If a writer has great vision and depth, the play's themes will loom important. If not, theme will not be provender for thought, reflection and emotional involvement. Instead, theme will be only topic. In either case, theme is not what a play means, nor is expression of theme the "purpose" of a play.

2.4 Diction

Diction means the choice of words used in a play. Discourse in drama must be clear since the language must be immediately understood by the listener because there is no turning back the page, no pause to weigh and consider a line before continuing to the next for audience in a theatre. In order to attract audience, the dialogues must be interesting despite the need for simplicity and economy, capturing the spirit of life and character.

In addition, the dialogues should be appropriate for the character and the situation and dynamic enough to show the character's relationship to others, reflect the progression of the action, indicate what is happening inside the characters and reveal their suffering, growth or decline. A dramatist's diction may have his own style; for instance, Shakespeare is famous for his poetic and lyrical language.

2.5 Music

Music here refers to all of the auditory aspect of a play, including sound effects, songs, instrumental music played in a play and the tonal pattern of the spoken word, which can intensify the story and strengthen the theme. There are two dominant pieces of music in *A Street Car Named Desire*, the polka[21] music and the blue piano which sharpen the conflicts between Blanche and Stanley. Polka is used to represent Blanche's imaginative memory of her dead husband and her recollection of the southern culture while blue piano is used to embody the spirit and vitality in Stanley and the reality Blanch is facing.

2.6 Spectacle

Spectacle refers to the visual elements in a play which affect the audience's visual organs such as words, silence, sound effects, background music, facial expressions, gestures, movements across the stage, lighting, groupings, shadows, shapes and costumes, all of which tell the audience something. For example, before Blanch is raped and driven mad in *A Street Car Named Desire*, creating a sense of menace by the use of lurid reflections on the walls around Blanche has a strong impact on the audience.

2.7 Convention

Convention means out of reality tricks that the playwrights and directors use to further the communication, and to solve the problems in representing reality that are posed by a particular artistic medium such as asides, flashback, freeze actions and soliloquies. In a comedy like *Twelfth Night*, the asides and speeches let the audience in on the joke. For instance, audience can watch Malvolio's rambling soliloquy about marrying Olivia alongside Toby, Andrew, and Fabian, hidden in the box hedge and they become part of the action, too. Then they want to see him get what he deserves.

2.7.1 Aside

The aside is a familiar convention in drama, tracing its use back to its earliest appearance in Greek tragedy in Euripides, Aeschylus and Sophocles. Dramatic plays or dramas consist entirely of dialogue, which makes it more difficult for a writer to express what characters are thinking and what their actions, motives and thoughts are. One device that gets around that difficulty is the aside.

An aside is a short speech from a character that is spoken directly to the audience. The other actors on stage can physically hear the words, but as their characters they pretend as if nothing were being said. The audience understands that the speech is meant for them only. Usually, an actor holds his hand to his cheek in a gesture of private conversation to the audience as if not being heard by other characters on the stage.

The aside became a very popular technique in the Elizabethan Era, during which time, the structure of theaters began to change. A three-sided platform stage became common, which allowed the audience to be much closer to the actors. This more intimate setting made asides more realistic than in the previous Greek amphitheater setting, in which actors had to practically shout in order for the whole audience to hear the dialogue. In *Macbeth*, the title character had given into his violent ambition and murdered the king in order to take over the throne. However, Macbeth met resistance from other leaders and so he planed to kill them. In Act 4, he learnt that one such man, Macduff, had fled the country. He then had this aside:

Time thou anticipat'st my dread exploits:
The flighty purpose never is o'ertook
Unless the deed go with it. From this moment
The very firstlings of my heart shall be
The firstlings of my hand[22]. And even now,
To crown my thoughts with acts, be it thought and done:

The audience learnt that Macbeth regretted waiting to attack MacDuff. His speech actually went on to announce that he would still attack Macduff's castle and murder his whole family. Through this speech, the audience could see just how immoral Macbeth had become. He struggled with his first decision to murder the king, but now he had no problem killing a whole innocent family. Through this aside, his transformation to an ambitious, violent man was transparent.

2.7.2 Flashback

A flashback is an interjected scene that takes the narrative back in time from the current point in the story. Flashbacks are often used to recount events that happened before the story's primary sequence of events to fill in crucial backstory. In the opposite direction, a flashforward reveals events that will occur in the future. Both flashback and flashforward are used to create suspense in a story, develop a character or add structure to the narrative. An ancient example occurs in the *Odyssey*, in which the main action is told in flashback by Odysseus to a listener.

2.7.3 Freeze Action

Freeze actions, simply, mean some characters stop in action while others continue. Freeze frame is also a drama medium term used in which, during a live performance, the actors or actresses will freeze at a particular, pre-determined time, to enhance a particular scene or to show an important moment in the play like a celebration. The image can then be further enhanced by spoken word, in which each character tells their personal thoughts regarding the situation, giving the audience further insight into the meaning, plot or hidden story of the play. This is known as thought tracking, another drama medium term. Directors use this to capture special moments that are considered particularly significant.

The 1970s television series of *Wonder Woman* has its episodes end with a freeze-frame of Diana Prince smiling.

2.7.4 Soliloquy

Soliloquy is a private speech by one character to the audience as if the character were thinking aloud. That is, he is a character speaking his thoughts out for the audience to hear. The lines can be directed either to the audience or, more often, the character is just speaking to himself. When Hamlet contemplates suicide, he talks to himself about the pros and cons "To be, or not to be, that is the question." This is a soliloquy because he is speaking his thoughts aloud for the benefit of the audience and not to another character.

It is a device often used in drama when a character speaks to himself or herself, relating thoughts and feelings, thereby also sharing them with the audience, giving off the illusion of being a series of unspoken reflections. If other characters are present, they keep silent or are disregarded by the speaker.

Soliloquy is distinct from a monologue. A monologue is, literally, half of a dialogue. Namely, it is one character speaking to another without getting a response. When Henry V delivers his speech to the English camp in the Saint Crispin's Day speech "we few, we happy few, we band of brothers", it is a monologue since he is speaking to other characters.

Soliloquies used to be frequently used in dramas but went out of fashion when drama shifted towards realism in the late 18th century.

Section 3 Qualities of a Fine Play

When reading, readers can go back and pause to think if they don't understand it. But a play addresses its ultimate audience in a different way. The words are designed to become a performance in a play. So they need to be dealt with differently.

Now most people go to the theatre to be entertained rather than to be improved and by picking out elements from past models of dramatic writings, it is possible to arrive at a formula for the delivery of such entertainment: simple action, easily recognizable characters, intrigue and secrets, points of crisis and entanglement and of course a just conclusion.

3.1 Credibility

Credibility is the most important aspect of a fine play. The internal consistence of actions must flow logically from the characters, the situation and the theatrical context the playwright provides. That is, the playwright must make the characters and situations believable and logical to the audience. If not, the audience will not go to theatre or leave before the story ends.

3.2 Intrigue

Intrigue refers to an air of mystery or surprise created in a play which is necessary for the audience to want to know how it will all turn out. A good play should have the quality that makes audience curious to see what happens next.

3.3 Speakability

The dialogue must be able to be spoken by the actors. This involves accents, foreign accents and all aspects of speech.

The language of Greek tragedy is public, democratic and male talk, that is, the language of tragedy is in all senses of the term political in Ancient Greece. A second area that provides a major influence on the language of tragedy is ritual and the world of religion. Tragedy is performed as part of a festival of Dionysus and there has been extensive discussion about to what degree the Dionysiac frame affects the tragic life of the city reflected on stage. A third major influence on the language of tragedy is the world of the democratic law-court and Assembly. The 4th element, closely related to the third, is one which is more and more influential throughout the 5th century in all aspects of Athenian life, namely the new interest in the formal training and analysis of speech.

Tragic language, then, combines contemporary tropes and vocabulary of the public institution of the city with elements of heroic grandeur which stem both from the epic poetry of the past and the sacral splendor of religious rite:

Son of a noble father, when I myself was a young man,
I had a slow tongue and a hand ready for action.
But as things are, from trial and proof, I see that for man,
The tongue, and not deeds controls all.

3.4 Stageability

Stageability refers to the fact whether a play is appropriate for theatre group to produce the show. This involves sets, costumes, theatre techniques etc. The quality of dialogue that describes its ability to function in the context of a particular physical situation in which setting, physical action and spoken dialogue are inextricably entwined is of extremely importance. In fact, not all good stories are fit for stage, only few are.

3.5 Richness

The audience must care about the character and the character must have depth. The play should have dimension. Plays of richness appeal to people at different periods of time and of different cultural backgrounds and will never die, which has been proved by those plays of Shakespeare. Hundreds of people reading *Hamlet*, there will be hundreds of Hamlet.

3.6 Flow

The pacing of the dialogue and action should be neither too slow nor too fast. Within two and half hours, there should be a beginning, development, climax, and ending of a story.

3.7 Gravity

Gravity means the importance of the subject. Any celebration such as a party, a birthday, funeral, wedding or any event where human beings come together in a social situation is a favorite of contemporary audience. TV programs use this consistently.

A script of a play is a different form of literature. It is a document that outlines every aural, visual, behavioral and lingual element required to tell a story. Why "outlines"? Because play is a highly collaborative medium and the director, cast, editor and production crew will, based on the "outline", interpret the story their way when it is filmed. It is crucial to remember that play is a VISUAL medium. You don't tell your audience your story, you SHOW them on stage.

The audience viewing a movie not only want to be interested in and care about the people they see on the screen, they want to be PASSIONATE about them, whether they like them or not. Great heroes and heroines inspire us; great villains make us want to jump into the screen. It can be something personal or for the good of all (saving the world from aliens) but it must be powerful and grow more desperate as the story unfolds. Audience, as critics, makes a play a success or a failure. If plays are closely related to individual and personal issues and if plays reflect society and social issues profoundly, they will be fascinating and unforgettable to audience, paving way for the coming success.

Section 4 Modern Tragedy

In the 21st century, there are appearing more and more fascinating means for entertainment. But theatre still echoes in heart of some people, thus modern drama coming into our life. Do we have modern tragedy? People can't not come to an agreement actually.

4.1 Debates on the Existence of Modern Tragedy

If tragedy is a heroic vision of humanity celebrating the triumph of spiritual nobility over physical defeat and death, how can it exist in an age of common and ordinary people, not high born, noble or important who have to live with submission and conformity? In a pragmatic age that emphasizes scientific study of the facts and the practical solving of problems how can there be room for tragedy?

4. 1. 1 Denial of Modern Tragedy

It is easy to see the magnitude of tragedy in the periods such as Greek, Elizabethan and neoclassic times. But can tragedy seem exalted in the 20th century? Many critics say no and one of them George Steiner has written a book called *The Death of Tragedy*[23].

The reasons for declaring the death of tragedy are various and complicated. Firstly, tragedy has never reached the high level as it used to at modern time. In Ancient Greece, man was liberated from nature and in Renaissance man was freed from religion control when man found his own wisdom and strength. The two periods shone with great splendor in many aspects, especially in literature. Man mirrored in tragedy became the essence of the universe, the paragon of animals, showing a extremely strong longing for freedom and struggle for better life in fighting against hardships in life. But the great achievement in tragedy is a past. Many people have taken pains to revive tragedy, but failed. Secondly, the tragedy tradition in which Aristotle gave a systematic and highly theatrical elaboration dwarfs modern tragedy, which modern drama theorists and literary critics have not succeeded in defining. In modernist literature, the definition of tragedy has become less precise. They don't have a satisfying systematic and theatrical explanation of the nature, form, conveying mode, realistic function and essence etc., of modern tragedy.

4. 1. 2 The Affirmation of Modern Tragedy

It is true that the tradition of tragedy faces a lot of challenges in the 20th century because there have been sweeping changes in the world.

Tragedy may no longer exist in comparison with its former manifestations in classical antiquity. No matter how classic and applicable of Aristotle's definition of tragedy is, he only summarizes the traits of Ancient Greek tragedy. The concept of tragedy should be both classical and also modern. Actually, when compared to the drama of Greek antiquity and French classicism, Shakespeare's forms are richer but hybrid. Therefore, there are still many people stating that there is modern tragedy.

From the development point of view, Western tragedy falls into three stages: Ancient Greek Tragedy, Shakespeare Tragedy and French Classical Tragedy and Modern Tragedy with Henrik Ibsen as the representative.

Western modern tragedy, as a holistic system, involves three dimensions of human beings: modern social tragedy, modern spiritual tragedy and modern ontological tragedy. Generally, the trait and essence of Western modern tragedy spirit is predicament.

Modern tragedies and ancient tragedies might have a lot in common, but the typical hero in a modern tragedy should be more like the rest of us because people in modern time are ordinary and common just like one of us. People at modern time, no matter where he is born, whether poor or rich, West or East, have to face natural predicament, social predicament, spiritual predicament and ontological predicament. With the development of civilization, people are more subject to conformity, chaining themselves day by day. After all, the predicament that nobody can escape is between man himself and his survival.

The survival predicament of modern people is actually the survival predicament in ontology. People will not obtain freedom or happiness unless they free themselves from survival predicament. However, people are always trapped in survival predicament and they cannot get rid of it, which is actually an existence paradox in human ontology. People cannot flee from this surviving predicament but fall into one predicament or another. It is in this sense that we can say tragedy is eternal. If a traditional tragedy presents struggles against the hardships and sacrifice of men when trapped in a crisis of survival predicament in a miniature stage, then modern tragedy is more focused on people's inexplicable spiritual fighting and possible hope in despair on a more open stage.

God has died, so has tragic hero in classical sense, but tragedy still exists. New changes and elements, as well as new tragedy samples and attitudes emerge in the process of the heritages and development of modern tragedy.

A modern tragedy, though, might not have the "noble" character that a true Greek tragic character would have;. for example, Arthur Miller's *Death of a Salesman* would not be considered a true Greek tragedy because (1) the protagonist is only a salesman and not a very good one at that and (2) even though he dies at the end, he really doesn't ever truly confess and regret his faults before he dies.

The most fundamental change has been the rejection of Aristotle's dictum that true tragedy can only depict those with power and high status. Arthur Miller's essay *Tragedy and the Common Man*[24] (1949) argues that tragedy may also depict ordinary people in domestic surroundings. British playwright Howard Barker[25] has argued strenuously for the rebirth of tragedy in the contemporary theatre, most notably in his volume *Arguments for a Theatre*.

While classical tragedy generally involves heroic people in simply awful situations (often of their own making), modern tragedy places everyday people in similar quagmires in a contemporary setting. The tragedy *Oedipus Rex* is about a young prince who gets involved in a prophecy that foretells he will kill his father and marry his mother. When that improbable scenario comes true, the king needlessly blinds himself, abdicating his throne and leaving Thebes in chaos. Henrik Ibsen's play *A Doll's House* certainly fits the definition of a modern tragedy. The tragic heroine, Nora is an everyday woman. She is special in that she is very attractive and has lots of admirers, but she is still, for her time period, quite a typical woman in a typical house, in a typical financial situation, with a typical husband and raising typical children. Her tragic downfall begins taking place when she decides to commit fraud to rescue her husband, a decision that anyone in a similar situation can make. The plot of the tragedy spirals from there and Nora becomes subjected to blackmail, must confide in her husband and learns that he is not the genuinely caring, selfless person she believes him to be, all of which are events that can happen to anyone.

In the modern world where God has died, the desolation of people's existence in an absurd world, the disillusionment of idealism caused by losing faith and modern civilization, the indignation expressed by hopeless people when struggling against the social oppression and exclusion, the loneliness of the individual being at a loss in a technology-orientated world and the sluggish caused by a transition from meaningful life and world to meaningless life and world, all of these show the tragedy of life. Facing the tragedy of life, however, people endeavor to find hope in desperation and encourage optimism when falling into pessimism, as well as endowing meaninglessness with meaningfulness, which offers good materials for modern tragedy.

Anyway, the need for tragic drama continues to exist. After all the cures of the doctor, there is still disease; after all the sessions with the psychiatrist anguish and defeat still come to the healthiest minds and cosmic loneliness finds even the busiest man. Even if man's power were to increase until he could shake the planets from their course, still his achievement would fall short of his dream. Disappointment, defeat and death, the inescapable pain and terrors are with people at modern time as surely as they were with Sophocles and Shakespeare — two very fortunate successful well-adjusted men.

God is dead, but people have to live.

Aristotle repeatedly emphasizes the "elevation and cultivation" function of tragedy in *Poetics*, which shows the maximum value of tragedy is to ennoble human spirit. Modern tragedy also has the function of informing people of being strong when encountering problems.

4.2 Tragedy in China

Generally China is not as famous as some Western countries for tragedy works. Yet, China does have some tragedy classics such as *The Orphan of China*, *Snow in Midsummer*, *The Palace of Eternal Youth* and *The Peach Blossom Fan*[26].

The Orphan of China is the first Chinese play known in Europe by a French missionary — Joseph de Premare[27]. In 1732, he translated the drama into French in Guangzhou and illuminated his motivation in the preface: Hoping the European would perceive the degree of Chinese civilization and moral sense. He deleted the libretto, just used the two words "he sings" or "she sings" to represent the content of the song and he didn't give the definite explanation because he thought that it was so difficult for Europeans to understand the songs.

The Orphan of China was adapted by Thomas Hatchett who published an adaptation of the play in English with the change of the ending significantly so that the play conformed to classical conventions of the three unities. Later, Voltaire adapted it as L'orphelin de la Maison de Tchao (*The Orphan of Zhao*, 1755) with juice of love story which was disliked by British Arthur Murphy, who spent two years rewriting the story with the title *The Orphan of China*, which succeeded in Britain and also in America.

4.3 Three Kinds of Tragic Characters of Modern Tragedy

Three kinds of tragic characters have emerged in the Western struggle to change the environment: the hero who is ahead of his time, the heroic little man who salvages a modicum of choice and the frustrated rebel who turns destructive.

When writers at modern time look at the appalling slums of the new industrial cities, they realize that the job of rebuilding will take generations and that, in the meantime, the individual in such an environment would be defeated no matter how hard he struggles. In this belief they find a modern tragic hero — not a hopeless victim but an individual who sees what is wrong with society and gives his life in the effort to change it though useless. There is no reconciliation or justice in the hero's defeat, as in classic tragedy, but instead the audience takes on the guilt of the injustice and the responsibility for rectifying it.

The greatest hero of this kind is Joan of Shaw's *Saint Joan*[28], who is an ordinary humble-born girl from the countryside. Wronged and unjustly treated with a death ending, she still chooses to fight for her country and people who misunderstand her. Far more deeply tragic, however, are plays that assume that progress will never solve all social problems and that a man must struggle to define his own individuality even in the midst of unsettled and contradictory social forces.

Arthur Miller's *Death of a Salesman* (1949) heads the list of plays that achieve tragedy on the modest scale by finding dignity in the struggle of the little man. Miller treats the salesman with respect.

Modern tragedy, in which the protagonist is often a common or middle class person, not high born, noble or important is unlike Greek tragedy. Ordinary people exemplify basic issues of social and personal conflicts. The "tragic sense" in the 20th century West countries seems to mean a despairing or deeply uncertain view, which is very different from what it meant in Ancient Greece and in Elizabethan England. This uncertainty is not merely about the cosmos but even abut character of identity. As a result, many modern plays are peopled by the "characterless" whose character is seen as unstable and blurred, torn and divided — the reflection of the reality of the modern world.

Section 5 Plays Adapted to Films

The number of theatre-goers has been declined since there are more ways for entertainment such as watching movies, television, travelling etc. But plays are still appealing to many people, including some directors. So quite a few plays have been adapted into movies, some of which are quite successful while some are not. Anyway, theater and movies have their particular glamour. In order to help students to get some understanding of famous plays, those adapted into movies are listed in the following. Actually, some plays have been adapted into movies many times by different directors at different times.

5.1 Shakespeare's Plays

Many of Shakespeare's plays have been adapted into movies.

Hamlet is directed by Laurence Olivier in 1948.

Macbeth is directed by Orson Welles in 1948 too.

Othello is directed by Oliver Parker in 1995.

*The Merchant of Venic*e is directed by Michael Radford in 2004.

A Midsummer Night's Dream is directed by Michael Hoffman in 1999.

As You Like It is directed by Kenneth Branagh in 2006.

Twelfth Night is directed by Trevor Nunn in 1996.

King Lear is directed by Trevor Nunn in 2008.

Romeo and Juliet is directed by Baz Luhrmann in 1996.

5.2 Sheridan's Plays

The School for Scandal is directed by Michael Langham in 1975.

The Rivals is directed by Rachel Kavanaugh in 2006.

5.3 Oliver Goldsmith's Plays

She Stoops to Conquer is directed by Max Stafford-Clark in 2003.

5.4 Oscar Wilde's Plays

The Importance of Being Earnest is directed by Oliver Parker in 2002.

An Ideal Husband is directed by Oliver Parker in 1999.

A Woman of No Importance is directed by Bruce Beresford in 2009.

5.5 G. B Shaw's Plays

Mrs. Warren's Profession is directed by Ákos Ráthonyi in 1960.

Heartbreak House is directed by Anthony Page in 1986.

Pygmalion is directed by George Cukor in 1964.

Just name a few of them for readers to refer to.

重难点解读

[1] 全世界是个舞台，
男男女女只是演员而已；
他们都有其退场和登场；
人生在世扮演着多种角色。
……

这是威廉·莎士比亚的戏剧《皆大欢喜》(梁实秋译成《如愿》)里面随老公爵被流放到 Arden 森林里的大臣 Jaques 说的话。

[2] **Andrei Serban**：安德瑞·塞班(1943—)。罗马裔美籍舞台剧导演，以创新性和反传统的舞台演出而出名。

[3] ***The Alchemist***：《炼金士》。英格兰文艺复兴剧作家、诗人和演

员本·琼森的社会讽刺喜剧。其剧作遵循古典主义原则，并有强烈的道德倾向，剧中对当时社会恶劣风气和习俗的尖锐批评曾使他两次被捕入狱。

[4] *Lady Windermere's Fan*：《温德密尔夫人的扇子》，又译《温夫人的扇子》、《少奶奶的扇子》。王尔德的作品。

[5] *The Comedy of Errors*：《错误的喜剧》。莎士比亚的戏剧作品。

[6] *The Cinderella*：《灰姑娘》。灰姑娘的故事原在欧洲民间广为流传，后来才由法国作家夏尔·佩罗和德国的格林兄弟加以采集编写。在多种语言包括法语、德语、意大利语、瑞典语，甚至汉语、斯拉夫语、凯尔特语中都有不同版本的类似故事，尤以格林的最为著名。

[7] *Merchant of Venice*：《威尼斯商人》。莎士比亚的戏剧作品。

[8] Victorian Period：维多利亚时代。维多利亚女王是第一个以大不列颠与爱尔兰联合王国女王和印度女皇名号称呼的英国君主。在位63年期间(1837—1901)，被认为是英国工业革命和大英帝国的峰端，是英国最强盛的"日不落帝国"时期。到第一次世界大战开始的1914年，英国都称为维多利亚时代，1914年以后，英国开始走向衰落。

[9] *Show Boat*, *West Side Story*：《演艺船》、《西区故事》。《演艺船》是美国早期音乐剧的代表，是奥斯·汉姆斯特恩作词兼编剧，吉罗姆·科恩作曲的音乐剧，是至今仍在上演的优秀音乐剧中最早的一部，标志着现代音乐剧的兴起。这部不朽的剧作在密西西比河上一条轮船上展开，记述了从1880年到1927年生活在该船上的歌舞团演员三代人的生活、爱情、欢乐以及忧伤。《西区故事》是一部美国戏剧作品，最早以音乐剧形式在百老汇和伦敦西区剧院上演，后经过改编拍成电影并获得多项奥斯卡金像奖殊荣，成为最著名的歌舞片之一，其内容改编自莎士比亚著名的爱情悲剧《罗密欧与朱丽叶》，但在背景与剧情上，都以当时的纽约移民社群为参考，使描述故事的过程充满了现实与讽刺的意味：种族歧视、青少年犯罪、暴力和文化代沟等。

[10] ***Cats***：《猫》。作曲家安德鲁·洛伊·韦伯根据 T. S. 艾略特的诗集《老负鼠的猫经》(Old Possum's Bode of Practical Cats)及其他诗歌所编写的史上最成功的音乐剧之一，自 1981 年在伦敦首演以来，被译成二十多种文字在全世界演出，总计在纽约演出了7 485场，在伦敦演出了8 949场。

[11] ***The Black Crook***：《黑钩子》。根据浮士德的故事改编而成的情节剧，1866 年在纽约尼布罗花园(Niblo's Garden)首演，演出档期创下了当时的纪录。此后短短两年内被多次搬上百老汇，并在全国范围内巡演。

[12] ***The Capture of Miletus***：《米利都的陷落》。悲剧诗人普律尼科司(492 BC)根据波希战争而写的剧本，再现了波斯人在米利都的暴行和战败者的悲惨遭遇。此剧在雅典新任首席将军泰米斯托克利的资助下上演，然而，演出的效果却多少有些出人意料："全体观众都哭了起来。于是他们由于普律尼科司使他们想起了同胞的令人痛心的灾祸而对他课以一千德拉克玛的罚金，并且禁止此后任何人再演这出戏。"

[13] **the Persian War**：希腊波斯战争。地处海路要津的希腊城邦米利都成了抵抗运动的策源地，公元前 494 年 11 月，波斯人通过发动"拉德湾海战"将米利都攻陷。随后，波斯人对这个城市实行了特别严厉的惩罚措施："城中的男人大部分被杀死，所有的妇女和儿童都被作为奴隶带到波斯本土。米利都城可以说是被完全毁掉了。这个曾经诞生了人类历史上第一个哲学学派的城邦从此变成了一个普通的二等城邦。"血腥屠城让这个小亚细亚当年最繁华的商业城市变成了一片焦土。

[14] ***Oedipus Rex***：《俄狄浦斯王》。古希腊悲剧家索福克勒斯的代表作《俄狄浦斯王》的拉丁文表达。

[15] ***A Street Car Named Desire***：《欲望号街车》。美国戏剧家田纳西·威廉斯著名戏剧作品，首部电影版本拍摄于 1951 年，由马龙·白兰度和费雯丽主演。

[16] **Strindberg**：斯特林堡（1849—1912）。瑞典第一位国际知名的剧作家，近代剧坛大师之一，写了 60 多部戏剧和 30 多部著

作，其中《父亲》(1887)、《茱莉小姐》(1888)是当代脍炙人口的作品。

[17] *The Hairy Ape*：《毛猿》。是由美国戏剧之父的尤金·奥尼尔创作的一部兼有现实主义、表现主义和象征主义的戏剧。于1921年上演，全剧共八场。描述现代人类在丧失宗教信仰和自然的和谐以后对自我的寻求。

[18] *Endgame*：《终局》。是贝克特在创作了《等待戈多》之后用法语创作的又一部力作，也是贝克特本人最为钟爱的作品，却遭受较多冷遇。《终局》与《等待戈多》相似，都是通过简约的人物设置、彼此间偶尔的冲撞及低语、人与人之间麻木又无助的依赖，传递出人们内心深处的孤独与困境。《终局》这部作品很可能是存在主义文学作品中最灰暗荒凉的一部，同时也是最有趣的一部。

[19] *Mrs. Warren's Profession*：《华伦夫人的职业》。英国19世纪剧作家萧伯纳的代表剧作，华伦夫人出身贫寒，年轻时在姐姐引导下由卖淫而后开妓院，成了有钱人。

[20] *Arts Poetica*：《诗艺》。由美国作家，现代诗人阿齐博尔德·麦克利什(1892—1982)所著，他曾获得两次普利策诗歌奖。

[21] **polka**：波尔卡。该词在捷克语中为“半步”，大致分为急速、徐缓和玛祖卡节奏等三种类型，一般为二拍子、三部曲式，节奏活泼跳跃，在第二拍的后半拍上常作稍微停顿。波尔卡本是捷克农民舞蹈，19世纪中叶，传到英国和美国，与华尔兹一道取代了乡村舞和科蒂林舞。

[22]《麦克白》第四幕麦克白的独白：

时间啊，在我痛下狠手之前，竟然让你占了先机；除非行动迅速，不然心血来潮的意图就永远无法实现。从此刻起，我心里一想到什么，便马上动手去做。即便是眼下，我也要用行动完成我的意志，边想边干。

[23] *The Death of Tragedy*：《悲剧之死》。为法裔美国文学批评家、哲学家、作家和教育家乔治·斯坦纳的著作。斯坦纳曾任《经济学人》杂志编辑，后任教于普林斯顿大学、剑桥大学、

日内瓦大学等知名学府，教授比较文学课程。研究领域涉及文学理论、比较文学，并提出了重要的“翻译四步骤”理论。其主要作品包括：《托尔斯泰或陀思妥耶夫斯基》、《悲剧之死》(1961)、《巴别塔之后》、《马丁·海德格尔》、《何谓比较文学》等。2007年，获得阿方索·雷耶斯国际奖。

[24] ***Tragedy and the Common Man***：《悲剧与普通人》。美国戏剧家阿瑟·米勒的文章。

[25] **Howard Barker**：霍华德·巴克(1946—)。英国剧作家和诗人，发明了灾难剧(Theatre of Catastrophe)来描绘自己的作品，其剧本主要关于暴力、性、权欲和人的动机等。

[26] ***The Orphan of China***, ***Snow in Midsummer***, ***The Palace of Eternal Youth and The Peach Blossom Fan***：《赵氏孤儿》、《窦娥冤》、《长生殿》和《桃花扇》。中国著名悲剧作品。

[27] **Joseph de Premare**：马若瑟(1666—1736)。法国著名汉学家、耶稣会传教士。是第一个把中国历史悲剧《赵氏孤儿》传入法国的，全文发表在法国1783年出版的《中华帝国全志》中。1698年来华后，在中国语言文学、哲学等方面付出了30多年的心血。在汉学方面造诣极深，被后世学者公认为西方人汉语文学专家和易学专家中的佼佼者。其拉丁文手稿《汉语札记》堪称传世力作。

[28] ***Saint Joan***：《圣女贞德》。由英国现实主义戏剧家萧伯纳描写法国青年女爱国者贞德在英法百年战争中领导农民反抗英军被俘牺牲的一部悲剧。萧伯纳塑造了一个平民英雄形象。

Chapter 5 Ways to Appreciate Drama

What is Drama? No one has ever succeeded in defining it. Drama comes from the Greek root meaning "to act" or "to do". In theater, drama is presented by actors to audience. Drama means different things to different people. To some people, the entire world is a stage and all the men and women are merely players. They have their exits and their entrances. One man in his time plays many parts. Yet life in the world and life on the stage are not the same to many other people.

Section 1 Some Ideas about Drama

A play or drama is a series of actions, which occur when something happens that makes or permits something else to happen. Therefore, action is "something happening", one leading to the other. In drama, something is happening before our eyes, which means, drama portrays the present moment, but keep in mind that moment is full of promise and threat, pregnant with the future.

To some degree, a drama is like a series of dominoes with one event triggering the next and so on.

1.1 Audience

The audience are caught up and carried from crisis to crisis in a rhythmic pattern of tension and relaxation, swept to a climax by an irresistible momentum when watching a play, then leave at the end changed and thrilled by the sense of having gone through a great experience.

1.2 Why Watch Drama?

In Ancient Greece, watching drama was a must to get involved in community life politically and economically and going to theatre was a way of displaying one's membership of wealth or celebrity at a certain period of time. For example, going to a fashionable theatre in 1607, one went to the theatre as much to be seen as to see. For more people, going to theatre offers company pleasure. Audience can see deep into the lives of characters so like themselves yet so different — lives lived more intensely than their own. It seems they can begin the journey from which they can't return, thus being elevated and civilized. A play is, to a great degree, an extension of life. Many people are fond of going to theatre because of the therapy function. It is like a journey into the mind both for the artists relentlessly creating new artistic forms to give vent to their feelings and of great help to the others and the patient discovering the right turn by reenacting the scene where he takes the wrong one. Besides, theatre offers rich, deep experience, bringing the joy of enlightenment, a revelation that makes order of confusion and doubt and relating us to the great archetypal patterns of human purpose and destiny.

1.3 What Playwrights Say

Every dramatist's dream is his name and his play's title in lights on a downtown marquee and a line at the box office, even on a rainy day.

Bernard Shaw called on the theatre to take itself seriously as "a factory of thought, a prompter of conscience, an elucidator and a temple of the Ascent of Man." Andrei Serban, the brilliant young New York director said, "Theatre is a manifestation of the essence of life." That essence is more than pleasure in entertainment, more than role-playing, more than any personal emotion of love, hate, anger or jealousy. The essence of life is a deep sense of wonder and awe, of a common human destiny.

Section 2 Problems of Drama

Drama is a highly specialized form of literature which can do some things supremely well but which must handle matters in its own way. The novel is designed to address its audience directly: open it and you have everything you need in front of you. But a play-text addresses its ultimate audience indirectly; it is a set of instructions designed to be interpreted by theatre makers who will then stage the play before its own audience.

The play-text is quite a strange incomplete object. But at the same time you will find how exciting the activity of reading plays can be when the signals they contain are recognized for what they are. You are on a journey to discover more about the relationship between the two sorts of "play" — the script and the performance. The first thing to realize when you open a play-text is that the words in front of you are not designed to function in the same way as the words in a novel or poem. The words are designed to become a performance. So drama needs to be understood differently.

2.1 Characteristics of Drama

Drama depends almost entirely on what people do and what people say to each other on the stage. That is, the meanings, thought and feelings are expressed or reflected in the main externalized conduct in drama. Different from other literature forms, there is little or no place for "description" made directly by the author in play. The play consists almost entirely of words spoken directly by the characters, that is, through dialogues. The playwright can not give any direct comments on the meaning of an action, a situation, an expression, a gesture and so on. Secondly, there is little direct use of action that is purely mental or psychological which can be used frequently in novels. Some direct mental probing can be done as in Shakespeare's soliloquies, but in general this will have to be occasional and subordinate and dealt with in a skilful way. Finally, plays are often written in verse-form especially in relatively old times. And they can be read or seen in the form of stage-presentation.

2.2 Problem of Scope

In performance several tips can be turned on at the same time. Words, silences, sound effects, background music, facial expressions, gestures, movements across the stage, lighting, groupings, shadows, shapes and colors in the costume and decor, all of these may be telling us something. At the same time we are emotionally involved by the appearance, the voice and the personality of the actors. We may feel in sympathy with one, hostile to another. But unlike poems or novels, in which writers can make extensive use of descriptions and discussion and present their ideas in a variety of ways from different points of view, drama is a literature form with many limits.

2.2.1 Limit of Length

Playwrights are limited in the length of drama in most cases. Generally, a play, sticking closely to the present and bringing in the past only by suggestion, lasts for two to three hours during which there should be a dramatic situation. Dramatists have to find a special kind of situation — compact of its own nature or the exploding point of a conflict because drama which usually ignores earlier and later ramification works at the height of a situation. If a situation does not have or cannot be made to have some high point, it is not a good one for drama which needs tight and concentrated play. For example, Dickens' *A Tale of Two Cities*[1] is an excellent long novel but it is almost impossible to make a good dramatic version of it.

2.2.2 Limit of Number of Character

Dramatists are much more limited than the novelists in the number of characters they can use in a play. They have to center his main action on one character or two — thus selecting the right kind of "lead". If a dramatist uses as many characters as he wishes, they may be blurred because of inadequate treatment within the limited time. If he uses a small enough number to permit some fullness of presentation, he may not create the variety he desires, which is a great challenge to dramatists. Dramatists have to recognize clearly just what the issue is and whose actions are really significant, with the result that each character bears a greater symbolic weight than in a fiction.

2.2.3 Limit of Space

In addition, dramatists have no practically complete freedom in the use of space that the cinema and the novel can. A tightly concentrated piece of action and a limited number of characters of drama make it normally hard to spread over a dozen different places. Dramatists should make the audience feel that the presence of characters at given spots and their movement from one locality to another thoroughly logical. The ironic fact for him is that if he does this well, the audience don't notice it, but if he does it badly, the audience feel that he is moving characters about arbitrarily, thus interfering with the effectiveness of his play.

It is really a hard task to be a good playwright. To obtain maximum enjoyment and understanding, play lovers have generally more work to do on their own than do readers of a novel or a poem. This limitation is in another sense an advantage, for the play's lack of description and authorial presence offer its readers greater opportunity to exercise their own judgment.

2.3 Dialogue Problem

As mentioned above, there is little description in a play which consists almost entirely of words spoken directly by the characters, that is, through dialogues. Dramatists do everything in dialogues. So dialogues in a play are very important and are distinctive because a play depends on dialogues leading to problems. The characteristics of drama dialogues include progression, exposition, the use of informative devices, plausibility, naturalness and tempo.

2.3.1 Progression

Dialogues in a play lead on toward future action, that is, they are being progressive. In each scene the lines must not only develop the situation with which that scene is concerned, they must also quietly direct audience toward the future — quietly and yet rapidly.

2.3.2 Exposition

A playwright can not come onto the stage and give any direct comments on the meaning of an action, a situation, an expression, a gesture and so on in a play. So characters in a play must let the audience know what is what and they must do it while they are talking about something else. Characters cannot inform us directly either. As a result, the information is implied in lines which are looking ahead rather than back.

2.3.3 Use of Informative Devices

Of course, playwrights can turn to the use of informative devices such as aside or soliloquy to let audience know more, but these devices are limited too. For example, Ben Jonson managed this rather well in *Volpone*[2] in which Volpone, who was supposedly on his deathbed, was visited by a series of his relatives who hoped to be remembered in his will. Before these men came in, Volpone and his servant had a discussion about them. This discussion was a zestful relishing of the deception to be practiced upon the visitors. It's perfectly plausible, but at the same time it serves most usefully to inform the audience about the intentions and characters of the visitors and to prepare the audience for the visits and make them the more sharply aware of the fluent hypocrisies which both sides speak.

2.3.4 Plausibility

Dramatic dialogue, which is effective, is a specialized form of conversation, having some of the generic qualities of conversation. Dialogues should achieve "naturalness" which depends on what is included in the conversation and how it is said. Dramatists secure naturalness without admitting all the casualness and disorder of everyday speech and yet concentrate on the subject without becoming strained and uneasy. A character must not sound like an orator reading from a prepared manuscript.

2. 3. 5 Naturalness

Dialogues should sound natural in a play. Plays used to be written in poetic verses. What is natural at one time is not natural at another. For the same reason, what is natural for one person is not for another and what is natural for one person on one occasion is not natural for him on another. Generally, too much speed, too much slang, too much formality and too much ordinariness will undoubtedly ruin a scene. Poetic form used to be the standard in ancient and modern times till the 18th century in drama writing then shifted from poetry to prose, marking the decline of the tragic sense. What is sure is that speeches should be always appropriate to time, place and characters.

2. 3. 6 Tempo

Tempo refers to the movement, the quality by means of which the dialogue gives us the sense of moving forward. Dramatists give to his dialogue the quality that will make it seem to move at a desirable speed and so allot his limited space that audience will not feel he has wasted any of it on less important materials.

Undoubtedly, the very fact of drama's limitations gives drama a special kind of concentration of effect which helps drama gain the precision and exactness essential in literature, first, by the very act of eliminating everything but a bare central theme and second, by dealing with that theme in the most expressive but at the same time the most controlled kind of language.

Section 3 Drama vs Other Literary Forms

Like fiction and poetry, drama can present a situation which stimulates readers' imagination, thus leading them to apprehend the meaning latent in it. But drama is different from poetry and fiction to a great degree. Poetry is able to use characters to speak and fiction is capable of dialoguing a good deal, but drama is able to do nothing else.

3.1 Drama vs Fiction

Does drama just occur to you or does novel just occur to you? Are there any big differences between them? Let's come to a story first.

3.1.1 A Specific Story

The salesmen decided to have a rest for the night. They chose a hotel and checked in.

Collins said, "Sure there's a corkscrew in there. You'll find it chained to the wall. All hotels have them." And Menefee answered from the bathroom, "Well, there's not one in here. Look for yourselves if you boys don't believe me." "That's a fine way to treat drummers[3]," said Red Smith, "I'll write and complain to the management." He got up and stretched himself. "I'll look in the closet," he said. "Maybe I'll find something to open it with in there."

Menefee came back into the room and put the unopened bottle on the dresser, his head drawn backward and turned at an angle, his eyes squinting up. He ground out the cigarette that had been burning between his relaxed lips. "You boys keep our pants on," he said, "I'll go down and borrow a corkscrew off a bellhop." He put on his coat and went into the hall, closing the door behind him.

Collins sat back and rested his legs on the vacant chair, looking lazily over his shoulder at Red Smith. Red was pulling out drawers noisily or standing tiptoe to peer at shelves just above his head. Then he stopped, picked up something and came into the room with it. It was a sheet of hotel stationery covered with writing and it had been crumpled into a ball and thrown into the closet.

Red opened the sheet and smoothed it flat and when he had read it, he passed it to Collins, a peculiar look on his face. "Read this, Wade," he said. Collins read slowly, the paper held close to his eyes. At the right of the sheet and commencing it, was the following entry: "Cash on hand \$ 17.45." Then to the left, were the following entries:

Expenses babies funeral (about)	\$ 148.00
Wifes hospital bill (about)	65.00
Owe to grocery store	28.17
Back Rent (2 mo. — make it 3)	127.25
Incidentals	25.00
	\$ 394.42

A litter further down the paper was the following: "Will borrow 400 dollars from Mr. Sellwood." This sentence was repeated, like an exercise in penmanship, over and over until the paper was filled with it. At first the words were written boldly, heavily and there were places where the pen had broken through the paper behind the determination of the writer; but as the writing progressed, the man seemed less sure of himself as if his courage and his certainty were fading away. The sentences were more perfect here, with an occasional mended letter, they were written more slowly, as if each letter were pondered. The last sentence was not finished at all. It dwindled thinly into wavering illegibility.

Collins had read the thing through and sat with it in his hands. He said sympathetically, "Tough! Tough!" then added, "He knew he couldn't work it out. He knew he was fooling himself; so he crumpled up the paper and threw it in the closet."

Red sat down, resting his elbows on his knees, his bright coppery hair shining in the light. Suddenly he had a picture of a shabby little man sitting in this same cheap hotel room, going over his problem over and over and finding no answer to it. Finally he said, "Don't you suppose Mr. Sellwood let him have the 400 bucks after all? Why not?"

Collins sighed, the Masonic emblem[4] resting on his fat stomach, rising with his breath. He spoke mockingly, "Of course not, Little

Sunshine. Of course not! Maybe our friend went to see Mr. Sellwood all right, but Mr. Sellwood said that times were hard right then and he had a lot of expenses of his own. I guess that's about the way it worked out. "

Red lifted his alert face. "I think you're wrong, Wade, I think everything worked out all right." But Collins shook his head. "Not a chance, young fellow!" he said. "Not a chance!"

Red replied, "Just the same, I think Mr. Sellwood let him have the 400 bucks. He was an old friend of the family, you see. Then he got a good job for this fellow that paid more money and this fellow came back home almost running. He came up the steps at the time to tell his wife. Everything worked out fine for them after that."

"Maybe he met Santa Claus on the way home," said Wade heavily, "and old Santa slipped the money in his stocking." Then he said more seriously, "The fellow who wrote that is sitting in some other cheap hotel tonight still figuring and still trying to find an answer, but he won't because there isn't any answer for him to find."

The door opened then and Menefee stood before them, a corkscrew in his hand. "Everything's okay," he said. "Everything is all set." "We'll leave it to Menefee," said Red. "Give him the writing, Wade and let's see what he thinks." Collins passed over the paper and Menefee examined it carefully as if he did not understand it before he looked at the two men, puzzled a little. "What's it all about? This doesn't make sense to me." Collins shook his head. "Good old Menefee. Trust him!"

Red laughed a little and said earnestly, "Don't you see the point, Menefee?" Menefee read the thing through again, turned the paper over and examined the writing once more. "I'm damned if I do," he said helplessly. Then a moment later he added triumphantly, "Oh sure, sure, I see the point now! Sure I do. It's added up wrong." Red looked at Collins and they both laughed. "It's added up wrong!" said Menefee, indignant and a little hurt. "8 and 5 are 13 and 3 are 21. 7 makes 28 and 5, 33 not 34 like it is here." But Collins and Red continued to laugh and to shake their heads.

"All right," said Menefee. "I'm dumb; I admit it." He pulled in his lips and spoke in a high quavering voice, "Come on, boys, let your poor old grandmother in on the joke!" He picked up the bottle and poured three drinks into three tumblers, grumbling a little to himself. "I never saw such superior bastards in all my life as you two are," he said.

3.1.2 The Method of the Story

This story is quite appealing to readers by turning upon a rather simple contrast: the misfortunes of the earlier occupant and the relative well-being of the three salesmen, desperation of his evening and the casual gaiety of theirs, the indifference which we may expect of them and the actual sympathy which they show, the different responses to and understanding of the note, contrast between Menifee and the other men — creating the final effect — his lack of understanding leading to the amusement of the others and to his irritation at their amusement, thus the ending of the story not on a note of sadness but on one of ironic amusement.

The writer of the story skillfully links the earlier occupant and the present three salesmen through the same hotel room, depicting the scene of two totally different types of evening spent by people under wholly different circumstances. The story writer is objective, using no device to help pump up sympathy. But the sharp contrast he prefers and the pathetic document he describes in details speak for itself, showing amount of sympathy.

3.1.3 The Story as Drama

How about converting this story into a play? According to the characteristics of drama which is highly limited in the number of characters, places and length of time, this story seems to be a good drama. There is a single scene in a hotel room. The only three characters can speak most of the lines almost as they are given in the story with Menefee going out and returning at the proper time. There are no serious mechanical problems for adapting the story into a good drama, but we will soon be aware that something is missing, that is, the dramatic version is a good deal less effective than the story version. Why? Why can not a story that is so like drama work very well as drama?

Read the story again and carefully and we will find this story has the characters on a situation. The characters talk about a situation instead of participating in it. As a result, we have a kind of photographic glimpse of static characters. Drama apparently works with greater success when characters act out a situation themselves instead of merely viewing it.

Secondly, when adapting, we have to leave out one of the most important "character" of all — the crumpled sheet of paper. Although it can not speak a word, it means so much and tells readers so many things that without it the implied meaning is totally lost. Of course, some characters could tell us about it, but this second-hand presentation would deprive it of almost all vitality. In addition, we have to leave out the line " 'Will borrow 400 dollars from Mr. Sellwodd' is first written boldly and heavily, then less confidently and finally its last form was left unfinished and it dwindled thinly into wavering illegibility", which also undermines the meaning of the story a lot. Finally, we have to leave out the insight into Red's mind which the author uses: Suddenly he had a picture of a shabby little man in this same cheap hotel, going over his problem over and over and finding no answer to it, which shows clearly what a dramatist cannot do — giving a direct, immediate account of mental operation of characters.

From the discussion, we can find that novel is able to describe setting and properties of all kinds, to look both at the outer world of things and the inner world of the mind, to shift easily from present to past and from place to place while drama demands a more overt form of action and presents the difference of attitude in an actual clash of characters, where the words are not merely descriptive but are accompaniments of action or indications of action to come. Words in a play is designed to become a performance. The dialogue is busy doing a lot more than telling a story. It is creating images and movements in a stage world.

Limited a lot, a playwright or at least the producer has some advantages over the novelist in presenting setting. One glance at the stage by the audience will take in what might take the novelist hundreds of words to convey to readers. Setting can provide for the occurrence of simultaneous events.

3.2 Drama vs Poetry

Drama and poetry can be combined. Great drama in the plays of Shakespeare is also great poetry. Yet, the poem differs sharply from both fiction and drama in the ways in which it gets its effects. Poems have less of overt action than drama and less development of characters in the usual sense of the word. Poetry uses imagery, rhythm, symbols and statements as the words of the author of some character, spoken to himself or to someone else. But drama depends almost entirely on what people do and what people say to each other. Meanings, thought and feelings must in the main be externalized in conduct.

Section 4 Ways to Appreciate Drama

It's easy to say, with Aristotle, that a play's main ingredients are plot, character, thought, diction, music and spectacle. But they are results, not first steps. They are what you have to find, not how you have to find them. Then how to find them?

A play's plot is the product of other elements. Character, particularly in drama is not where analysis starts, but where it ends. On stage or in real life character is amorphous, shifting and intangible. Understanding character requires analysis of its components — concrete and palpable components. Don't even think about a play's thought until you understand the concrete elements of which the play is composed of. Then where to start to appreciate drama?

4.1 Conflict

All literature involves a certain amount of conflict. Yet, drama tends to highlight conflict. The fact that it does so often to emphasize conflict is in accord with its special potentialities. As we've seen that drama, compared with some other arts, is limited in its ability to change scene, to show the slow development of characters and to show a character from as many points of view as a novel can. But drama can deal powerfully with characters in conflict — problems do come to a head at a particular time and conflicts occur in a particular place.

4.1.1 Drama Conflicts

It is not exaggerating to say that conflict is the essence of drama. Drama in all age is as William Archer[5] stated aptly in play-making, "a representation of the will of man in conflict with the mysterious powers of natural forces which limit and belittle us: it is one of us thrown living upon the stage there to struggle against fatality, social law, one of his fellow mortals, himself, the ambitions, the interests, the prejudices, the folly, the malevolence of these around him." Paying attention to conflict in a play is one of good ways to help people to appreciate drama.

Yet, conflict in drama is not a general crash of one thing into another. Dramatic conflict is distinct from other kinds of conflict. A novel's conflict might be free will versus destiny and a poem's conflict might be youth versus old age or the city versus the country. But a play's conflict is a particular kind of interaction, deeply rooted in and inalienable from real life human behavior. It is a kind of an obstacle, which means any resistance to one's having what he wants. What he wants and what resists his having it work against each other to create dramatic conflict. An obstacle can be anything. Often it stems from what someone else wants. For example, You want to be king. But the obstacle is that you have to sty king. Obstacle can also stem from circumstances or one's own inabilities or misgivings or from chance or fate. In every case, the obstacle must be something you are willing to fight. If you are not, you do nothing. So there's no action and the audience will go to sleep.

4.1.2 Types of Dramatic Conflicts

Ibsen's themes suggest man's unending conflict between duty to himself and duty to others. Conflicts that occur frequently in drama include four major ones.

4.1.2.1 One Against Himself

One wants your collection of stamps, but he knows that stealing is wrong and he has difficulty bringing himself to do it. If he wants the stamps badly enough he will try to overcome the obstacle (his moral stance against stealing). The conflict is between one and his own reservations — one against himself. In *Hamlet*, there also exists the conflict — Hamlet against Hamlet. "To be or not to be, this is a question" is a question Hamlet asks himself again and again. He wonders what to do. From the viewpoint of his father who is murdered, he should revenge for him, but Claudius is his uncle and his step father and also the King of the country. For Hamlet, there is no choice but to be in a state of feigned madness, which causes his hesitation and melancholy. Another example is the inner conflict in *Death of a Salesman*. The confusion and frustration of Willy Loman is caused by his inability to face and understand the realities of modern society and his fruitless struggle for success against his real feelings. Willy's most prominent delusion is that success is dependent upon popularity and having personal attractiveness. Willy builds his entire life around this idea and teaches it to his children. In a war with his own inner self, he refuses to accept what he really is — ordinary, average and unremarkable. Ultimately his inner and outer conflicts destroy him.

4.1.2.2 One Against Other Individuals

The conflict one against other individuals means one wants your stamps, but you guard them with great carefulness. This conflict is between one and you — one against another individual. Hamlet versus Claudis in *Hamlet* is a obvious example. Firstly, to revenge for his own father, Hamlet has to kill Claudis, his step father who kills the ex-king to be the king. Claudis has to continue the killing. On the one hand, he is afraid of the possibility that Hamlet will figure out the truth and on the other he is also scared that Hamlet will be the new king. Willy Loman versus his sons in *Death of a Salesman*, Faustus versus Mephistophilis[6] in *The Tragical History of Doctor Faustus*, Shylock versus Antonio in *The Merchant of Venice* and so on all belong to this kind of conflict.

4.1.2.3 One Against Society

One stole your stamps. Now he is wanted by the F. B. I., hunted like a dog. He broke the law; now society's wrath hounds him. His adversary is not you; he is fighting for his freedom and he is fighting against society. In *Merchant of Venice* there exist many conflicts, one of which is Shylock against society. Shylock is a Jew who is faced with severe racial prejudice. Shylock endures much of Antonio's abuse over a long period of time. This can be seen by the sheer volume of disgraces he has bore. Here is what he says about whites once: "He hath disgraced me half a million, laughed at my losses, mocked at my gains, scorned my nation, thwarted my bargains, cooled my friends, heated mine enemies..." In *Othello*, there also exists the conflict between Othello and the society. Othello is referred to as a "Moor", a term used during the English Renaissance to refer to dark-skinned people in general. He believes in what Iago has said because of his distrust of the society. In that society, people look down upon the black. So he believes Iago and acts madly. The tragedy is caused by the society.

4.1.2.4 One Against Fate or Universe or Natural Forces or God

This is a hard battle to win! It is man against the sheer cliff of a mountain or Lear's howling "Blow winds" at the storm or Macbeth's refusing to accept his fate, crying "Lay o, Macduff!" It is not a conflict likely to result from one's stealing your stamps. In Ancient Greek drama the conflict is usually between "one against fate". Before the 20th century the conflict centers around "one against reality" while in the Absurd drama, the conflict includes uncertainty and disillusion of modern men.

To sum up, when appreciating drama, what should not be ignored is a character's want which may be opposed by some hindrance — by some obstacle. A character talks to maneuver another character or characters in such a way that the obstacle to the want is removed. To understand a line of dialogue we must know what the speaker wants and how the speaker intends the words spoken to overcome the obstacle to what is being wanted.

Keep in mind, for some playwrights they can have several conflicts at the same time. The confrontation of two minds can create conflict as tense and exciting as a physical fight on stage.

4.2 Dialogue

Dialogue in drama is doing more than telling a story. It's creating images, movement and a stage world. Thus, dialogue must be dynamic, advancing the plot, delineating character or getting a laugh.

4.2.1 Dialogue Functions

Dialogue in drama is different from casual conversation in our daily life. It has certain functions such as conversational exchange between characters, information as to time and place, information about action, actual enactments and information about characters. We can now stand back a little and see just what is designed to deliver to the audience at any one time.

4.2.2 Types of Dialogue

In order to show the functions of dialogue in drama, let's come to see the types and differences of some other dialogue examples to help us to sense the differences of dialogue in drama and in some other situations.

4.2.2.1 Courtroom Dialogue

The following is the courtroom dialogue in the trial in which the physician of a murdered man is being questioned by the Defense Attorney[7], Biggs.

"Was blood from the wounds on Laurel's head stopped or flowing when you examined the body?" Biggs asked.

"Stopped." the doctor replied.

"What was the condition of Sir Henry's face? Was it bloody?"

"There was a small clot of dry blood on the nostril and upper lip. There might have been a little oozing from a wound, but I am not sure."

Biggs handed Armbruster a photograph of the body showing a streak of blood across the face. "The body must have been moved," the physician stated emphatically. "Blood will not flow uphill out of the ear and nostrils."

Jury Jacob Stone interrupted the questioning to ask the doctor if there was any indication of the body being lifted.

"I did not examine it sufficiently to answer that question," Armbruster replied.

"Would you say that the burns you saw would have prevented Sir Henry from moving from the bed?" the juror continued.

"So, Sir Henry would have been capable of moving if the burns

preceded the blows."

"*Did he move after the blows?*" *Stone asked.*

"*In my opinion, Sir Henry did not move himself after the blows were struck,*" *the doctor added.*

"*How long would it have taken a normal healthy person to die then?*" *Justice Sir Claude Weeks asked.*

"*A normal healthy person does not die,*" *Armbruster responded candidly. The courtroom roared with laughter, including the white-wigged, red-robed Weeks.*

……

This dialogue may convey a certain excitement and even exhibit a mild tension— qualities which one expects of true drama, but still it is not drama. Why?

This kind of exchange of lines could go on and on for 300 pages and we would still be essentially just where we had started. We would have a few more facts about a murder, but nothing more. Such a dialogue does not push forward the plot nor portray characters. Such questions and answers can go on indefinitely and we will still know practically nothing about the attorney, the jurymen, the judge or the witnesses.

4.2.2.2 A Private Conversation

Then let's examine a conversation between people. The participants include Bossuet, a famous bishop and the Duchess de Fontanges, mistress of Louis XIV (B refers to Bossuet while F means Fontanges in the following).

B: Mademoiselle[8], *it is the King's desire that I compliment you on the elevation you have attained.*

F: O monseigneur[9], *I know very well what you mean. His Majesty*[10] *is kind and polite to everybody. The last thing he said to me was,* "*Do not forget to compliment Monseigneur the Bishop on the dignity I have conferred upon him, of almoner to the Dauphiness. I desired the appointment for him only that he might be of rank sufficient to confess you, now you are Duchess. Let him be your confessor, my little girl. He has fine manners."*

B: I dare not presume to ask you, mademoiselle, what was our gracious reply to the condescension of our royal master.

F: Oh! Yes, you may! I told him I was almost sure I should be ashamed of confessing such naughty things to a person of high rank, who writes like an angel.

B: The observation was inspired, by your goodness and modesty.

F: You are so agreeable a man, I will confess to our directly, if you like.

B: Have you brought yourself to a proper frame of mind, young lady?

F: What is that?

B: Do you hate sin?

F: Very much.

B: Are you resolved to leave it off?

F: I have left it off entirely since the King began to love me. I have never said a spiteful word of anybody since.

B: In your opinion, mademoiselle, are there no other sins than malice?

F: I never stole anything; I never committed adultery; I never conveted my neighbor's wife; I never killed any person, though several men have told me they should die for me.

B: Vain, idle talk! Did you listen to it?

F: Indeed I did, with both ears; it seemed so funny.

B: You have something to answer for, then.

F: No, indeed, I have not. I have asked many times after them and found they were all alive; which mortified me.

B: So, then! You would really have them die for you?

F: Oh, no, no! But I wanted to see if they were in earnest or told me fibs; for, if they told me fibs I would never trust them again. I do not care about them; for the King told me I was only to mind him.

B: Lowest and highest, we all owe to His Majesty our duty and submission.

F: I am sure he has mine; so you need not blame me or question me on that. At first, indeed, when he entered the folding-doors, I was in such a flurry I could hear my heart beat across the chamber; by degrees I cared little about the matter; and at last, when I grew used to it, I liked it rather than not. Now if this is not confession, what is?

B: We must abstract the soul from every low mundane thought. Do you hate the world, mademoiselle?

F: A good of it; all Picardy[11] *for example. Nothing is uglier and oh, my life! What frightful men and women!*

B: I would say, in plain language, do you hate the flesh and the Devil?

F: Who does not hate the Devil? If you will hold my hand the while, I will tell his so — I hate you, beast! There now. As for flesh, I never could bear a fat man. Such people can neither dance nor hunt, nor do anything that I know of.

B: Mademoiselle Marie-Angelique de Scoraille de Rousille, Duches de Fontanges! Do you hate titles and dignities and yourself?

F: Myself! Does anyone hate me? Why should I be the first? Hatred is the worst thing in the world because it makes one so very ugly.

B: To love God, we must hate ourselves. We must detest our bodies if we would save our souls.

F: That is hard; how can I do it? I see nothing detestable in mine! Do you? To live is easier...

F: ... And now let me tell you, my lord, you compose such pretty funeral sermons, I hope I shall have the pleasure of hearing you preach mine...

B: To me the painful duty will, I trust, be spared: I am advancing age; you are a child.

F: Oh, no! I am 17.

B: I should have supposed you younger by two years at least...

......

Is this conversation like drama ? This conversation is like drama, yet it is not drama. Why?

From the conversation, we can see two characters develop before us — devotion to a heavenly master and devotion to an earthly master. Duchess is extremely naive. On the one hand, she is completely candid and without hypocrisy at her pleasure in her own charms in a long way from adult vanity. On the other hand, her simplicity is such that she misses the real point of all the questions. She is well-meaning but tactless and she jumps to conclusion. She is completely literal-minded, unable to understand such simple and well-known figures of speech as 'the world', 'the flesh' and 'devil'. There is little creation of characters. But there is no plot, no real action taking place and no conflict. The scene displays the character, but we don't see them in action. The relationship between them is casual and formal. In addition, the conversation does not have the directness and continuity which it would have as part of a play. Drama needs central action which binds the parts together, unifies them and gives them direction.

4. 2. 3 Relation of Dialogue to Action

Drama portrays the present moment, but that moment is full of promise and threat, pregnant with the future. There might be delay, but the critical moment does arrive, thus a fate determined, a choice made and a door closed forever. That is why dialogue in drama must be dynamic — a stimulus to further action.

The action develops and moves forward. However, it moves forward, not peacefully but with a sense of strain and conflict. There is struggle, forces coming into collision and decisions being made. The action is not only meaningful but has the tensions of active conflict within it.

In a play every scene except the last is looking ahead. The play must be progressive. A play is a series of actions. A play is not about action, nor does it describe action. A play is action. Then what is action? Action occurs when something happens that makes something else happen. At first, reading a play this way is difficult like learning to drive a standard shift car.

Dialogue is the formal principle of drama. It has some relation to real speech, but the character of that relation will vary greatly. Playwrights in Ancient Greece were called poets. Drama was written in verse. Shakespeare used blank verse in his plays — a kind of poetic dialogue. Dialogues aim at reproducing with high accuracy the cadences and patterns of actual speech that can be seen in many modern plays.

4. 2. 4 Relation of Dialogue to Character

Dialogue often establishes stage character through idiolect. Social groups also share a common way of speaking. This goes beyond accent. In plays sociolect quickly establishes the character's social origin or status. Clearly, idiolect is often at work in comic characterization and sociolect in making stereotypes. Dialogue establishes personality too — conveying feelings, desire and character etc. What one says is determined by his age, social position, experience, education, where he grows up, in what environment he grows up and what he wants. So reading between the lines is really important in appreciating drama.

4. 3 Character

Dramatists express ideas through their characters' words and gestures, translating thoughts, feelings and psychological conditions of their characters into the concrete and tangible dialogue and action. Characters almost always "stand for" or act as representatives of something in a play. They may typify a social class like Willy Loman in Miller's *Death of a Salesman* or a moral position like Bonario in Jonson's *Volpone*. They may represent a fundamental drive like greed like Volpone in *Volpone*. The most important thing about a character in a play might be their behavior or the choices they make in life, that is, they may stand for a particular sort of ethics.

It is impossible to analyze characters objectively. We can agree with each other on plot because it's all in the script and usually unambiguous. We can more or less agree on a play's thought. But rarely can two readers see precisely the same character because individual judgment is involved. Characterization is partly in the eye of the beholder, because we always judge others in terms of our individual selves. Analyzing character is another good way to start appreciating drama because character offers great interpretive latitude.

4.3.1 Character — Changing

Character in drama changes a lot. There are two sorts of change a character might undergo. They might change in themselves — becoming more humble, wise or generous or they might change their situation — becoming married, dead or prosperous. In *A Doll's House*, Nora develops from being naive and childish into a mature woman who can clearly see that she has been living a lie. She becomes committed to her own self-discovery. Her situation changes from a security, which is also, however, a trap, to a liberty which is also, however, a step into the dangerous unknown. Besides, she loses her children. In George Bernard Shaw's *Pygmalion*[12], a duchess is made out of a flower girl and a woman is made out of a duchess. The experience of *Pygmalion* is the experience of discovering new possibilities and the qualities in Higgins and Eliza as the play progresses. In Arthur Miller's *Death of a Salesman*, Willy Loman finally realizes he is stupid to commit himself so deeply to the phony values of salesmanship, losing the capacity to discriminate between a line of patter and a serious promise. His dilemma is fighting for what is impossible or destroying it, neither of which he can do. Without any choice, he destroys himself, hoping his son especially the elder son can do it for him and his family. We feel sorry for him as we do for a caged leopard.

4.3.2 Causes of the Change

Character will change in drama. What causes the changes? The first step in delving into character is to find out what the character wants, what is in the character's way (obstacle) and what the character does or is willing to do to satisfy the want. This step, of course, comes after the obvious such as name, age, sex, station and situation.

Character analysis and development are highly specialized in drama. But we have got to know character in drama is revealed in one way — action, that is, what a person does or deeds.

Character consists of all the qualities, traits and features that create the nature of a person and distinguish that person from another person. Generally, character answers "Who am I?" The minimum answer is name. "Who are you?" asks the doctor. The patient gives a name — for the circumstances, a sufficient answer. The maximum answer is endless. The patient could elaborate forever, telling who he is for hours, days, and even months. Somewhere between the minimum and the maximum falls the amount of information necessary to create character in literature.

4.3.3 Subjectivity and Mystery

We have got to know character in drama is revealed in action. Keep in mind actions on stage that most richly reveal character work in the same way as actions do in real life. You must find them out yourself because how I interpret what I see differs from how you interpret what you see. Much of what I perceive is based on who I am, not just who you are. Objective analysis of character is not possible.

Characterization is partly in the eye of the beholder because we always judge others in terms of our individual selves. Thus, character offers great interpretive latitude because rarely can two readers see precisely the same character based on individual judgment, thus a good start for play analysis.

Section 5 Play-Reading as a Pleasure

A novel or a poem is neither more nor less than the words it consists of, but a script is obviously less than a play, while a production is obviously more. Reading a script can be all the more enjoyable if we remember that it isn't intended for reading. We see words; we imagine sounds and pictures. When we go to the theatre, we hear words and sounds, but we see people and backgrounds; when we read, we sue our eyes on the element that is invisible in performance. During Shakespeare's lifetime, it was natural to talk of hearing a play.

When we read a play the experience tends to be more intellectual and less emotional than it is in the theatre and we are more disposed to interpret, more eagerly on the look-out for explicable relationships between the component parts of the text.

The richness of Shakespeare's, Chekhov's and the best of Ibsen's text lies partly in ambiguities which only the careful reader can fully explore. Where to put the stress then?

I think the meaning and the experience — what the writer wrote, are what we should put the stress on when reading a play.

One of the greatest advantages a reader has over audience is that he's closer to the writer's original work. Not necessarily closer to his original conception, but there, printed on the page, are the words the playwright chooses in the order he arranges them. The rhythms that rise up from the page are his rhythms, designer's way of dividing up the space. If we get the impression contrary impulses, this is an illusion thrown up not by an actor's timing but by the playwright's words and rhythms. These can be squeezed by a bad production into a wrong-headed interpretation. With a new play, unless we can read it for ourselves, we may find it hard to make up our minds whether production and acting are doing justice to what the writer has written.

The danger for the armchair reader of a play is to have the meaning but miss the experience. Approach to the experience restores the meaning. A play begins in personal experience and its main intention is to convey experience — not necessarily the same, but necessarily not unrelated — to an audience. The reader is like the actor in that he cannot fully enter into what the text is offering unless he can relate it to his own experience. He may be drawing on his previous experience as a reader, on memories of family life and love affairs and on stories their people have told him about their experience, but the play will make sense to him only if he can take it over from the writer, appropriate it and savor it by empathizing.

Imagine a performance as vividly as you can. A play is written orally and visually. Pay attention to the effect of colors, costumes, groupings and positions. In the cultural situation we are now in, television is one of many pressures which tend to make us use our imagination less. It is easier to tune in to a serial than to read a play. But when we do — as when we listen to a play on the radio — we find that there is great pleasure to be derived from allowing our imagination to do the work of contributing all the visual elements.

We close the book, feeling friendlier than before with the rest of us, for these individuals have shared our journey. We have seen deep into the lives of characters so like ourselves yet so different. Our journey has widened our sympathy and deepened our compassion. We are more civilized. When reading a play, keep the following tips in mind.

(1) Try to remind yourself of what the set might look like, what sort of atmosphere it would evoke, how the action would fill the space and

how the impacts — separately or simultaneously — would affect the audience. Read all stage directions especially carefully.

(2) With sound effects, try to imagine the quality of the sound and the way it might help the development towards a climax.

(3) Try to make your mind as receptive as possible to the growth of the play's rhythms and the relationships between them.

(4) Don't take the words at their face value. Try to understand the "Hidden" meaning of the dialogue. Their main function may be to make it possible to reach through them to what lies underneath.

(5) Try to think less in terms of character than of identity and of the way it is presented physically.

(6) Never psycho-analyze the motivations of the characters as if they were real people.

(7) Take time to explore the ambiguities of a script and don't try to close questions the playwright wants to remain open. You can have it both ways.

(8) Explore and exploit all the opportunities of mental theatre. The best actors and the best equipped theatres in the world all have their limitations. Your imagination can do everything you allow it to. Be generous with it.

(9) Look out for the silences, whether they're signposted by stage direction or not. Unanswered question, ignored requests, broken blank verse lines and changes of tone are no less significant than "Pause" or "Silence".

(10) A play does not always mean what the writer means it to mean. The meaning is the resultant force that emerges from the words, the silences and all the other elements and from all the relationships that develop between them.

The psychologically oriented pilgrim who returns from his theatre journey sees the experience as a journey into the mind. Jus read a play as a pleasure if you like.

重难点解读

[1] **Dickens' *A Tale of Two Cities***：狄更斯的小说《双城记》。狄更斯(Charles John Huffam Dickens，1812—1870)，维多利亚时代英国最伟大的作家，也是一位以反映现实生活见长的作家，狄更斯有生之年已享有空前的名声，在20世纪时他的文学作品受到评论家和学者广泛的认可。《双城记》是一部以法国大革命为背景所写的长篇历史小说，是世界文学经典名著之一，书名中的“双城”指的是巴黎与伦敦。

[2] ***Volpone***：《福尔蓬奈》(也有译为《狐狸》)。英国文艺复兴时期剧作家本·琼森的代表作之一，福尔蓬奈是一个威尼斯绅士，他假装重病卧床去欺骗贪求他财产的亲友们。他们轮流去往福尔蓬奈的家里，给他带来昂贵的礼物，希望能成为这无儿无女的绅士的财产继承人。

[3] **drummers**：旅行推销员(美)。

[4] **Masonic emblem**：共济会的会徽。共济会最早出现于18世纪的英国，至今已遍布全球。共济会是一种准宗教的兄弟会，基本宗旨倡导博爱和慈善，追求个人美德与完善社会。会员包括众多著名人士和政治家，申请者一般为有神论者，相信万物间存在着一位神，而其反对者则认为共济会主要是富人和权贵的阴谋组织，有着不为人知的统治世界的秘密计划，比如世界新秩序等。

[5] **William Archer**：威廉·阿彻(1856—1924)。苏格兰戏剧批评家，易卜生戏剧翻译者。

[6] **Fsustus versus Mephistophilis**：浮士德对梅菲斯特费利斯。这两个人是英国文艺复兴早期克里斯托弗·马洛的名剧《浮士德博士的悲剧》中的人物，浮士德博士学识过人，但对权力、财富与知识有着永不满足的欲望，他把撒旦的第一助手梅菲斯特费利斯召唤来，并与魔鬼签订了契约，把自己的灵魂抵押给魔鬼，换取二十四年为所欲为的岁月，但梅菲斯特费利斯要来收取他的灵魂。

[7] **Defense Attorney**：被告辩护人。指接受被追诉一方委托或者受法院指定，帮助犯罪嫌疑人、被告人行使辩护权以维护其合法权益的人。

[8] **Mademoiselle**：小姐。法语对女士的称呼，相当于英语的"Miss"。

[9] **monseigneur**：阁下(法语)。

[10] **His Majesty**：陛下。这是一个固定用法，对国王的称呼，如果直接对话，则用"Your Majesty"。

[11] **Picardy**：皮卡第。法国的27区之一，位于法国北部，下属三个省：埃纳省、瓦兹省和索姆省。

[12] **Pygmalion**：《皮格马利翁》(也有译为《卖花女》和《窈窕淑女》)。英国剧作家萧伯纳的作品。皮格马利翁是希腊神话中塞浦路斯的国王，用自己出神入化的技艺雕刻出一个美丽的象牙少女雕像，结果无可救药地爱上了它。后来他请求美神阿芙洛狄忒赐予这座雕像生命，于是皮格马利翁得偿所愿。在此基础上，"皮格马利翁效应"也流行开来，皮格马利翁效应(Pygmalion Effect)，也译为"毕马龙效应"、"罗森塔尔效应"或"期待效应"，由美国著名心理学家罗森塔尔和雅格布森在小学教学上予以验证提出。暗示在本质上，人的情感和观念会不同程度地受到别人下意识的影响，人们会不自觉地接受自己喜欢、钦佩、信任和崇拜的人的影响和暗示。

Chapter 6 Playwrights

There are so many famous playwrights in both Britain and the United States, like bright stars in the sky. Because of the class hour limit and hardness of reading scripts of plays in the original in Shakespeare's time and before, this book just focuses on several modern British and American playwrights, which of course can't reveal the real situation of drama both in Britain and the United States at different periods of time, but this will reduce the difficulty in reading plays in the original for students and the author hopes that a wise man hears one word and understands two.

Section 1* George Bernard Shaw

George Bernard Shaw was born in 1856 and died in 1950, being awarded both a Nobel Prize in Literature[1] and an Oscar[2], for his contribution to literature for his work on the film *Pygmalion* (adaptation of his play of the same name) respectively. Of course, he was greatly influenced by the time he experienced.

1.1 Social and Historical Background

With the development of capitalism, there arose a powerful working class. From the thirties of the 19th century, the struggle between the workers and capitalists became the fundamental contradiction in English social life. In the years 1839, 1842 and 1848, the Chartist Movement[3] urged Parliament to adopt three great petitions, asserting the rights of ordinary people. Of these, the best known was the final petition, with six million signatures (although a number of these were later found to be fake), presented to Parliament on 10th April 1848 after a huge meeting. During the century after the end of the movement, most of the Chartist demands were passed into law, thus capitalism witnessing a period of rapid growth. Monopoly capitalism replaced free competition and played a decisive role in economic life. Meanwhile, colonial expansion which went on throughout the 19th century had now made the British Empire the leading imperialist power of the world. But the prosperity soon ended owing to depressions and crises in the seventies and eighties, which, in turn, sharpened the class contradictions. So the late 19th century witnessed another upsurge of workers' movements in England. The English working-class movement reached a new height in the years 1911-1914. Three great strikes, railway men, coal miners and London transport workers, which were ended only by government intervention, paralyzed much of the country's industry. Germany, a newly-emerged imperial power, together with Austria and Italy formed the Triple Alliance[4], crying for the re-division of the world which had been completed by the end of the 19th century. Britain, France and Russia also formed the Triple Entente[5]. The capitalist Europe was thus divided into two hostile camps for the sake of their respective interests. The contradictions between the imperialist countries grew into such great tension between the Triple Alliance and the Triple Entente that it soon led to the outbreak of World War I, a war causing immense losses for both sides. German Empire collapsed and signed *Treaty of Versailles*[6] which made Germany have a deep sense of injustice while Britain spent all her wealth, no longer the most powerful in the world. Italy turned to the Triple Entente but got nothing except the collapse of economy after the war while Austria broke into pieces. The October Revolution[7] in 1917 in Russia became impetus of national liberation movements all over the world. These great political, economic and military upheavals had a powerful impact upon the cultural life in Britain. The 1930s were called the Red Decade as many British intellectuals turned to the Left, to Marxism and communism.

1.2 The Irish Dramatic Movement

Ireland has made special contributions to English literature by bringing up a considerable number of illustrious writers and poets such as Swift[8], Yeats and Goldsmith etc. It is also interesting to note that nearly all the important English dramatists of the 18th and the 19th centuries are Irish-born. In 1898, under the leadership of William Butler Yeats and Lady Augusta Gregory[9], an attempt was made to establish an Irish Literary Theatre, called the Abbey Theatre, which performed works by Irish dramatists. In his lecture delivered to the Royal Academy of Sweden on receiving the Nobel Prize, Yeats chose as his theme "the Irish Dramatic Movement" because he believed that the English committees would never have sent his name if he had written no plays, no dramatic criticism or if his lyric poetry had no quality of speech practiced upon the stage. About the Irish Dramatic Movement, he said that the great mass of the Irish people were accustomed to political speeches and read little, so from the very start they had felt that they needed a theatre of their own. It was not, however, until he met in 1896 Lady Gregory, that such a theatre had become possible. Lady Gregory was the director of the Abbey Theatre and also a dramatist herself. She wrote many peasant comedies, displaying an insight into peasant character and full of pleasant humor.

In the creation of poetic drama W. B. Yeats played a major role. The necessities of the Irish Renaissance[10] drove him to think more precisely on the creation of drama whose effects would remain after the fall of the curtain. He wanted to create a drama which would move the hearts and minds of men in such a way that they would leave the theatre with a new understanding of their nature and fate. Although the reputation of W. B. Yeats as one of the preeminent writers of the 20th century rested primarily on his poetry, drama and the theatre were among his abiding concerns. Indeed, in 1917 he wrote, "I need a theatre I believe myself to be a dramatist." A practicing dramatist himself, Yeats had strong convictions about the goals of the Irish theater and the appropriate plays to be produced.

1.3 George Bernard Shaw' Life

George Bernard Shaw was born on the 26th of July 1856, in Dublin[11]. Shaw's childhood was troubled. His father, an unsuccessful businessman, was a drunkard, which made him a teetotaler. His mother was a musician of talent. He went to the Wesleyan Connexional School, then to Dublin's Central Model School, ending formal education at the Dublin English Scientific and Commercial Day School. At the age of 15, he started to work as a clerk in a land agent's office after middle school, experiencing the wealth gap. In 1876 when he was 19 years old, he went to London, joining his sister and mother. He was jobless for 9 years, but had much self-education. Greatly influenced by Fabian Society[12], the English reformist organization, he joined the Fabian Society, a middle-class socialist group and served on its executive committee from 1885 to 1911. He also took an active part in the socialist movement and studied carefully works of Marx and Engels[13].

1.4 His Career

Shaw began his literary career by writing music and theatre criticism and novels, including the semi-autobiographical *Immaturity*[14] without much success. He wrote some novels first — *An Unsocial Socialist*[15] for example, then turned to the theatre, first working as a dramatic critic, then writing plays for the stage. He was against "art for art's sake". Instead, he used the stage to criticize the evils of capitalism. In 1895 Shaw became a drama critic for the *Saturday Review*[16]. Shaw wrote music, art and drama criticism for *Dramatic Review*[17], too. His music criticism was collected in *Shaw's Music*. In 1898, Shaw married the wealthy Charlotte Payne-Townshend. They settled in the Hertfordshire village of Ayot St. Lawrence in 1906. Shaw died there, aged 94, from chronic problems exacerbated by injuries he incurred by falling from a ladder.

1.5 His Works

Although his first profitable writing was music and literary criticism, and later also famous as an essayist, novelist and short story writer, Shaw's main talent was for drama. He wrote more than 60 plays.

Shaw's plays, like those of Oscar Wilde, were fraught with incisive humor, which was exceptional among playwrights of the Victorian Era; both are remembered for their comedy. However, Shaw held that art should serve social purposes by reflecting human life, revealing social contradictions and educating the common people. He was against the credo of "art for art's sake" held by Oscar Wilde and condemned the "well-made" but cheap and hollow plays. Shaw's wittiness should not obscure his important role in revolutionizing British drama. In the

Victorian Era, the London stage had been regarded as a place for frothy, sentimental entertainment. Shaw made it a forum for considering moral, political and economic issues, possibly his most lasting and important contribution to dramatic art. In this, he considered himself indebted to Henrik Ibsen, who pioneered modern realistic drama, meaning drama designed to heighten awareness of some important social issues. His plays can be roughly divided into four major periods.

1. 5. 1 Plays

Nearly all Shaw's writings address prevailing social problems, but have a vein of comedy which makes their stark themes more palatable. Issues which engage Shaw's attention include education, marriage, religion, government, health care and class privilege.

1. 5. 1. 1 *Plays Unpleasant*

Plays at his early period were called *Plays Unpleasant*[18] because these plays were intended not to entertain their audience as traditional Victorian theatre was expected to but to raise awareness of social problems and to censure exploitation of the laboring class by the unproductive rich, satirizing that ill-gotten money was squeezed out of poor and suffering people. *Widowers' Houses* (1892) was the first play by George Bernard Shaw to be staged, and also one of three plays Shaw published as *Plays Unpleasant* in 1898. The other plays in the group were *The Philanderer* and *Mrs. Warren's Profession*

Mrs. Warren's Profession (forbidden at theater then) is a play written by Shaw in 1893. Despite its title, the play barely touches the theme of prostitution with the story centering on the relationship between Mrs. Warren, an ex-prostitute and her prudish daughter, Vivie. Mrs. Warren is a middle-aged woman whose Cambridge-educated daughter, Vivie, is horrified to discover that her mother's fortune is made by managing high-class whorehouses. The two strong women make a brief reconciliation when Mrs. Warren explains her impoverished youth, which originally leads her into prostitution. Vivie forgives her mother until learning that the highly profitable business remains in operation. Shaw said he wrote the play "to draw attention to the truth that prostitution is caused, not by female depravity and male licentiousness, but simply by underpaying, undervaluing and overworking women so shamefully that the poorest of them are forced to resort to prostitution to keep body and soul together". The play focuses on the conflicts related to the "new women" of the Victorian Era — issues arising because middle-class girls want greater social independence in work and education. Other themes include criticism of the sexual triteness of the times and a want for greater social sexual awareness along with equality in the workplace for working women

1.5.1.2 *Plays Pleasant*

Candida, *Arms and Man*, *The Man of Destiny* and *You Never Can Tell* consist of his *Plays Pleasant*[19], appearing when capitalism enteres imperialism with powers in arm race. *Candida* satirizes the liberal talkers and preachers of "Christian socialism"; *Arms and Man* condemns militarism and wars.

1.5.1.3 *Three Plays for Puritans*

Three Plays for Puritans[20] (published 1901) is Shaw's third series of plays, including *Caesar and Cleopatra*, *The Devil's Disciple* and *Captain Brassbound's Conversion*. *Caesar and Cleopatra* is based on historical facts, assailing bourgeois morality and *The Devil's Disciple* derides the much lauded puritan piety.

1.5.1.4 The Most Creative Period

Since the 20th century Shaw has written more influential plays as his experience and popularity increased. His plays and prefaces became more voluble about reforms he advocated, without diminishing their success as entertainments, including *Man and Superman* (1903), *How He Lied to Her Husband* (1904), *Major Barbara* (1905), *The Doctor's Dilemma* (1906) and *Getting Married*[21] (1906), all of which display Shaw's matured views, for he was approaching 50 when he wrote them.

The first of his new plays to be performed at the Court Theatre, *John Bull's Other Island*[22] (1904), while not especially popular today, made his reputation in London when King Edward VII[23] laughed so hard during a command performance that he broke his chair.

Major Barbara describes the cannon king destroying millions of lives for making profits. Major Barbara is a major in the Salvation Army[24] (a reformist Christian organization). Never ashamed of killing so many people by selling cannons, Andrew is happy to get money in an easy way.

Andrew: ... sell arms to all men who offer an honest price for them, without respect of persons or principles; to Royalist and Republican, to Communist and Capitalist, to Protestant and to Catholic, to burglar and to policeman, to black man and white man and yellow man, to all sorts and conditions, all nationalities, all faiths, all follies, all causes and all crimes.

The first Undershaft wrote up in his shop **If God Gave the Hand, Let Not Man Withhold the Sword.** The second wrote up **All Have the Right to Fight: None Have the Right to Judge**. The third wrote up **to Man the Weapon, to Heaven the Victory**. The fourth had no literary turn, so he didn't write up anything; but he sold cannons to Napoleon under the nose of George the Third. The fifth wrote up **Peace Shall Not Prevail, Save with a Sword in Her Hand**. The sixth, my master, was the best of all. He wrote up **Nothing Is Ever Done in This World Until Men Are Prepared to Kill One Another If It Is Not Done**. After that there was nothing left for the seventh to say. So he wrote up, simply, **Unashamed** [25].

... Think of my business! Think of the widows and orphans! The men and lads torn to pieces with shrapnel and poisoned with luddite! The oceans of blood, not one drop of which is shed in a really just cause! The ravaged crops! The peaceful peasants forced, women and men, to till their fields under the fire of opposing armies on pain of starvation! The bad

blood of the fierce little coward at home who egg on others to fight for the gratification of their national vanity! All this makes money for me: I am never richer, never busier than when the papers are full of it.

Barbara: I was happy in the Salvation Army for a moment. I escaped from the world into paradise of enthusiasm and prayer and soul saving; but the moment our money ran short, it all came back to Badger: it was him who saved our people; he and the Prince of Darkness, my papa. Undershaft and Badger: their hands stretch everywhere: when we feed a starving fellow creature, it is with their bread, because there is no other bread; when we tend the sick, it is in the hospital they endow; if we turn from the churches they build, we must kneel on the stones in the street they pave. As long as that lasts, there is no getting away from them. Turning our backs on Badger and Undershaft is turning our backs on life.

Barbara: I felt like her when I saw this place —felt that I must have it, that never, never, never could I let it go; Only she thought it was the houses and the kitchen ranges and the linen and china, when it was really all the human souls to be saved: not weak souls in starved bodies, crying with gratitude for a scrap of bread and treacle, but fullfed, guallsome, snobbish, uppish creatures ... That is where salvation is really wanted.

……

The Salvation Army, for instance, as shown in *Major Barbara*, fights drunkenness; yet one of its greatest contributors is Badger, a whiskey distiller, who furnishes yearly thousands of pounds to do away with the very source of his wealth. Bernard Shaw, therefore, concludes that the only real benefactor of society is a man like Undershaft, Barbara's father, a cannon manufacturer, whose theory of life is that powder is stronger than words.

By the 1910s, Shaw was a well-established playwright. New works such as *Fanny's First Play*(1911), *Pygmalion*(1912) and many others were written, most of which had long runs in front of large London audience. Several of his plays formed the basis of musicals after his death — most famously the musical *My Fair Lady* — it was officially adapted from the screenplay of the film version of *Pygmalion* rather than the original stage play (keeping the film's ending).

Pygmalion, according to an Ancient Greek myth, was the King of Cyprus, good at sculpting and uninterested in women. However, he found himself in love with his sculpture, Galatea, and he caressed her and offered her with all the gifts women like. At the end, Venus[26] realized his wish and turned Galatea into a real woman. Shaw's *Pygmalion* (performed 118 times on end) had a poignant satire on high life, showing what upper class had such as grace, right clothes etc., could be bought with money.

Shaw's outlook was changed by World War I, which he uncompromisingly opposed despite incurring outrage from the public as well as from many friends. His first full-length piece, presented after the War, written mostly during it, was *Heartbreak House*[27] (1919) showing the decline of modern civilization. A new Shaw had emerged — the wit remained, but his faith in humanity had dwindled. In 1934 Shaw published *Saint Joan*, a historical play devoted to the great daughter of the French people, Joan of Arc and her struggle for the liberty of her country. *The Apple Cart*[28] dealt with the theme of rivalry between the U. S. A and England in the political arena and criticized bourgeois parliamentary system. In one of his last plays *Too True to Be Good*[29] Shaw again dwelt on the decay of the bourgeois system. In the same play he depicted the birth and growth of new progressive forces in the world.

1. 5. 2 His Novels and Essays

Shaw wrote five unsuccessful novels at the start of his career between 1879 and 1883 — *Immaturity*, *An Unsocial Socialist*, *Love Among the Artists*, *the Irrational Knot* and *Cashel Byron's Profession*[30], all of which were eventually published.

In addition, he wrote many essays such as *Maxims for Revolutionists*

(1903), *Preface to Major Barbara* (1905), *On Going to Church* (1905), *How to Write a Popular Play* (1909), *Dictators, Let Us Have More of Them* (1938) and *Everybody's Political What's What?* (1944), etc. He was most angered by what he perceived as the exploitation of the working class. An ardent socialist, Shaw wrote many brochures and speeches for the Fabian Society. He became an accomplished orator in the furtherance of its causes, which included gaining equal rights for men and women, alleviating abuses of the working class, rescinding private ownership of productive land and promoting healthy lifestyles. For a short time he was active in local politics, serving on the London County Council.

1.6 His Style

Structurally and thematically following the great tradition of realism, Shaw deals with contemporary social problems with his pen, portraying his situations frankly and honestly and intending to shock his audience with a new view of society. He is a humorist, which helps him succeed in attracting audience though in Shaw it is often the ideas that really matter. He knows well how to achieve theatrical effect, in which his unique talent for wit, music, surprise and paradox greatly assists, pouring great doses of melodrama, farce, preaching, prophecy and, above all, high spirits and wit into his plays. He is able to construct the tightest well-made plot, the most dazzling comic mélange or the most complicated Chekhovian structure, championing Ibsen because he is not a "mere artist" but a practical man seeking to reform the world through drama. More typically is the sting of his dialogue and the freshness and topsy-turvy unpredictability of his characters.

He believes that theatre is not candy shop. Drama is not for entertaining people, but criticizing ill society. It's a tool for education and propaganda with new ideas and discussion that are closely related to reality.

1.7 Comments on Him

Of him, his friend **Sean O'Casey** [31] wrote:

He set down a lamp in the theatre that has ever since been a light to our feet and a guide to our path ... Let those who write plays today throw a wider chest than Shaw's, in either poetry or prose — if they can ... He was a great playwright ... This silvery thread of laughter runs through all of Shaw's plays and most of his writing, weaving a delightful decoration into his keen thought and thrusting satire. This joking sage has been a godsend to England (and to Ireland, too) for his wisdom, his love of truth and freedom, his gay spirit and fearless conduct have been a banner before us, a banner and a bugle band leading the slow, the certain, the glorious ascent of man.

The great writer of China, Lu Xun compared Shaw and Ibsen by thinking that Shaw had a more profound insight into and criticism of the dark side of the capitalism.

1.8 His Position

Shaw is of course a great representative of Irish writers first of all. He is a leading figure in the 20th century theater, playing an important role in revolutionizing British drama — a tool for education instead of entertainment. As a freethinker, supporter of women's rights and an advocate of equality of income, he believes that if drama is to be significant, it must lead the audience to action, rejecting the idea that the opinion of the majority should serve as a basis for action.

He is the only person to have been awarded both a Nobel Prize in Literature and an Oscar (1938) for his contributions to literature and for his work on the film *Pygmalion* respectively. The citation of the Nobel

Prize Committee praised his work as "... marked by both idealism and humanity, its stimulating satire often being infused with a singular poetic beauty". Shaw wanted to refuse his Nobel Prize outright because he had no desire for public honors, but accepted it at his wife's behest who considered it a tribute to Ireland. He did reject the monetary award, requesting it be used to finance translation of fellow playwright August Strindberg's works from Swedish to English and asking the committee depart the prize and money, saying "I can forgive Alfred Nobel for inventing dynamite, but only a fiend in human form could have invented the Nobel Prize."

He liked Ibsen but disliked Shakespeare, saying "With the single exception of Homer, there is no eminent writer, not even Sir Walter Scott, whom I can despise so entirely as I despise Shakespeare when I measure my mind against his." He even expressed the idea that he was so intolerant of Shakespeare that sometimes he felt only digging Shakespearean body and throwing stones on would alleviate the aversion because that was the only way to make Shakespeare and his admirers understand.

Why did he so despise Shakespeare? Firstly, they were living at different periods of time, facing different problems. Secondly, what he took pains to advocate in plays was what Shakespeare ignored or did not pay enough attention to in his plays — criticizing that Shakespeare should have inculcated more sense of morality in his plays. That was why he gave praise to *Hamlet* in which the protagonist hesitated to kill.

Shaw's great contribution is to widen the scope of high comedy beyond the personal relationships of lovers, parents and friends to show characters involved in social, political and philosophical problems. In his witty discussion of poverty, wealth, power and religion Shaw anticipates by half a century the time when the world would try to use power to abolish poverty and money to help individuals find a higher spiritual life.

Besides, the Shaw Festival[32], an annual theater festival in

Niagara-on-the-Lake, Ontario[33], Canada, began as an eight-week run of *Don Juan in Hell*[34] (as the long third act dream sequence of *Man And Superman* is called when staged alone) and *Candida* in 1962 and has grown into an annual festival with over 800 performances a year, dedicated to producing the works of Shaw and his contemporaries.

Shaw is also remembered as one of the pivotal founders of the London School of Economics and Political Science[35] (LSE), whose library is now called the British Library of Political and Economic Science[36]. The Fabian Window, designed by Shaw, hangs in the Shaw Library in the main building of the LSE.

Section 2 Samuel Beckett

Samuel Barclay Beckett (1906—1989) was an Irish novelist, playwright, theatre director and poet, who was born in Dublin but lived in Paris for most of his adult life and wrote in both English and French. Beckett is widely regarded as among the most influential writers of the 20th century. He is considered one of the last modernists. As an inspiration to many later writers, he is also sometimes considered one of the first postmodernists. He is one of the key writers in what Martin Esslin called the "Theatre of the Absurd". He always refused to appear on radio or television or give newspaper interviews and declined to comment on his works. He died in Paris of respiratory problems in 1989.

2.1 Literary Background

Modernism in English literature prevailed during the 20s and 30s of the 20th century. Modernist poetry was a break with the 18th century Romanticism while modernist fiction had a trend drifting away from the tradition of the 19th century realism, emphasizing characters' psychological activities with D. H. Lawrence[37] as one of the pioneers.

2.1.1 Stream of Consciousness

"Interior monologue" originated in France as an application of modern psychological knowledge to literary creation in the late 19th century. It was influenced by the psycho-analytic theories of Sigmund Freud, a famous psychologist, later famous as "Stream of Consciousness", one of the modern literary techniques in the 20th century. The writing style was first used in 1922 by the Irish novelist James Joyce who explored the existence of subconscious and unconscious elements in the mind — emphasizing the characters' mental and emotional reactions to external events rather than the events. This way of writing broke through the bounds of time and space, abandoning the conventional usages of realistic plot structure, characterization and description. Very soon, Britain became the center of the novels of stream-of-consciousness and in the United States William Faulkner successfully advanced this technique.

2.1.2 James Joyce

James Joyce (1882-1941) was an Irish novelist of the "stream of consciousness" school. He lived in France, Italy and Switzerland as a voluntary exile. Most of his life, he lived in poverty mainly because of his eye disease. *A Portrait of the Artist as a Young Man* was his first novel which was largely autobiographical. *Ulysses*, his most famous novel told through recording the characters' mental activities by using a new way of writing of "stream of consciousness", changing the old style of fictions and creating a strange mode of art to show the chaos and crisis of consciousness of that period.

In literature, "stream of consciousness" has been used as a special narrative technique. The assumption was that in the mind of an individual at a given moment his or her stream of consciousness was a mixture of all the levels of awareness, an unending flow of sensations, thoughts, memories, associations and reflections. If the exact content of the mind (consciousness) was to be described at any moment, then these varied, disjointed and illogical elements should find expression in a flow of words, images and ideas similar to the unorganized flow of the mind. The way of writing of "stream of consciousness" came into the highest point of modern literature later.

James Joyce had great influence on Samuel Beckett who was his student, assistant and had a life-long friendship with.

2.2 Beckett's Works

Samuel Beckett's career as a writer was roughly divided into three periods. His early works up until the end of World War II in 1945 was generally considered to have been strongly influenced by the works of his teacher as well as friend James Joyce. From 1945 to early 1960s, regarded as his middle period, he wrote what were probably his most well-known works, including four major stage plays *En attendant Godot*, *Fin de partie*, *Krap's Last Tape* and *Happy Days*[38]. These plays are often considered, rightly or wrongly, to have been instrumental in the so-called "Theatre of the Absurd", dealing in a very blackly humorous way with themes similar to those of the roughly contemporary existentialist thinkers — the subject of despair and the will to survive in spite of that despair in the face of an uncomprehending and indeed, incomprehensible world, though Beckett himself cannot be pigeonholed as an existentialist.

Throughout the 1960s and into the 1970s, Beckett's works exhibite an increasing tendency — already evident in much of his works of the 1950s — towards compactness that has led to his works sometimes being described as minimalist. The extreme example of this, among his dramatic works, is the 1969 piece *Breath*, which lasts for only 35 seconds and has no characters.

2.3 Theatre of the Absurd

The term "Theatre of the Absurd", coined by Martin Esslin in a book of the same name with Beckett and his *Waiting for Godot* as centerpieces of the book, has been applied to a wide range of plays that bear some similar characteristics such as characters caught in hopeless situations and forced to do repetitive or meaningless actions, dialogue full of clichés, wordplay and nonsense and plots being cyclical or absurdly expansive. They are either a parody or dismissal of realism and the concept of the "well-made play".

Generally speaking, character and emotion in Absurd plays range from one-dimensional and lack of feeling to multidimensional and sensitive feeling. In view of the fact that Absurd characters frequently seem involved in pointless activity devoid of traditional plot action, it is best not to ask what has happened in the past and what comes next, but rather, what is happening now? Neither the actor nor the audience can rely on cause and effect and logical sequence of motivated action. We can only be amused or shocked by the often grotesque nature of the spontaneous movement.

Actually, most characters in Absurd plays are based on realism. However, at some point in the play the authors usually distort reality by dehumanization or by having inanimate objects take on life. Absurdist playwrights utilize many of the alienating techniques of Epic Theatre[39]. For Beckett, absurdity means a life lived in isolation and despair.

2.3.1 *Waiting for Godot*

Waiting for Godot is Samuel Beckett's masterpiece in which the characters wait for someone named Godot, who never arrives, Beckett's translation of his own original French version, *En attendant Godot* and is subtitled (in English only) "a tragicomedy in two acts". Some people think this play is likely related to his personal experience. He was wounded one night in 1938 by a person on his way home. Leaving hospital, he went to prison to visit the guy and asked why only to get the answer "I don't know". Maybe the answer reflected the absurdity of reality. This play earned him father of "Theatre of the Absurd" with anti-traditional characteristics. Just opposite from "well-made" traditional ones, this play has no plot. It is just waiting, no development, no conflict and no ending. During the waiting, there are repetitive or meaningless actions. One likes taking off his hat, peers inside it, feels about inside it, knocks on the crown, blows into it and puts it on again; another likes sitting on a low mound, trying to take off his boot. He pulls at it with both hands, panting. He gives up, exhausted, rests, tries again, constantly asking for radish, carrots to eat and even waters for the chicken bones thrown away by Pozzo. Some critics think the first one stands for man's brain and soul which is empty; the second represents body and flesh — the basic need is what man focuses on. Secondly, the play also demonstrates the limit of language by using repeated same dialogues, meaningless dialogues and dialogue without purpose to show inability to communicate such as nonsense, nothing to communicate such as long silence and unwillingness to communicate such as simple or evasive answers. What is more, the main protagonist Godot never shows up — the biggest mystery, arousing limitless discussion and debates.

The play was refused at first by many big theatres in Paris for the lack of traditional dramatic elements. It was performed in California in 1957 for over 1,000 prisoners who lived a life in isolation and despair with flood of comments in the newspapers in the prison. Then more and more were shocked by the play though feeling it strange. It was the feeling of uncertainty it produced, the ebb and flow of this uncertainty — from the hope of discovering the identity of Godot to its repeated disappointment — that was the essence of the play. The writer became famous overnight at the age of 47 and the play was translated into over 20 different languages and watched by over 5 million audiences, becoming the most significant English language play of the 20th century.

Godot's absence, as well as many other aspects of the play has led to many different interpretations since the play's premiere.

Who is the protagonist, Godot? Is he God? Actually, he's not. Beckett said "if I wanted Godot to be God I would have called him God". He also said that he had no idea who Godot was, but he didn't think that his identity was significant to the play. Actually, the importance of the play is the "waiting for" part and not the identity of the character. Whether Godot is meant to suggest the intervention of a supernatural agency or whether he stands for a mythical human being whose arrival is expected to change the situation or both of these possibilities combined, his exact nature is of secondary importance. Through the "complex of waiting", the play, profoundly reveals the embarrassing situation of human beings who live in the absurd world and feel disoriented; it also reveals the suffering, anxiety, pessimism and hopelessness of modern Westerners.

Waiting for Godot is highly symbolic, acutely implying the living condition of modern people: "the vagrant" in the play implies the history of human beings. Since human beings have been plunged onto the earth, especially when God (father of spirit) passed away, they have become vagrant; "the wild countryside" symbolizes spiritual wildness; "nightfall" means human beings have come to the end, a dark circumstance; "the various boring behavior" demonstrates human's behavior counting for nothing and is boring as smelling the stinking boots and shabby hats and attempting to commit suicide by hanging oneself; "the confused and obscure utterance" represents the so-called probe and pry in thought and spirit, meaning just the behavior of "uttering". The two tramps here are people who have been deprived of human nature by capitalism. Joy and capability fail them. They are feeling at lost. When the old God is dead (the collapse of traditional values), people expect to see the appearance of the new God to save them who never shows up. They can do nothing but wait in anguish.

2.3.2 *Endgame*

Endgame, a one-act play with four characters was originally written in French, too, entitled *Fin de partie* as was his custom then translated into English by himself. It was published in 1957 and considered along with such works as *Waiting for Godot* to be his most important works. Its protagonists Hamm, an aged master who is blind and not able to stand up and his servant Clov, who cannot sit down exist in a tiny house by the sea although the dialogue suggests that there is nothing left outside — no sea, no sun, no clouds. The two characters, mutually dependent on each other keep fighting for years and will continue to do so as the play progresses.

2.4 Comments on Him

Of all the English-language modernists, Beckett's works represent the most sustained attack on the realist tradition. He, more than anyone else, opens up the possibility of drama and fiction that dispense with conventional plot and the unities of place and time in order to focus on essential components of the human condition. Many major 20th century composers have created musical works based on his texts. Beckett's works also have an influence on many visual artists. In addition to being inspired by Beckett's literary world, they also draw a number of portraits of Beckett and illustrate several of his works.

Some early philosophical critics praise him, one for his revelation of absurdity, the other for his works' critical refusal of simplicities; others condemn him for "decadent" lack of realism. He may have devalued language as an instrument for the communication of ultimate truths, but he has shown himself a great master of language as an artistic medium.

He is one of the most widely discussed and highly praised of the 20th century authors, inspiring a critical industry to rival that which has sprung up around James Joyce.

Section 3 Harold Pinter

Harold Pinter (1930—2008), one of the most important and influential English writers of his generation, is often grouped with other major absurdist playwrights such as Eugene Ionesco and particularly his mentor, Samuel Beckett, though on the surface his plays seem well-made realistic plays about ordinary people. Pinter also is prolific as a screenwriter, director and actor. In addition to crafting film versions of several of his own plays, he adapted works by Franz Kafka (*The Trial*), F. Scott Fitzgerald (*The Last Tycoon*), Ian McEwan (*The Comfort of Strangers*), Margaret Atwood (*The Handmaid's Tale*) and John Fowles (*The French Lieutenant's Woman*)[40] and penned original scripts.

In 2002, Pinter was made a Companion of Honor by the Queen for services to Literature and in 2005 awarded the Nobel Prize for Literature, the highest honor available to any writer in the world. In announcing the award, Chairman of the Swedish Academy said that Pinter was an artist "who in his plays uncovers the precipice under everyday gossip and forces entry into oppression's closed rooms".

3.1 His Life

Harold Pinter was born on the 10th of October 1930 in the London borough of Hackney, son of a Jewish dressmaker. Growing up, Pinter met with the expressions of anti-Semitism[41] and had indicated its importance for his becoming a dramatist. At the outbreak of the Second World War, he was evacuated from London at the age of nine, returning when twelve. He said the experience of wartime bombing when he would at times open the back door and "find garden in flames" had never lost its hold on him. Back in London, he attended Hackney Grammar School where he played Macbeth and Romeo among other characters in productions directed by Joseph Brearley. This prompted him to choose a career in acting. In 1948, he was accepted at the Royal Academy of Dramatic Art[42]. In 1950, he published his first poems. In 1951 he was accepted at the Central School of Speech and Drama[43]. That same year, he won a place in Anew McMaster's famous Irish repertory company, renowned for its performances of Shakespeare. Pinter toured again between 1954 and 1957, using the stage name of David Baron. Between 1956 and 1980, he was married to actor Vivien Merchant. In 1980, he married the author and historian Lady Antonia Fraser.

He was a rebel from an early age, declaring himself a conscientious objector and refusing to do then-compulsory military service — experiencing the terrors caused by war when young. He published poetry under the name "Harold Pinta" and emerged as a playwright with *The Birthday Party* (1957), in which the intruders Goldberg and McCann entered the retreat of Stanley, a young man who was hiding from childhood guilt. Influenced by Samuel Beckett, Pinter once said of language, "The speech we hear is an indication of that which we don't hear. It is a necessary avoidance, a violent, sly and anguished or mocking smoke screen which keeps the other in its true place."

Since 1973, Pinter has won recognition as a fighter for human rights, alongside his writing. He has often taken stands seen as controversial as an unrelenting critic of the U. S involvement in Iraq and of the government of Prime Minister Tony Blair[44]. His most recent speech was given on the anniversary of NATO's bombing of Serbia[45] at the Committee for Peace in the Balkans Conference, at the Conway Hall June 10th 2000. His reputation as an outspoken critic of American foreign policy and his own government under Prime Minister Tony Blair added a tinge of controversy to Pinter's winning the Nobel for Literature in 2005.

3. 2 His Works

Harold Pinter's writing career span over half a century.

He began with his first play, *The Room*, *first produced* in 1957, followed by another one-act play *The Dumb Waiter*[46], firstly produced in 1959. Then he wrote full-length plays such as *The Birthday Party* (1958), *The Caretaker* (1958) and *The Homecoming* (1964) etc., which established him as a commercial and critical success. His later plays include *Old Times* (1971), *No Man's Land* (1975), *Betrayal* (1978; film, 1983), *Mountain Languag*e (1988), *Moonlight* (1993) and *Celebration* (2000).

Pinter also remained socially engaged, supporting the rights of other artists and people in all fields. Pinter's writing also included poetry, screenplays, stories and essays and could have a decided political bent. In 2004, he earned the prestigious Wilfred Owen[47] prize for a series of poems opposing the war in Iraq. In his acceptance speech, Pinter described the war as "a bandit act, an act of blatant state terrorism, demonstrating absolute contempt for the concept of international law."

3. 2. 1 His Versatility

Pinter wrote 29 stage plays, 26 screenplays, many dramatic sketches, radio and TV plays, poetry, some short fiction, a novel and essays, speeches and letters. He also directed almost 50 stage, TV and film productions of his own and others' works. Among his best-known screenplays are those for *The Servant*(1963), *The Accident*(1967), *The Go-Between*(1971) and *The French Lieutenant's Woman*[48](1981, based on the novel with the same name of John Fowles).

But he is best known as a playwright and screenwriter.

3. 2. 2 *The Birthday Party*

The Birthday Party is a full-length play and one of Pinter's best-known and most-frequently performed plays. After its hostile London reception that almost ends Pinter's playwriting career, it goes on to be considered "a classic".

The Birthday Party is about Stanley Webber, an erstwhile piano player in his 30s, who lives in a rundown boarding house run by Meg and Petey Boles, in an English seaside town. Two sinister strangers, Goldberg and McCann, who arrive supposedly on his birthday and who appear to have come looking for him, turn Stanley's apparently innocuous birthday party into a nightmare.

Like many of Pinter's other plays, very little of the expository information in *The Birthday Party* is verifiable; it is often contradicted by the characters and otherwise ambiguous and therefore one cannot take what they say at face value. For example, in Act One, Stanley describes his career, saying "I've played the piano all over the world," reduces that immediately to "All over the country," and then, after a "*pause*", undercuts both hyperbolic self-representations in stating "I once gave a concert". While the title and the dialogue refer to Meg's planning a party to celebrate Stanley's birthday: "It's your birthday, Stan. I was going to keep it a secret until tonight," even that "fact" is dubious as Stanley denies that it is his birthday: "This isn't my birthday, Meg", telling Goldberg and McCann: "Anyway, this isn't my birthday. No, it's not until next month," adding, in response to McCann's saying "Not according to the lady, Meg."

In this play as in his other plays, behind the surface symbolism, in the silence between the characters and their words, Pinter opens the door to another world, convincible and familiar — the part we hide from ourselves. The threat or fear comes from others or oneself.

3.3 Comments on Him

Pinter's dramas often involve strong conflicts among ambivalent characters, fighting for verbal and territorial dominance. He is stylistically marked by theatrical pauses and silences, comedic timing, provocative imagery, witty dialogue, ambiguity, irony and menace. He is also thematically ambiguous, raising complex issues of individual human identity oppressed by social forces and vicissitudes of memory. Most of his works, just like him are considered complex and contradictory.

Pinter's story and dialogues are closely related to reality, but wholly he has already achieved a certain mystery. The strangeness of his method — based on melodramatic suspense — matches the mystery of his message. Pinter's use of language is so distinctive that it earns its own adjective, "Pinteresque". His work — represented on Broadway last season by an acclaimed revival of 1967's *The Homecoming*, which wins the Tony Award[49] in its original production — is psychologically and rhythmically complex, distinguished by stark pauses. But the tension, desperation and dark humor in forming Pinter classics such as *The Homecoming*, *The Caretaker* and *Betraya*l derive much from a fascination with the more personal politics of human behavior and alienation.

Pinter is described as a "Comedy of Menace[50]" and as an example of the Theatre of the Absurd with such features as the fluidity and ambiguity of time, place and identity and the disintegration of language. There is little expository information, often contradicted by the characters and one cannot take what they say at face value. Yet it is about a private, obsessive work about time past; about some vanished world, either real or idealized, into which all but one of the characters readily escapes. People can also sense a yearning for some lost Eden[51] as a refuge from the uncertain, miasmic present in his works. His is not an empty universe, but one full of undefined menace. It is a world of insiders versus outsiders, stirring one of our most primitive fears, the fear of an invader breaking into our home and driving us out. Extraordinarily, he evokes a realm of nameless terror where no value or identity is substantial or secure.

Pinter said, "There are no hard distinctions between what is real and what is unreal, nor between what is true and what is false. A thing is not necessarily either true or false; it can be both true and false." "I believe that these assertions still make sense and do still apply to the exploration of reality through art. So as a writer I stand by them but as a citizen I cannot. As a citizen I must ask: What is true? What is false?"

Section 4 Eugene O'Neill

Eugene O'Neill is widely acclaimed "founder of the American drama".

4.1 The Modern Period of American Literature

This is a period of spiritual wasteland, but a full blossoming of literary writings in the United States.

4.1.1 World Wars' Impact on American Literature

The pre-war world was another country — a world worth fighting for. But to more and more people, wars meant violence, devastation, blood and death. The 20th century witnessing two world wars was a period of social breakdown — a transformation from order to disorder, a sense of unease and restlessness, a decline in moral standard and a waste of spiritual wasteland because of the destroyed civilization, individual powerlessness and hopelessness with resulting feelings of fear, loss, disorientation and disillusionment. Therefore, "seizing the day" or "enjoying the present" was pervasive with people.

4.1.2 Historical and Cultural Backgrounds after World War II

The two world wars exerted a tremendous influence on the mentality of Americans, changing man's view of himself and the world. The following Korean War and the Vietnam War made the gap between people and the government wider. Many people, scared by the misuse of modern science and technology, started to question the role of science in human progress and reconsidered the nature of man and man's capacity for evil. Some no longer believed in God, finding life a big joke or an absurdity and the world more disintegrating and fragmentary. As a result, people became more estranged and despondent.

4.1.3 American Literature between the Two World Wars

America experienced a spiritual crisis, but a full blossoming of literary writings at this period of time — the second American Renaissance[52] with a lot of expatriates leaving America and forming a community of writers and artists in Paris. Young writers who experienced the war found modern warfare not glorious or heroic, but disillusioned and disgusted by the frivolous, greedy and heedless way of life in America. They wrote from their own experience and experimented new modes of thought and expression, some becoming prominent figures in American Literature such as F. Scott Fitzgerald and Ernest Hemingway — representatives of the Lost Generation[53]. The leading spokesman of the Imagist Movement was Ezra Pound[54], while Faulkner created his own mythical kingdom and Robert Frost[55] revealed profound truth with simplicity.

4.1.4 Features of Modern American Literature

Modern American literature attempted to convey a vision of social breakdown and moral decay, trying to develop techniques that could represent a break with the past — discontinuity and fragmentation.

Generally, a typical modern work began arbitrarily, advanced without explanation and ended without resolution. It was no longer a record of sequence and coherence. Instead, they were only fragments drawn from diverse areas of experiences such as shifts in perspective, voice and tone — the biggest one was from the external to the internal, from the public to the private, from the chronological time to the psychological, from the objective description to the subjective projection with a more detached and ironic tone.

4.1.5 American Drama

To say that American drama began in 1916 when the Provincetown Players[56] produced Eugene O'Neill's first play was to write off the efforts of the 19th century playwrights too ruthlessly to be just. Native American drama emerged in the play *The Great Divide*, first presented under the title of *The Sabine Woman* at the Garrick Theatre in Chicago on April 12, 1906 by William Vaughn Moody[57], completely in the spirit of the times. George M. Cohan[58] was writing American musical comedies. But it was true that there were no great masters in theatre comparable to such major figures in fiction as Herman Melville[59] or James but the late 19th century realists made tentative attempts to place realistic drama on the American stage: carrying out some dramatic experimentation around the turn of the century.

American drama began the process of developing itself into a department of American literature equal in significance to both poetry and the novel with the stimulus coming from the naturalistic, symbolic and critical drama of Europe and possibly moved by the vigorous stirrings in American poetry and fiction.

America experienced a renaissance of drama in the 1920s. The theatre of the Depression[60] was not depressing at all. Drama at this time was preoccupied with social concerns with new plays keeping appearing all through the 40s and in the post-war years — entering a new phase in its development when diversity became one of its salient features from the end of the 60s.

4.2 O'Neill's Life

Eugene O'Neill (1888-1953) was born in a hotel room overlooking the Times Square on Broadway in New York into a theatrical family James O'Neill. His father was a well-known touring actor. He grew up in New London, Connecticut, spending his early years on theatrical road tours with his parents and having a succession of religious boarding schools. He was kicked out of Princeton University[61] one year later after a drunken prank, after which he arranged a secret marriage which ended with failure at 21 years old. Then he went to sea and voyaged South America and South Africa, making friends with the lowest of society and getting to know life better. In 1912, he attempted a suicide, leading to physical breakdown, thus staying at a sanitarium for months. Recovering from tuberculosis in a sanatorium where he cultivated an interest in play writing, he joined the famous Professor George Pierce Baker's "47 Workshop[62]" at Harvard to learn writing better in 1914. His first performed play *Bound East for Cardiff*[63] in 1916 marked the beginning of his long and successful dramatic career, thus ushering in the modern era of the American theatre.

In 1936, he won Nobel Prize in Literature. Besides, he received the Pulitzer Prize 4 times.

4.3 His plays

Drama at the time that was melodramatic and divorced from reality disgusted O'Neill. He was the first to introduce into American drama the techniques of realism, associated with Russian playwright Anton Chekhov, Norwegian playwright Henrik Ibsen and Swedish playwright

August Strindberg. He wrote only one comedy: *Ah, Wildernes*. All his other plays involved some degree of tragedy and personal pessimism. He wrote over 40 plays including the most famous *Beyond the Horizon*, *The Emperor Jones*, *Anna Christie*, *The Hairy Ape*, *Desire under the Elms*, *Mourning Becomes Electra* and *Long Days Journey into Night*[64], etc.

4.3.1 *The Emperor Jones*

The Emperor Jones was a play telling the tale of Brutus Jones, an African-American man who killed a man, went to prison, escaped to a Caribbean island where he established himself as emperor, running an abusive, corrupt dictatorial regime. The revolt of local people forced him to flee and hide in the forest where eventually the troops of a native chief, found him and killed him with a silver bullet that had been specially made. It was O'Neill's first play to receive great critical acclaim and box-office success and the one that launched his career, displaying an uneasy mix of expressionism and realism, also characteristic of several other O' Neill plays, including *The Hairy Ape*.

4.3.2 *Long Day's Journey into Night*

Long Day's Journey into Night is a 1956 dramatic play in four acts, which is widely considered to be his masterwork. The play, somewhat autobiographical won the Pulitzer Prize for Drama in 1957. The play covered a fateful, heart-rending day from around 8: 30 am. to midnight, in August of 1912 at the seaside Connecticut home of the Tyrones — the autobiographical representations of O'Neill himself, his older brother and their parents at their home, Monte Cristo Cottage. His earlier frustrated characters managed to retain some faith in life, with the misfits in this play having nothing but night stretching before them, thus the mood of sheer despair indicating any illusion he has cherished about life evaporating completely.

The four characters, parents and two sons in the play suffered frustration and wished to escape from the harsh reality — James (Father) looking for solace in cups and Mary (Mother) and sons seeking the protection of the fog which they hoped would screen them from the intrusion of the world outside. They met and tormented one another and themselves until midnight.

Father was angry with the mother for her drug addiction while mother angry with the father for his failure to offer her a home; father with his sons for being good for nothing and sons with their parents for not being good parents — all were torn in a war between love and hate. Love gave way to hate, day to night and hope to despair. This play is a metaphor for O'Neill's life long endeavor to find truth and the way to acceptance. The former he finds, namely the faithless, fragmentary nature of modern life whereas the latter he does not — all passing into night.

4.3.3 *Strange Interlude*

Strange Interlude[65] was an experimental play, which he finished in 1923, but was not produced on Broadway until 1928, when it won the Pulitzer Prize for Drama. It was one of the few modern plays to make extensive use of a soliloquy technique, in which the characters spoke their inner thoughts to the audience. Some productions had the actors carry masks to distinguish their spoken dialogue from their soliloquies while most productions allowed the distinction to be made through acting style alone. The soliloquies in *Strange Interlude* mostly took the form of relatively brief side comments, not of lengthy speeches in the Shakespearean manner. The meaning of the title was suggested by the aging Nina in a speech near the end of the play, "Our lives are strange dark interludes in the electrical displays of God the Father".

Nina Leeds, the daughter of an Ivy League[66] professor, devastated when her adored fiancé' was killed in World War I. Nina embarked on a series of sordid affairs before determining to marry an amiable fool, Sam

Evans. While pregnant with Sam's child, Nina learnt a horrifying secret known only to Sam's mother — insanity ran in the Evans family and could be inherited by any child of Sam's. Realizing a child was essential to her own and to Sam's happiness, Nina decided on a "scientific" solution by aborting Sam's child and conceiving a child with the physician Ned. She tried her best to let Sam believe that the child was his. The plan backfired when Nina and Ned's intimacy led to their falling passionately in love. Twenty years later, Sam's "son" Gordon Evans approached manhood, with only Nina and Ned being aware of the boy's true parentage.

4.4 Comments on Him

Eugene O'Neill is unquestionably America's greatest playwright, widely recognized as the founder of the American drama and a major figure in world literature. As a tireless experimentalist in dramatic forms and theater techniques, he takes drama away from the old traditions of the last century and roots it deeply in life, being equally adept in the styles of realism and expressionism. He borrows freely both from the best traditions of European drama and from modern literary techniques such as the stream-of-consciousness device with the help of which he manages to reveal the emotional and psychological complexities of modern man.

Thematically, he deals with the basic issues of human existence: life and death, illusion and disillusion, alienation and communication, dream and reality, self and society, revealing tragic sense of modern man helpless and impotent in a faithless and fragmentary nature of modern life. He is a critic of American society and society as a whole, never ceasing attempt to improve his art in step with the spirit of the times.

He is a sensitive artist, concerned with the problem of modern man's "belonging". To him man is rootless in an indifferent and impersonal universe.

Section 5 Arthur Miller

Arthur Miller (1915-2005) is an American prominent figure in American theatre, writing a total of 17 plays. He doesn't win Nobel Prize in literature, yet he wins a lot of influential prizes such Pulitzer Prize, New York Drama Critics' Circle[67] award and Tony Award several times. He is regarded as a moralist, "the conscience of America", one among American playwrights who have most consistently focused on social matters.

5.1 His Life

Arthur Asher Miller was born on October 17, 1915 in Harlem, New York City, the second of three children of Isidore and Augusta Miller Polish Jewish immigrant, a clothing manufacturer who migrated to the United States from Austria-Hungary at the turn of the 20th century. In the Wall Street Crash of 1929, the family lost almost everything and moved to Gravesend, Brooklyn. As a teenager, Miller delivered bread every morning before school to help the family. After graduating in 1932 from Abraham Lincoln High School, he worked at several menial jobs to pay for his college tuition. Wanting to go to the University of Michigan[68] because of being attracted by its theatre program, he persuaded Michigan (in Ann Arbor) that his talents surpassed his high-school grades and he was indeed admitted. At the University of Michigan, Miller first majored in journalism and worked as a reporter and night editor for the student paper, the Michigan Daily. It was during this time that he wrote his first play, *No Villain*. Miller switched his major to English and subsequently won the Avery Hopwood Award[69] for *No Villain*. The award brought him his first recognition and led him to begin to consider having a career as a playwright. Miller enrolled in a playwriting seminar taught by the influential Professor Kenneth Rowe, who instructed him in his early forays into playwriting. In 1937, Miller wrote *Honors at Dawn*, which also received the Avery Hopwood Award. In 1938, Miller received a BA in English. After graduation, he joined the Federal Theater Project[70], a New Deal agency established to provide jobs in the theater. He chose the theater project although he had an offer to work as a scriptwriter for the 20th Century Fox[71]. However, Congress, worried about possible Communist infiltration, closed the project in 1939. Miller began working in the Brooklyn Navy Yard while continuing to write radio plays which made him concentrate on the words and realize what the power of a good sentence was. In 1940, he married Mary Grace Slattery who studied at the same university. Miller was exempted from military service during World War II because of a high-school football injury to his left kneecap.

Miller died of heart failure after a battle against cancer, pneumonia and congestive heart disease at his home in Roxbury, Connecticut. He died on the evening of February 10, 2005 (the 56th anniversary of the Broadway debut of *Death of a Salesman*), aged 89, surrounded by family and friends, interred at Roxbury Center Cemetery in Roxbury.

5.2 His Works

Miller was often in the public eye, particularly during the late 1940s, 1950s and early 1960s, a period during which he testified before the House Un-American Activities Committee[72] (HUAC), received the Pulitzer Prize for Drama and was married to Marilyn Monroe[73] less than a month after his divorce from ex-wife. In 2002 he received the Prince of Asturias Award and the Jerusalem Prize[74] in 2003.

Miller was applauded in Hollywood and in New York theater circles when he refused to name names before HUAC, saying "I could not use the name of another person and bring trouble on him", a courageous act in an atmosphere of horror during the McCarthyism[75] era. As a result, he was found guilty of contempt of Congress in May 1957, sentenced to a $500 fine or thirty days in prison, blacklisted and disallowed a US passport. Two years later, the courts dismissed his contempt of Congress citation. He spoke against the Vietnam War in 1965 at the first teach-ins on the subject at the University of Michigan. He was also active in local political affairs in Connecticut and was elected to serve as a delegate to the Democratic National Convention in 1968. Besides, he accepted the presidency of PEN International, the association of poets, editors, essayists, novelists and other literary figures in 1965, becoming increasingly active in defending the rights of writers.

Miller wrote *The Man Who Had All the Luck* (1940), which was produced in New Jersey in 1940 and won the Theatre Guild's National Award. The play closed after 4 performances with disastrous reviews. In 1946 Miller's play *All My Sons* (1949), the writing of which had commenced in 1941, was a success on Broadway (earning him his first Tony Award, for Best Author) and his reputation as a playwright was established. *The Price* (1968) was produced on Broadway during the 1967-1968 season — his last solid critical and commercial hit. *The Misfit* (1961), the screenplay was a 1961 movie directed by John Huston and starring Monroe, to whom he was married at the time — composed as a gift to his wife, who found herself increasingly tormented by personal demons and drug abuse. *After the Fall* (1964), his most overtly autobiographical play, brought him a storm of criticism when it was produced in 1964, shortly after Monroe's death because the play, which had been written soon after the collapse of their marriage, implied a search for understanding of his responsibility toward Monroe, of her inability to cope and of his failure to help her. He insisted that he was dealing with large human themes and professed surprise when critics noted the resemblance between Monroe and Maggie, the drug-addicted, blond-wigged protagonist in the play and was accused of capitalizing on

Monroe's fame and defiling her image.

But his reputation rests on a handful of his best-known plays, the dramas of guilt and betrayal and redemption that continue to be revived frequently at theaters all over the world.

5.2.1 *The Crucible*

He broke with Elia Kazan[76], the talented stage and film director, over his decision to give names of former members of the American Communist Party of the Group Theater to HUAC because of unwillingness to risk his promising career in Hollywood for the Communist cause that he had come to despise. Distressed by the sight of former friends giving evidence against other former friends as a result of McCarthyism, Miller decided to write a play about this situation: "What I sought was a metaphor, an image that would spring out of the heart, all-inclusive, full of light, a sonorous instrument whose reverberations would penetrate to the centre of this miasma." After speaking with Kazan about his testimony Miller traveled to Salem, Massachusetts to research the witch trials[77] of 1692. *The Crucible*, in which Miller likened the situation with the HUAC to the witch hunt in Salem in 1692, opened at the Beck Theatre on Broadway on January 22, 1953. Though widely considered only somewhat successful at the time of its initial release, today *The Crucible* is his most frequently produced work throughout the world. It was adapted into an opera by Robert Ward, which won the Pulitzer Prize for Music in 1962. Today it is studied in high schools and universities, because of its status as a revolutionary work of theatre and for its allegorical relationship to testimony given before HCUA during the 1950s.

The play was adapted for film twice, by Jean-Paul Sartre as the 1957 film *Les Sorcières de Salem* and by Miller himself. Miller's adaptation earned him an Academy Award nomination for Best Screenplay based on previously produced material, his only nomination.

The play has also been presented several times on stage and television.

In his autobiography he recalled that at one performance of *The Crucible*, upon the execution of the leading character, John Proctor, people "stood up and remained silent for a couple of minutes, with heads bowed" — he hoped it would be seen as an affirmation of the struggle for liberty, for keeping one's own conscience.

5. 2. 2 *Death of a Salesman*

In 1948 Miller built a small studio in Roxbury, Connecticut. There, in less than a day, he wrote Act I of *Death of a Salesman*. Within six weeks, he completed the rest of the play, one of the classics of the world theater. *Death of a Salesman* premiered on Broadway on February 10, 1949 at the Morosco Theatre, directed by Elia Kazan. The play was commercially successful and critically acclaimed, winning a Tony Award for best author, the New York Drama Circle Critics' Award and the Pulitzer Prize for drama. It was the first play to win all three of these major awards. The play was performed 742 times, acclaimed as a modern American masterpiece in its first reviews; translated into 29 languages and performed even in Beijing, China.

The play was mostly told from Willy Loman's point of view, showing previous parts of Willy's life in his time shifts, sometimes during a present day scene. It did this by having a scene begin in the present time and adding characters onto the stage that only Willy could see and hear, representing characters and conversations from other times and places. One example of this was during a conversation between Willy and his neighbor Charley. During the conversation, Willy's brother Ben came on stage and began talking to Willy while Charley spoke to Willy. When Willy began talking to his brother, the other characters did not understand who he was talking to and some of them even began to suspect that he had "lost it." However, at times the scene broke away from Willy's point of view and focused on the other characters, Linda,

Biff and Happy. During these parts of the play, the time and place stayed constant without any abrupt flashbacks while the play took Willy's point of view. The play's structure resembled a stream of consciousness account: Willy drifted from his living room, downstage, to the apron and flashbacks of an idyllic past and also to fantasized conversations with Ben. The use of these different "states" allowed Miller to contrast Willy's dreams and the reality of his life in extraordinary detail; and also allowed him to contrast the characters themselves, showing them in both sympathetic and villainous lights, gradually unfolding the story and refusing to allow the audience a permanent judgment about anyone. When in the present the characters abided by the rules of the set, entering only through the stage door to the left; however, when audience visited Willy's "past", these rules were removed, with characters openly moving through walls. Miller's mobile concurrences, however, rather showed highly subjective memories. Furthermore, as Willy's mental state deteriorated, the boundaries between past and present were destroyed and the two started to exist in parallel, the use of these particular theatre techniques making the play a real tragedy.

In the late 1980s, after his autobiography was published, Miller reflected in an interview on the course he had taken in life. "It has gone through my mind how much time I wasted in the theater, if only because when you write a book you pack it up and send it off," he said. "In the theater, you spend months casting actors who are busy in the movies anyway and then to get struck down in half an hour, as has happened to me more than once." But when asked how he wanted to be remembered, he did not hesitate. "I hope as a playwright," he said. "That would be all of it", showing his love and devotion to drama.

5.3 Comments on Him

Arthur Miller continues the trend of the 30s. While many dramatists of that period are bent on recording the shock of opposing forces such as capital and labor, democracy and fascism, he examines the individual in his moral behavior under specific social pressures. His central theme is about man's obligation of assumed responsibility in the community of his fellow men which is bluntly projected in *All My Sons* and much more subtly treated in *Death of a Salesman*. He spends his whole life seeking answers to what he sees around him as a world of injustice, seeing plays as a way to change America and putting it: "that meant grabbing people and shaking them by the back of the neck." That is why in his work, there is almost a conscious need to be a light into the world.

He is considered by both audience and scholars one of America's greatest playwrights and moral voice of American stage. After his death, many respected actors, directors and producers pay tribute to him, some calling him the last great practitioner of the American stage and Broadway theatres darken their lights in a show of respect. Miller's alma mater, the University of Michigan opened the Arthur Miller Theatre in March 2007. As per his express wish, it is the only theatre in the world that bears Miller's name. Miller's papers are housed at the Harry Ransom Humanities Research Center at the University of Texas at Austin[78]. Arthur Miller is also a member of the American Theater Hall of Fame, inducted in 1979.

重难点解读

[1] **Nobel Prize in Literature**：诺贝尔文学奖。瑞典化学家、工程师、发明家、军工装备制造商和炸药的发明者诺贝尔在 1895 年 11 月 27 日写下遗嘱，捐献全部财产3 122万瑞典克朗，并设立基金，每年把利息作为奖金，表彰那些对社会作出卓越贡献、或作出杰出研究、发明以及实验的人士，文学奖就是其中之一。爱尔兰剧作家萧伯纳，“因为作品具有理想主义和人道主义”而获得 1925 年诺贝尔文学奖。

[2] **Oscar**：奥斯卡。美国学院功绩奖，通称奥斯卡金像奖、奥斯卡奖或奥斯卡，每年由美国电影艺术与科学学院组织与颁发，旨在鼓励优秀电影的创作与发展。该奖项不仅是美国电影业界年度最重要的活动，亦是目前世界上最受瞩目的电影奖之一。萧伯纳的戏剧《卖花女》(*Pygmalion*)曾于1938年翻拍成黑白电影，由Wendy Hiller饰演卖花女伊莱莎·杜立德；1956年，此剧改编为音乐剧《窈窕淑女》(*My Fair Lady*)，由朱莉·安德鲁斯饰演伊莱莎；后音乐剧拍成同名电影，改由奥黛丽·赫本饰演伊莱莎。1963年公映赢得最佳影片在内的八项奥斯卡大奖。

[3] **the Chartist Movement**：宪章运动。19世纪30—50年代英国发生的争取实现人民宪章的工人运动，是世界三大工人运动之一。1832年英国议会改革为工业资产阶级打开进入议会的大门，在这一改革斗争中起过巨大作用的人民群众仍处于无权地位。他们决心进行独立的政治斗争，争取新的选举改革。1836年伦敦工人协会成立，提出年满21岁的男子普选权等6条要求，并于1838年5月8日以《人民宪章》(*the People's Charter*)名称发表，宪章运动由此得名。宪章拥护者在全国各地集会、游行，要求实现宪章。1839年运动进入第一次高潮，同年5月在请愿书上签字的人超过了125万，1842年的经济危机促使第二次宪章运动高潮的到来，同年2月宪章派向议会递交了新请愿书，签名人数达300多万。除要求普选权外，还提出废除新济贫法、限制工时和实行政教分离等要求。1848年出现第三次高潮，约197万人在请愿书上签名。这三次运动都被政府镇压。1848年后，运动逐渐衰落。

[4] **the Triple Alliance**：同盟国。由德意志帝国、奥匈帝国和意大利结成的军事同盟，以对抗协约国，意大利虽是同盟国，但后来英国、法国及俄国与意大利签订密约，承诺给予意大利某些土地，意大利于1915年加入了协约国而对抗同盟国，三国同盟瓦解。第一次世界大战末，美国加入协约国，同盟国最终失败。在第一次世界大战时，加入同盟国方面作战的，

还有保加利亚和土耳其。

[5] **the Triple Entente**：协约国。第一次世界大战中以英国、法国、沙皇俄国为主的国家联盟，还包括南斯拉夫等弱小的欧洲国家。它与以德国、奥匈帝国为中心的同盟国集团形成了第一次世界大战的对立双方。第一次世界大战中后期，美国、日本，以及中国北洋军阀政府等一些国家也先后加入协约国集团，而俄国在十月革命爆发后退出了战争。最终，协约国赢得了第一次世界大战的胜利。

[6] ***Treaty of Versailles***：《凡尔赛条约》或《凡尔赛和约》。是第一次世界大战后，战胜国(协约国)对战败国(同盟国)的和约，其主要目的是惩罚和削弱德国。协约国和同盟国于1918年11月11日宣布停火，经过巴黎和会长达6个月的谈判后，于1919年6月28日在巴黎的凡尔赛宫签署条约，标志着第一次世界大战正式结束，得到国际联盟的承认后，于1920年1月10日正式生效。中国因巴黎和会对于中日青岛问题无法解决，进而爆发全国反日的“五四”运动，没有签署凡尔赛条约，但与德国另签订和约；美国因其国会表决多数反对，也未签凡尔赛条约。

[7] **The October Revolution**：十月革命(又称布尔什维克革命、俄国共产革命)。指1917年列宁领导的武装起义，前苏联、中国等社会主义国家及组织普遍认为，十月革命是经列宁和托洛茨基领导下的布尔什维克领导的武装起义，建立了人类历史上第二个无产阶级政权(第一个是巴黎公社无产阶级政权)和由马克思主义政党领导的第一个社会主义国家——苏维埃俄国。

[8] **Swift**：斯威夫特(Jonathan Swift，1667—1745)。爱尔兰讽刺文学大师，以《格列佛游记》和《一只桶的故事》等作品闻名于世。

[9] **Lady Augusta Gregory**：奥古斯塔·格雷戈里夫人(1852—1932)。爱尔兰剧作家，致力于爱尔兰文艺复兴运动，1899年与叶芝等人在都柏林建立爱尔兰民族文学剧院。1902年组成爱尔兰民族戏剧学会，继而管理1904年开放的艾比(阿贝)剧院并为其写戏，直至1928年退休。她在35年的创作生涯中创

作和翻译了40部反映爱尔兰人民生活、历史和幻想的喜剧、通俗历史剧和神话剧，尤以运用爱尔兰西部方言的独幕喜剧见长。剧作有《散布流言》、《月出》、《旅人》、《龙》等。她还参与了叶芝的一些剧本的创作。

[10] **the Irish Renaissance**：爱尔兰文艺复兴。19世纪末至20世纪20年代，爱尔兰人的民族意识普遍高涨，纷纷要求摆脱英国的殖民统治，实行自治，1937年通过新宪法宣告独立。与政治上的民族独立运动相呼应，一些爱国作家为复兴爱尔兰的民族文学语言、艺术而创作了大批表现爱尔兰人民生活、反映民族精神的作品，形成了一个蔚为壮观的文艺复兴运动。

[11] **Dublin**：都柏林。爱尔兰共和国的首都，也是爱尔兰最大的城市，靠近爱尔兰岛东岸的中心点，位处都柏林郡的丽妃河河口、都柏林地区中心。由于有很多高技术企业的聚集，都柏林有欧洲硅谷之称。

[12] **Fabian Society**：费边社。20世纪初英国的一个工人社会主义派别，其传统重在务实的社会建设，倡导建立互助互爱的社会服务。尽管费边社本身并未创建一套完整的社会福利理论，但是在他们的社会实践中，明显地贯穿着期望通过社会各阶层的平等，包括平等的财产、社会地位和政治权利的分配而达到自由，由实践平等和自由的理念达到社会合作和互爱的人际关系的理念。这是英国工人群众对福利国家制度最早、最直接的要求。

[13] **Engels**：恩格斯(Friedrich Von Engels，1820—1895)。德国哲学家，马克思主义创始人之一，是卡尔·马克思的挚友，被誉为"第二提琴手"，为马克思创立马克思主义提供了大量经济上的支持，在马克思逝世后，帮助马克思完成了其未完成的《资本论》等著作，并且领导国际工人运动。

[14] ***Immaturity***：《未成熟》(1879)。萧伯纳的第一部小说，遭到多家出版社的拒绝。

[15] ***An Unsocial Socialist***：《业余社会主义者》。萧伯纳的长篇小说，尖锐地批判了资本主义。

[16] *Saturday Review*：《星期六评论》。英国杂志。

[17] *Dramatic Review*：《戏剧评论》。英国杂志。

[18] *Plays Unpleasant*：《不愉快戏剧集》。萧伯纳 1892 年正式开始创作剧本，这是其第一个戏剧集(1898)，其中包括《鳏夫的财产》(*Widowers' Houses*)、《华伦夫人的职业》(*Mrs. Warren's Profession*)、《荡子》(又译《好逑者》，*The Philanderer*)三个剧本。

[19] *Plays Pleasant*：《愉快戏剧集》(1898)。包括《康蒂坦》(*Candida*)，《武器与人》(*Arms and Man*)，《风云人物》(*The Man of Destiny*)和《难以预料》(*You Never Can Tell*)，是萧伯纳第二个时期的戏剧作品。

[20] *Three Plays for Puritans*：《为清教徒写的戏剧》。萧伯纳的第三个剧集，包括《恺撒和克莉奥佩特拉》(1898)、《魔鬼的门徒》(1898)和《布拉斯庞德上尉的转变》(1899)。

[21] *Man and Superman*, *How He Lied to Her Husband*, *Major Barbara*, *The Doctor's Dilemma and Getting Married*：《人与超人》(1903)、《他是如何对她的丈夫撒谎》(1904)、《芭芭拉少校》(1905)、《医生的两难选择》(1905)和《结婚》(1906)。萧伯纳 20 世纪早期戏剧。

[22] *John Bull's Other Island*：《英国佬的另一个岛》。萧伯纳的戏剧作品。

[23] King Edward VII：爱德华七世(1841—1910)。英国国王(1901—1910)。维多利亚女王和阿尔伯特亲王之子，曾在牛津与剑桥大学就读，1863 年与丹麦克里斯蒂安九世之女亚历山德拉结婚，对赛马、游艇比赛尤感兴趣，在位期间大力恢复因女王长期孀居而显得黯淡的英国君主制度之荣光。

[24] the Salvation Army：救世军。1865 年成立，以军队形式作为其架构和行政方针，并以基督教作为信仰基本的国际性宗教及慈善公益组织，以街头布道和慈善活动、社会服务著称，其创办人希望能够把基督教传给穷困的人，并透过了解穷人们物质及心灵之需给予帮助。其国际总部位于英国伦敦，在

全世界有几千个分部，约有成员两百万，其中以美国人较多。救世军及旗下的组织基本上不会涉及任何国家的政治和政策，而其成员亦无种族之分，故在世界各地可与其他国际救援机构和政府合作。

[25] 本处及本段中黑体部分指兵工厂的几任领导所信奉的格言：第一任领导的名言："如果上帝赋予人类手，人不要拒绝刀剑"；第二任："所有人都有权利去战斗，但无人有权做出判决"；第三任："武器归人，胜利归上苍"；第四任没有文采，什么都没写，但他在乔治三世的鼻子底下把武器卖给了拿破仑；第五任："除了一手持剑，和平不好降临人间"；第六任(我师父)："在这个世界上想要干成一件事就要让人们做好互相残杀的准备"；第七任没什么可写了，只写了："不知羞耻"四个字。

[26] **Venus**：维纳斯。爱神、美神，同时又是执掌生育与航海的女神，对应于希腊神话的阿芙洛狄忒(Aphrodite)。

[27] ***Heartbreak House***：《伤心之家》(1919)。萧伯纳的戏剧作品。

[28] ***The Apple Cart***：《苹果车》(1930)。萧伯纳的戏剧作品。

[29] ***Too True to Be Good***：《真相毕露》(1932)。萧伯纳的戏剧作品。

[30] ***Love among the Artists*, *the Irrational Knot* and *Cashel Byron's Profession***：《艺术家的爱情》、《无理之结》和《凯雪尔·拜伦的职业》。萧伯纳的戏剧作品。

[31] **Sean O'Case**：肖恩·奥凯西(1880—1964)。原名约翰·凯西，爱尔兰剧作家，其都柏林三部曲《枪手的影子》、《朱诺与孔雀》和《犁与星》)真实地再现了爱尔兰独立运动中城市劳工阶层的面貌，表现了爱尔兰民族的典型性格。

[32] **Shaw Festival**：萧伯纳戏剧节。萧伯纳戏剧节是与莎士比亚戏剧节齐名的世界知名戏剧节，莎士比亚戏剧节是在莎士比亚的家乡小镇 Stratford 举行，而萧伯纳戏剧节则是在旅游胜地尼亚加拉湖畔小镇举行，让观众在欣赏戏剧之外，还可以轻松度假。据记载，早在 1962 年，一名当地律师把尼亚加拉湖

畔小镇的旧法院的集会大厅改成了剧院，在周末上演 8 场萧伯纳的两个剧目，演出大受欢迎。第二年，萧伯纳戏剧节正式与观众见面，并成为北美最大和最成功的戏剧节。

[33] **Niagara-on-the-Lake，Ontario**：安大略省的尼亚加拉湖畔小镇。曾是 19 世纪英国殖民时期北部加拿大最初的首府，镇上有很多英式建筑，也是加拿大风景最为优美的小镇之一，被评为世界上最美的小镇。

[34] ***Don Juan in Hell***：地狱的唐璜。萧伯纳《人与超人》中最长的第三幕。

[35] **the London School of Economics and Political Science (LSE)**：伦敦政治经济学院。1895 年由费边社成员萧伯纳等人创办，学院于 1900 年成为伦敦大学(University of London)的一部分，今天的 LSE 是伦敦大学最著名的学院之一，也是英国金三角名校和罗素大学集团成员。校友及教员之中包括 17 名诺贝尔奖获得者，42 名政府或国家元首，31 名英国下议院议员及 42 名上议院议员。

[36] **the British Library of Political and Economic Science**：英国政治经济图书馆。伦敦政治经济学院的主图书馆，图书馆位于葡萄牙街，伦敦政治经济学院主楼的北面，是全球最大的社会科学类图书馆。始建于 1896 年。

[37] **D. H. Lawrence**：戴维·赫伯特·劳伦斯(1885—1930)。20 世纪英国文学中最重要的人物之一，也是最具争议性的作家之一。主要成就包括小说、诗歌、戏剧、散文、游记和书信。

[38] ***En attendant Godot*, *Fin de partie*, *Krapp's Last Tape and Happy Days***：《等待戈多》(*Waiting for Godot*, 1949)、《终局》(*Endgame*, 1957)、《克拉普最后的录音带》(1958)和《幸福的日子》(1960)。贝克特的戏剧作品。

[39] **Epic Theatre**：史诗剧。史诗剧的概念源于作为诗歌实践的理论家布莱希特。史诗剧主要在于表明这种戏剧希望观众，一点也不要紧张地跟随情节的发展而逐步放松心情。史诗式的戏剧正是布莱希特所追求的，1929 年他在剧本《马哈哥尼城

的兴衰》的注释中提出了他戏剧主张的雏形，他把自己所追求的戏剧称为叙事诗体戏剧，或称非亚里士多德式戏剧，而将他所反对的戏剧称为戏剧体戏剧，或称亚里士多德式戏剧。叙事诗体戏剧又译为叙事戏剧或史诗戏剧，其基本特点是形式的自由朴实、舒展大度和表现手法的叙述性，它要求逼真地展现广阔的生活面貌，揭示社会发展的规律，强调通过戏剧的欣赏可以起到给予观众的娱乐作用和认知作用。

[40] **Franz Kafka (*The Trial*), F. Scott Fitzgerald (*The Last Tycoon*), Ian McEwan (*The Comfort of Strangers*), Margaret Atwood (*The Handmaid's Tale*) and John Fowles (*The French Lieutenant's Woman*)**：弗兰兹·卡夫卡(《判决》)、弗朗西斯·司科特·菲茨杰拉德(《最后一个大亨》)、伊恩·麦克尤恩(《只爱陌生人》)、玛格丽特·阿特伍德(《侍女的故事》)和约翰·福尔斯(《法国中尉的女人》)。卡夫卡是奥地利小说家，欧洲著名的表现主义作家，其作品大多用变形荒诞的形象和象征直觉的手法，表现被充满敌意的社会环境所包围的孤立、绝望的个人。菲茨杰拉德是20世纪美国最杰出的作家之一，以《了不起的盖茨比》而出名。麦克尤恩是英国文坛当前最具影响力的作家之一，一度投身于20世纪60年代的反文化运动，后来对这一反理性主义的文化思潮感到厌倦，于1974年在伦敦定居下来。阿特伍德是加拿大著名女小说家、诗人、文学评论家，曾四次被提名英国布克奖，2000年终于以小说《盲刺客》摘得这一桂冠。福尔斯是当代英国著名小说家之一，代表作《法国中尉的女人》，被改编成电影，其《收藏家》和《魔法师》也被成功地改编成了电影。

[41] **anti-Semitism**：反犹太主义。闪米特人或称闪族人，亦称“塞姆人”，起源于阿拉伯半岛的游牧民族。阿拉伯人、犹太人都是闪米特人。生活在中东、北非的大部分居民，就是阿拉伯化的古代闪米特人的后裔。反犹太主义是对仇恨犹太人或犹太教的思想与行为的总称，其在各个不同历史时期有不同的动机和表现形式。虽然犹太人与阿拉伯人同属闪族，但通

常反闪族主义指的是反犹太主义。

[42] **Royal Academy of Dramatic Art**：皇家戏剧艺术学院(英语简称 RADA)。位于英国伦敦，被普遍认为是世界上最著名的戏剧学校之一，也是英国历史悠久的戏剧学校之一，建于 1904 年。

[43] **the Central School of Speech and Drama**：中央演讲和戏剧学院。伦敦大学下的一个组成学院，由艾尔西·福格蒂创立于 1906 年，长久以来在戏剧高等教育中保持中心地位，2005 年并入伦敦大学。著名校友包括劳伦斯·奥利佛和哈罗德·品特。主要提供戏剧表演方面的教育。2008 年科研评估将该学院评为“世界领先”及“国际一流”学院。《卫报》排名将其列在专业机构类第六位、戏剧和舞蹈类第九位。

[44] **Tony Blair**：托尼·布莱尔。英国首相、议员、中东问题特使。1997 年 5 月，工党在英国大选中以压倒多数的选票击败连续执政达 18 年之久的保守党。年仅 44 岁的布莱尔出任政府首相，成为 20 世纪以来英国最年轻的首相，并在 2001 年和 2005 年再次当选首相。

[45] **NATO's bombing of Serbia**：北约对塞尔维亚的轰炸。北大西洋公约组织(The North Atlantic Treaty Organization)，简称北约组织或北约，是美国与西欧、北美主要发达国家为实现防卫协作而建立的一个国际军事集团组织。1949 年 3 月 18 日美国和西欧国家公开组建北大西洋公约组织，于同年 4 月 4 日在美国华盛顿签署《北大西洋公约》后正式成立。1949 年 8 月 24 日，北大西洋公约组织条约经各国陆续批准后开始生效，其最高决策机构是北约理事会，理事会由成员国国家元首及政府高层、外长、国防部长组成，总部设在比利时的布鲁塞尔。1966 年 7 月 1 日，法国退出北大西洋公约组织一体化军事机构。塞尔维亚是一个欧洲国家，位于欧洲东南部，巴尔干半岛中部的内陆国，与黑山、波斯尼亚与黑塞哥维那、克罗地亚、匈牙利、罗马尼亚、保加利亚、马其顿、科索沃及阿尔巴尼亚接壤。

[46] ***The Dumb Waiter***：《送菜升降机》。哈罗德·品特的作品。

[47] **Wilfred Owen**：威尔福莱德·欧文。反战诗人，25岁英年早逝，生于1893年。虽然一直自视为反战分子，仍于1915年10月入伍，1917年1月加入法国曼彻斯特军团，其间，开始将他的战争经验写成诗，1915年夏，因被诊断患有弹震击(战争精神病的一种)而遣返英国。他写下了一系列的诗篇。1918年8月，欧文返回其被授予十字勋章的西线战场，同年，遭机关枪扫射身亡，一周后，停战协定被签订。

[48] ***The Servant*** (1963), ***The Accident*** (1967), ***The Go-Between*** (1971) **and *The French Lieutenant's Woman***：《仆人》、《事故》、《送信人》和《法国中尉的女人》。品特的电影剧本，其中，《送信人》一片获得1971年第24届戛纳国际电影节金棕榈奖。

[49] **Tony Award**：托尼奖。全称为安东尼特·佩瑞戏剧奖(The Antoinette Perry Award for Excellence in Theatre)。是世界上最著名和最大型的戏剧和音乐剧大奖。美国表演艺术共有三项大奖：电影奥斯卡奖、电视艾美奖和舞台表演"托尼奖"。托尼奖是美国舞台表演的最高奖和纽约百老汇最高奖，由全美戏剧联盟和全美制作人联盟颁发，每年的颁奖晚会和奥斯卡金像奖一样向全世界转播。"托尼奖"成立于1947年，获奖作品的评选由"托尼奖提名委员会"、"美国演员联盟董事会"、"美国戏剧家同业会"、"美国舞台导演和编舞协会"、"美国舞美设计家联合会"、"美国舞台新闻管理和代理协会"、"美国舞台表演协会"和观众代表(共701票)表决产生。

[50] **Comedy of Menace**：威胁喜剧。指因其戏剧情节常发生在一个完全无辜的境遇下，主人公平淡地聊一些日常生活的话题，最后发展成一个具有威胁性的荒诞状况，将人物性格的对立、权力的撕咬、情感的隐现冲撞成激烈的戏剧。这种特点的戏剧是由英国戏剧大师品特创立的，其早期剧作《房间》、《生日晚会》、《送菜升降机》都是这种威胁戏剧的代表之作。有人把他划归于萨缪尔·贝克特那样的"荒诞派戏剧"，而他却

自称是“威胁喜剧”，因为其作品强调了一种普遍存在的“威胁”，这种威胁既来自外部，也来自自身。

[51] **Eden**：伊甸园。根据《旧约》创世纪记载，上帝耶和华照着自己的形象造了人类的祖先男人亚当，再用亚当的一根肋骨创造了女人夏娃，并安置第一对男女住在伊甸园中。伊甸园在《圣经》的原文中含有乐园的意思。

[52] **the second American Renaissance**：第二次美国文学中兴。美国著名思想家、文学家爱默生在美国形成其国民性的时代是美国文学第一次文艺复兴，第二次文艺复兴始于美国将要作为一个统一的、强大的民族在国际上扮演重要角色的时期。伴随着这种角色的转换，美国文学已不再满足于摆脱英国文学的传统，而要在世界文学之林占有自己的一席之地。20 世纪二三十年代，美国文坛大匠如云，7 个诺贝尔文学奖获得者在此期间发表了他们的主要作品：作家刘易斯、赛珍珠、福克纳、海明威、斯坦贝克，剧作家奥尼尔和诗人 T·S·艾略特。正是这些文学家，以及许许多多与他们一起活跃于二三十年代美国文坛的作家和诗人，如费茨杰拉德、安德森、庞德、弗洛斯特、多斯·帕索斯、法雷尔等，引导着美国文学走向真正的成熟和真正的繁荣。

[53] **the Lost Generation**：迷惘的一代，又称迷失的一代、失落的一代。通常指在第一次世界大战期间成年的一代人。海明威在其创作的小说《太阳照常升起》中使用了“迷惘的一代”作为题词，从而使这一名称广为人知。

[54] **Ezra Pound**：埃兹拉·庞德。美国著名诗人，意象派诗歌运动(Imagist Movement)的代表人物。意象派诗歌运动是 1909—1917 年的一些英美诗人发起并付诸实践的文学运动，是当时盛行于西方的象征主义文学运动的一个分支，其宗旨是要求诗人以鲜明、准确、含蓄和高度凝练的意象生动而形象地展现事物，并将诗人瞬息间的思想感情融化在诗行中，反对发表议论及感叹。庞德从中国古典诗歌、日本俳句中生发出“诗歌意象”的理论，为东西方诗歌的互相借鉴作出了卓越

贡献。

[55] **Robert Frost**：罗伯特·弗罗斯特(1874—1963)。20 世纪最受欢迎的美国诗人之一，曾赢得 4 次普利策奖和许多其他的奖励及荣誉，被称为“美国文学中的桂冠诗人”。

[56] **the Provincetown Players**：普罗文斯顿剧社。1915 年，一些志同道合的艺术家和作家在美国马萨诸塞州普罗文斯顿组成一个非商业性的戏剧团体，旨在打破当时操纵在纽约百老汇几个资本家手中的商业化组织对戏剧的垄断，从而给美国剧作家提供一个自由表达思想的机会，此剧社发起人坚持上演艺术性较强的严肃戏剧，因而吸引了一大批作家和艺术家同他们合作。其中最重要的是奥尼尔、埃德蒙特·琼斯和麦克高温三人。剧社于 1922 年因内部分歧解散后，1923 年又重组并改名为实验剧院，更趋向于职业化。1925 年，剧社内部再次分裂，又进行改组。由于演出费用不断上涨和工会问题而使该剧社陷入困境，勉强维持到 1929 年而告解散。

[57] **William Vaughn Moody**：威廉·沃恩·穆迪(1869—1910)。美国剧作家及诗人。其代表剧为《分水岭》，第一次表演时起名为《萨宾的妇女》。

[58] **George M. Cohan**：乔治·M·柯汉(1878—1942)。美国音乐剧历史上第一位有影响的剧诗作者，百老汇剧诗艺术的奠基人。作为一个精力充沛、多才多艺的天才人物，剧诗作者只是柯汉的舞台身份之一。他在音乐剧的艺术旅途中尝试过多种角色，像作曲家、导演、制作人、剧作家等，其作为早期喜剧演员的经历更为人所熟知和津津乐道。

[59] **Herman Melville**：赫尔曼·梅尔维尔(1819—1891)。19 世纪美国最伟大的小说家、散文家和诗人之一，生前没有引起应有的重视，20 世纪 20 年代声名鹊起，被普遍认为是美国文学的巅峰人物之一。英国作家毛姆认为他的《白鲸》是世界十大文学名著之一，被誉为美国的“莎士比亚”。

[60] **Depression**：大萧条。指美国 1929 年至 1933 年之间的经济危机。

[61] **Princeton University**：普林斯顿大学。位于美国新泽西州，是著名的私立研究型大学，8 所常春藤高校联盟之一。学校于 1746 年在新泽西州伊丽莎白镇创立，是美国殖民时期第四所成立的高等教育学院，当时名为“新泽西学院”，1747 年迁至新泽西州，1756 年迁至普林斯顿，并于 1896 年正式改名为普林斯顿大学。

[62] **George Pierce Baker's "47 Workshop"**：乔治·皮尔斯·贝克的“四十七工作室戏剧班”。贝克(1866—1935)是美国著名的戏剧理论家和教育家，1916 年当选为美国艺术与人文科学院(文学部)院士，1905 年，开设“四十七工作室戏剧写作课”，1908 年创建哈佛戏剧俱乐部(Harvard Dramatic Club)，1912 年，成立“第四十七工作室”，为班上学生的戏剧作品提供表演平台，培养了许多杰出的戏剧人才，还 4 次获得普利策戏剧奖(Pulitzer Prize for Drama)。

[63] ***Bound East for Cardiff***：《东航加狄夫》。奥尼尔的戏剧作品。

[64] ***Beyond the Horizon*** , ***The Emperor Jones*** , ***Anna Christie*** , ***The Hairy Ape*** , ***Desire under the Elms*** , ***Mourning Becomes Electra*** **and** ***Long Days Journey into Night***：《天边外》(1920)、《琼斯皇》(1920)、《安娜·克里斯蒂》(1921)、《毛猿》(1922)、《榆树下的欲望》(1924)、《悲悼》(又译《悲悼三部曲》1931)和《进入黑夜的漫长旅程》(1956)。奥尼尔的戏剧作品。

[65] ***Strange Interlude***：《奇异的插曲》，奥尼尔的戏剧作品。

[66] **Ivy League**：常春藤联盟。美国东北部 8 所院校组成的体育赛事高校联盟。这 8 所院校包括：布朗大学、哥伦比亚大学、康奈尔大学、达特茅斯学院、哈佛大学、宾夕法尼亚大学、普林斯顿大学及耶鲁大学。

[67] **New York Drama Critics' Circle**：纽约戏剧评论界奖。是除普利策奖、托尼奖之外的又一项重要戏剧奖。每年 5 月份，由纽约市的报纸杂志、电视、广播等传媒的戏剧评论家们评选颁发，(不包括《纽约时报》)奖项有：最佳戏剧、最佳音乐剧、最佳外国戏剧、最佳新剧和特别奖等。

[68] **University of Michigan**：密歇根大学。创建于 1817 年，位于美国密歇根州，是美国历史上最悠久的公立大学之一，在世界范围内享有盛誉。密歇根大学建校以来，在各学科领域中成就卓越并拥有巨大影响，被誉为“公立常春藤”，与加州大学伯克利分校以及威斯康星大学齐名。

[69] **Avery Hopwood Award**：阿福瑞·侯伍德奖。詹姆斯·阿福瑞·侯伍德(1882—1928)，美国爵士时代最成功的戏剧家，死后，留下遗嘱将一大笔财产捐给母校密歇根大学，设立创意写作奖。米勒在该校学习期间，因创作《没有坏人》(*No Villain*)和《荣誉的真谛》(*Honors at Dawn*)两次获得该奖。

[70] **the Federal Theater Project**：联邦剧院项目。美国新政项目，其目的是为了资助大萧条时期的剧院和其他形式的艺术表演。

[71] **20th Century Fox**：二十世纪福克斯电影公司。美国最主要的电影、电视节目发行和制作公司之一，它是新闻集团的一个子公司。总部坐落在美国加州洛杉矶比弗利山庄西侧的世纪城。

[72] **House Un-American Activities Committee**：众院非美行为调查委员会。美国国会众议院设立的所谓“防范外国间谍”的机构。成立于 1938 年，1945 年成为常设委员会，是第二次世界大战后美国统治集团反共的重要工具，因迫害进步人士、破坏进步团体、镇压工人运动而臭名昭著。1952 年曾要求国会授予“战时”权力，以便能够任意传讯公民，遭到了国内外舆论及民众的强烈谴责。1969 年更名为：“国内安全委员会”，1975 年 1 月被撤销。

[73] **Marilyn Monroe**：玛丽莲·梦露(1926—1962)。美国 20 世纪最著名的电影女演员之一，36 岁过世，成为影迷心中永远的性感符号和流行文化的标志性象征人物，1999 年，美国电影学会选她为百年来最伟大的女演员。

[74] **Prince of Asturias Award and the Jerusalem Prize**：阿斯图里亚斯王子奖和耶路撒冷文学奖。前者创立于 1980 年，共设 8 个奖项，旨在奖励在科技、文化、体育和社会等领域有杰出贡献

的个人或团体，每年颁奖一次，获奖个人或团体可获 5 万欧元奖金。阿斯图里亚斯是西班牙的一个自治区，奥维耶多是阿斯图里亚斯自治区的首府。西班牙王储费利普是阿斯图里亚斯王子，也是基金会主席。后者用中东地区“耶路撒冷”城市命名，是以色列文学界的最高奖项，首次颁发在 1963 年，每两年颁发一次，表彰全世界优秀的文学作品和作家。

[75] **McCarthyism**：麦卡锡主义。1950—1954 年间美国参议员麦卡锡的美国国内反共、反民主的典型代表，它恶意诽谤、肆意迫害共产党和民主进步人士甚至有不同意见的人。从 1950 年初麦卡锡主义开始泛滥，到 1954 年底彻底破产的前后五年里，它的影响波及美国政治、外交和社会生活的方方面面。麦卡锡主义作为一个专有名词，也成为政治迫害的同义词。

[76] **Elia Kazan**：伊利亚·卡赞。希腊裔美国著名戏剧家和电影导演，以《推销员之死》、《欲望号街车》等影片闻名遐迩。自 20 世纪 30 年代起，执导过不少百老汇巨作，创作风格独特。1999 年被授予奥斯卡终身成就奖。20 世纪 30 年代曾短时间加入过共产党，后由于对斯大林主义僵化意识形态的不满脱离了共产党。50 年代，因涉及美国好莱坞政治“黑名单”事件、揭发他人的行为，结果令包括查理·卓别林、奥森·威尔斯在内的很多自由派导演、编剧流亡海外，但其导演事业仍如日中天，电影《天伦梦觉》、《娃娃新娘》、《天涯何处无芳草》等带给他不少荣誉。

[77] **the witch trials**：女巫案。1692 年，美国马萨诸塞州塞勒姆镇一牧师的女儿突得怪病，随后与她平素形影不离的 7 个女孩相继出现了同样的症状。从现代医学角度讲，这是“跳舞病”的一种表现。其病因是一种寄生于黑麦的真菌。当时人们普遍认为，让孩子们得怪病的真正原因，是来自村里的黑人女奴蒂图巴和另一个女乞丐，还有一个孤僻的从来不去教堂的老妇人。人们对这 3 人严刑逼供，“女巫”和“巫师”的数量一步步增加，先后有 20 多人死于该冤案，另有 200 多人被逮捕或监禁。1992 年，马萨诸塞州议会通过决议，宣布为所有受

害者恢复名誉。

[78] **Harry Ransom Humanities Research Center at the University of Texas at Austin**：美国得克萨斯大学奥斯丁分校的哈里·兰莎姆人文研究中心。该中心收集了 360 万文学手稿、100 万珍稀书籍、500 万幅照片以及十多万件艺术作品。

References

1. Ball, David. 1998. Backwards & Forwards — A Technical Manual for Reading Plays [M]. Southern Illinois University Press.
2. Brooks, Cleanth Brooks & Robert Bechtold Heilman. 1961. Understanding Drama: Twelve Plays [M]. Holt, Rinehart and Winston New York.
3. Jerry, Crawford, Catherine Hurst & Michael Lugering. 1995. Acting: in Person and in Style [M]. McGraw-Hill.
4. Eastrling, P. E. 1997. The Cambridge Companion to Greek Tragedy [M]. Cambridge University Press.
5. Esslin, Martin. 2004. The Theatre of the Absurd — Martin Esslin [M]. Vintage; 3rd.
6. Falb, Lewis W. & Chapel Hill. 1973. American Drama in Paris, 1945-1970 [M]. The University of North Carolina Press.
7. Hayman, Ronald. 1999. How to Read a Play [M]. Grove Press.
8. Hmmildon, Edith. 1993. The Greek Way [M]. W. W. Norton & Company.
9. Shepherd, Simon & Mick Walis. 2002. Studying Plays [M]. Bloomsbury USA.
10. Wager, Walter. 1968. The Playwrights Speak [M]. Delta Publications.

11. 刘海平，朱雪峰：英美戏剧：作品与评论［M］. 上海：上海外语教育出版社，2004.
12. 刘建军：基督教文化与西方文学传统［M］. 北京：北京大学出版社，2005。
13. 任生名：西方现代悲剧论稿［M］. 上海：上海外语教育出版社，1998.
14. 徐宝耕：西方文学：心灵的历史［M］. 北京：清华大学出版社，1990.
15. 徐光兴. 世界文学名著心理案例集［M］. 上海：上海教育出版社，2004.
16. 郑传寅，黄蓓. 欧洲戏剧文学史［M］. 武汉：长江文艺出版社，2002.